I0817631

THERE'S NO POINT IN DYING

FRANCISCO MACIEL

TRANSLATED BY
BRUNA DANTAS LOBATO

NEW VESSEL PRESS
NEW YORK

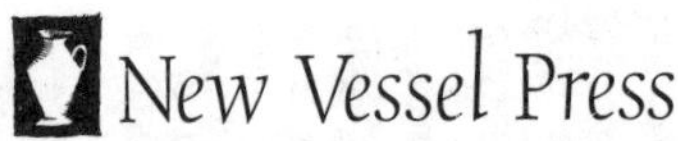

www.newvesselpress.com

First published in 2017 as *Não adianta morrer* by Editora Estação Liberdade

Published with the support of the Brazilian National Library Foundation,
of the Brazilian Ministry of Culture, and of the
Guimarães Rosa Institute of the Brazilian Ministry of Foreign Affairs.

Obra publicada com o apoio da Fundação Biblioteca Nacional, do Ministério da Cultura do Brasil, e do Instituto Guimarães Rosa, do Ministério das Relações Exteriores do Brasil.

MINISTÉRIO DA
CULTURA

MINISTÉRIO DAS
RELAÇÕES
EXTERIORES

GOVERNO FEDERAL
BRASIL
UNIÃO E RECONSTRUÇÃO

Library of Congress Cataloging-in-Publication Data
Maciel, Francisco
[Não adianta morrer, English]
There's No Point in Dying/Francisco Maciel; translation by Bruna Dantas Lobato.
p. cm.
ISBN 978-1-954404-39-7

Library of Congress Control Number 2025936992
I. Brazil—Fiction

Table of Contents

"And then man, tormented and unyielding, would run ahead of the fatality of things after a nebulous, elusive figure cobbled together out of scraps, a scrap of the intangible, another of the invisible, all sewn with flimsy stitches by the needle of the imagination; and this figure—nothing less than the chimera of happiness—either fled constantly or allowed itself to be caught by its train, upon which the man would clasp it to its breast, and then the figure would give a scornful laugh and vanish like an illusion."

—Joaquim Maria Machado de Assis,
The Posthumous Memoirs of Brás Cuba
(translator: Flora Thomson-DeVeaux)

"Some, finding the spectacle barbaric,
would rather (the fragile ones) die.
There comes a time when there's no point in dying."

—Carlos Drummond de Andrade,
"The Shoulders That Carry the World"
(translator: Bruna Dantas Lobato)

A HORSE AT THE DOOR

Dafé is running down Maia de Lacerda, it's 2:15 in the afternoon, and at 2:22 he's going to die. Tall, green eyes, coiled hair bleached bright yellow, he could've been whatever he wanted in life. Soccer player. Security guard. Gigolo. Star. He was meant to shine, he'd always thought. He was different, he was better. Then he made the wrong choices. Now he's running down Maia. Just a pipe dream.

He feels like he's soaring, but he isn't. He spent the last two days fucking and nuzzling. No sleep, not enough food, too much to drink. He's running on the sidewalk, on the left side of the street, past the parked cars, the trees, the lampposts. He's trying to get to São Roberto. He'll be safe then, he thinks. That's where the woman he's been banging lives, and though he told her they're done, that's where he's headed, sex is no help in a situation like this, only gets in the way. But that's where he's going. His mother Mirtes's would be safer, but he doesn't think of that.

It'd be faster if he went through the Bezerra de Menezes Spiritist Center, jumped over the back wall to São Carlos and ran down the steps to get to São Roberto. But he keeps running down the street.

Everyone here's a lame horse. That's what Guile Xangô says, and Guile Xangô is a nice guy, weird and smart, he's got a job, an address, identity documents. All the others are screw-ups, starving, one foot in jail. At least that part is true:

it's hard to find someone here who's never done time. People pretend they haven't. But when they're hammered and high on blow they brag about it. They're out and got nothing to show for it. No job, respect, dignity. They get wasted in seedy bars and snort white lines off black tables, the thin threads of their stupid lives going between their teeth. Life was better on the inside, they say. Then why not just stay there? Out here they got no rights, no respect. They're nobody. They're sick. They walked through the cell door right into a solid wall. They don't exist. They don't even know how much they don't exist. Everyone here's a lame horse, Guile Xangô says, and you know what you do to a lame horse? You put a bullet in it, kill it.

Dafé is still running down Maia, still feeling like he's soaring. If he ran into the Halley Hotel, ran up the stairs, locked himself up in a room, Pernambuco would help him, he wouldn't stand for cowardice, he'd be on his side. Dafé could stand a chance.

No one here has IDs. They work underground. They have marks on their skin instead. And he, Dafé, doesn't have any of those either. He's never liked tattoos. He's proud of his own skin, clear, unblemished. He's never fallen off his bike or his motorcycle. He's never fallen.

The truth is that everyone's gotten their marks right here in the present world. Guile Xangô has a historical explanation for this stuff. He says that all marks are inherited, like astral maps handed down from a past life. You believe this shit? It doesn't make sense. Guile Xangô loves to talk about how slaves got punished. Like at the whipping post. Everyone's feet swollen, all of today's twists and turns from the thrashings at that same post in their past lives. All the slaves back then were marked like cattle. They were cattle. The body parts that would get marked: thighs, arms, stomach, shoulders, chest, faces. The marks could be a cross, a bell, flowers, letters (BP, FC, N&B). That's what Guile Xangô keeps saying. Everyone here gets to be a slave again.

If you think about it (and you always think about it after talking to Guile Xangô) a lot of girls have these burn marks. Usually from boiling water. Mothers throwing hot water at their babies when they wouldn't stop crying. A child reaching for the stove and pulling down the kettle, a waterfall on her face. Another kid throwing water at a girl walking home up the hill after school, so she'd learn her lesson and never look at another woman's man. The ones with chemical burns from jealous cuckolded boyfriends like to show it off the most. They still wear tiny shorts, no matter that there's only a scar left and the faint idea that at some time they were desired.

Leo smashed Monstrinho's face with a bat. A trampled bloody chunk over his left eye and bare flesh under his right eye all the way down his chin. A beautiful scar. And the two of them go way back, served time together with Dentinho, Paula da Olívia, Pará da Lana. So many stab wounds between them. The bullet scars are more impressive: Monstrinho has at least twelve, entry and exit wounds. And two from bullets that didn't exit: a scar on his leg and another on his scalp. Everyone here has those marks too: from stabbings, gunshots, bats, hot water, acid. And marks from diseases, arms and legs broken in places that don't mend easy. Arms and legs maimed or crippled in car accidents, fingers lost to factories or lumber mills or machete fights, ears severed in some brawl.

And he's still running at a gallop. The best part is when Guile Xangô talks about the iron muzzle, the one Escrava Anastácia wears in the history books, made of zinc or tin sheets. It covers her whole face and has tiny air holes. Slaves had to wear it as punishment when they drank or stole food or ate earth or clay. Cachaça was the vice of choice for city slaves. Clay was more popular in rural areas. Men and women relished eating right out of anthills, with shards of clay pots, broken bits from perfume bottles. When they had the muzzle on, they tried to inhale particles off the ground as best they could. Like people nowadays snorting white powder, desperate to get their fix. (Imagine all these addicts dying to get something in their bodies with their mouths gagged.) Every drunk and junkie in the world, every single one of them is a child of Anastácia, Guile Xangô says. Can you believe it?

Dafé keeps running. If he crossed the street and turned on Professor Quintino, he'd see two cops standing outside Luiz's bar on Sampaio Ferraz, talking to the gambling mobster, they're nice guys. He knows one of the cops, Sargento Salgueirão, he's a friend, once he even gave Dafé some advice he ignored. Dafé remembers the cop lost his son in an accident, some five years ago, with his own gun in his own home. Soon this same cop will deliver Lana's baby inside that very police car, he'll win a medal and go crazy, lose his mind, a total lunatic. Dafé would be safe there.

And if he ran into Luiz's bar, he'd see the woman he loves (and pretends he doesn't) talking to Guile Xangô. At that very moment, she says to Guile Xangô, "I need a bump." She walks toward the bathroom, followed by an attentive collective gaze. On her way back, she walks through a fog of desire, a disdainful smirk in the corner of her lips, red like a matador's cape. She puts a coin in the jukebox and dances by herself. The men are like dogs watching a bitch in heat. Calves, thighs, ass, and the dogs on all fours, slobbering. She sways her arms, calves, hips, shakes her ass, rubbing it in. Then she sits back down, her naughty face shining with sweat, she reaches for Guile Xangô, touches his cheek with her hand and purrs, "You're so, so, I don't know, so . . . sweet!"

"If you call me sweet one more time, I'll beat you to a pulp!" Guile Xangô's eyes look cold, but then they warm up and he smiles. She bursts out laughing, her hand cupping her mouth, her whole body shaking, two fat tears puddling on her fingers.

"You always make me laugh. You know you're the only one who makes me laugh like this?"

Dafé would be jealous, but Guile Xangô would take one look at him and Dafé would see it's fine, the three of them would drink and drink until the sun came down.

He's running at a gallop down Maia de Lacerda. His lungs are burning, his legs getting heavy. The guys on the motorcycle have their helmets on. The one on the back carries a gun in his left hand. Dafé is on his left side too, making it easier for him to finish the job.

Guile Xangô gets it. Vovô do Crime, on the other hand, looks down on everybody. Even on Dafé. He was another weirdo. Dafé had seen what it was like to walk up the hill with him at least three times. The two of them side by side and voices shouting "Asshole" from the houses, shacks, bars, and stores. The Asshole must be on his way up the hill right about now and Dafé wishes he could be there with him again. But he's not. Up there, the Asshole will smoke and snort and talk to the kids in the Movement. They're his armed guards, his dragons of independence: the tougher ones call the Asshole Dr. Freud, and the younger ones call him Vovô do Crime, their Criminal Papa. They talk about philosophy, the streets, and they come up with plans for the day the favela comes to an end, they'll take over the city, burn shit to the ground, use the guts of the last priest in town to hang the last rich man. The Asshole will talk until he's exhausted. The troop shakes when he says God doesn't exist, and he doesn't laugh at any of their Jesus jokes. (Did you know Jesus was Brazilian? Because he was always performing miracles, he was poor, and was killed by his government.) The kids hold on to their guns when they hear him mention the devil. Dafé wishes he was up there with the Asshole. He'd be safe.

Dafé needs more air, he's sucking in air, his feet are hitting the ground and sending pain up his chest and then up to his head, still burning. He's burning up. If he ran toward the metro, through the vacant lot across the street from the station, if he did that, Dafé would also be safe. And he'd see the group of Angolans. Though he wouldn't know what was going on. Or maybe he'd know deep down, without fully knowing.

The Angolans stand around the phone booth outside the Estácio station. Someone found a way to call any number for free, some glitch, and they wait for their turn. More than twenty of them. Men, women, teenagers, children. They stand there from morning to night to morning again. But now they leave early. The military police warned them, a bunch of Black people huddled on a corner in the middle of the night can't be anything good. Now they stay there from morning to ten in the evening, eleven, midnight. They came to Brazil to try to escape their civil war and the colonial misery they'd inherited, but they were never slaves, they were never trafficked in slave ships. They don't have that mark. They haven't been pulled up by the roots.

Dafé is out of breath. He drags himself down that street like a lame horse. He can't think straight. He's starting to feel foreign to himself. He's ready to cross the street, continue his trip. His entire body hurts. But where is this heat on his back coming from, this hot sting on his back, and now this jabbing on his shoulder, and why is the sidewalk rushing up against him like this, turning into a wall?

He doesn't know, but somewhere he's still soaring, untethered, airborne, free, running, he'll make it, he will, at a gallop. He's turning on São Roberto, he's there, but São Roberto is now a dark well, the houses have disappeared, the steps have disappeared, and he wants to freeze time, even Dafé himself is disappearing, going faint, collapsing forever, goodbye.

OUT OF TIME

There are seven of them and they're sitting on the floor, in a circle. Manaus opens the bags and they each put in their piece. By his feet, three full pillowcases and a bundle of heavy weapons. They're leasing their guns to Dentinho. Manaus closes the bag and places it under his right thigh. To his left, on the floor, a small black pistol. Manaus looks down and his dark hair falls on his indigenous features. He's pissed and anything could happen. The women (there are three of them) are making the chow, talking and laughing.

"Go ahead, talk louder!" Manaus shouts at them in the other room.

The utter silence. The locked doors. The sheets covering the windows. The utter silence. Manaus moves his hair off his face with both hands like he's parting curtains. He grabs the pillowcases at his feet and dumps out their contents: rings, necklaces, bracelets, watches, earrings, gold, silver, pearls, costumes, foreign coins, CDs, a wig, five pairs of panties. He picks up a pair with the tips of two fingers and asks without looking at anyone:

"Who brought this?"

Manaus collects the CDs. Then he places them side by side. He gets up and steps on each one with the heel of his cowboy boot. Then he sits back down.

No one says a word.

Manaus looks at Panda, who scratches his head and stares at his feet.

"You said there'd be no one at the house," Manaus says. "But that wasn't true, was it?"

"The cook said they'd be out of town," Panda says.

"And what's more, the owner of that house is an army colonel," Manaus says. "Do you understand how bad you fucked up?"

"I never saw him in uniform the whole ten days I watched that house."

"And the cook? You fucked her and got her to tell you when they were traveling, but nothing else? What about the safe? You didn't ask shit about the safe?"

"But he had guns. We're loaded now, no need to . . . "

"I don't want to hear it."

The women's whispers and food smells are coming from the kitchen.

"What I wouldn't give to see what's inside that safe," Manaus says.

And Panda starts to describe how they dragged the safe from the office. The thunder from the safe falling down the stairs and how he spent half an hour trying to open that shit, until he thought of calling the man they found in the house that day, and the guy tried and everything, he said only the owner knew the combination, that he was only the wife's brother, the owner was on a trip. The effort they made to lift that safe, they wanted to load it into the van in the garage, but they couldn't get it off the living room floor.

Everyone laughs at this image. Even Manaus is laughing. The women are laughing in the kitchen, they don't even know why. Until the guys notice Manaus isn't laughing with them anymore. They go quiet and wait.

"And while we were fighting with that safe, Micuçu was in the bedroom fucking the woman," Manaus says.

"So what? She was hot," Micuçu says and laughs."Go ahead, laugh," Manaus says.

Nobody laughs. The utter silence.

Three knocks on the door. Manaus throws his RK 62 to Dafé and his Uzi to Beleco. Two knocks. Then three more quick knocks. Dafé opens the door and Dentinho comes in. Manaus's jacket is hiding the loot.

Dentinho looks at everybody, shaking his head. Manaus hands the weapons and a stack of bills to Dentinho.

"Dollars?" Dentinho asks, counting the money. "Anyone down?"

"I wanted them all to go down, but the man wouldn't let me," Micuçu says as he gets up.

Dafé hits Micuçu's face with his gun, and Micuçu stands there, begging Dentinho for protection, but he keeps counting the money. Then he leaves.

They all watch the blood run down Micuçu's face, soaking his shirt.

Dentinho hops on his motorcycle and says to Rafa, "You ever seen a haunted house before? That right there is one," Dentinho says, pointing. "No one in there lasts more than two weeks. They've fucked up and are out of time already."

THE FOUR MANDELAS

The four Mandelas are drinking beer and talking around a table. They're all Black, white-haired, tall, thin, young-looking for their age. That one is a lawyer and was head of a samba school at one point, and he talks more than the others. That one used to be an army sergeant, but he looks like a general and everyone talks to him like he's a commander. That other one is a cop and it's better not to know much more about his past. That one was a doctor, still is. Every Sunday the four of them drink at Luiz's bar, they talk and share old memories like it's a card game. They don't play cards.

They've been sitting there for a while already when Monstrinho comes in and stares at them. Monstrinho is a nasty man and says whatever he wants to say to anybody who'll listen. One day, he stood in the middle of the bar, pointed at them, and yelled, "I'm seeing four Mandelas." Luiz came from behind the bar to kick out the troublemaker. The men told Luiz it was fine, then told him to pour Monstrinho a beer.

It's become a weekly ritual. Every Sunday Monstrinho comes into Luiz's bar, opens his arms wide, and bows. "My four Mandelas!" Then he drinks his beer and leaves.

When the four Mandelas sit at their table right in the middle of the room, on Sunday mornings, Luiz's bar looks like a Spiritist Center. Everyone who comes into the bar stops by to argue, kiss their hand, talk, ask for advice. Most of the time the Mandelas sit there in silence, with their mysterious faces sculpted by time, carved in wood, not that they're wooden, that isn't it, but it's like time has carved a mask on each of their faces and people can see it on their skin, their posture, their knowing nods, an ancient wisdom.

Not wood, stone, it's like they're made of stone, that's it, like they're carved out of stone, and can withstand anything: wind, rain, time itself, other stones—wind, time, and rain wash their faces and leave no marks, just lightly polish the stone. They were born out of stone and sit there, stony brothers at the marble tabletop, permanent, eternal, tradition itself.

Pardal Wenchell is the first to stop by, and he's always talking about his childhood, the past, other lands, lost tribes, and sometimes, after too many beers, he starts speaking in a strange tongue, always paying reverent attention to the Mandelas. Only Pardal Wenchell can manage this level of warmth, attention, devotion, like they're all the same.

(Monstrinho is completely different: he invokes Exú and he's treated like a messenger, a delivery man, an errand boy, a postal worker, but also fondly.)

Not Seu Nonô. He's almost their age but not nearly as respectable. He treats the Mandelas the way a music teacher teaches a samba player who can only play by ear. He carries his guitar and leans it against the table like a challenge. It's part of the ritual. He asks for a round of beers for the Mandelas and a whiskey for himself (though he doesn't drink it). And thus begins a lesson about the importance of the art of patience.

Seu Nonô says that reading sheet music is essential, that Brazilian musicians can only play by ear, apart from Tom Jobim—Villa-Lobos's mediocre disciple, Bach's plagiarist—and that samba players are essentially banging on stuff, unacceptable to gather ten men in a samba school to play such melodically simplistic and poetically chaotic music. And Seu Nonô drums his fingers on the table, trying to show off his expert knowledge, and doesn't get even a wrinkle to budge on the Mandelas' stony faces.

Then Seu Nonô gets his guitar out of the case and tries to play a Spanish tune, his legs open wide, his guitar resting on his left leg, a lot of posturing for little result. "My fingers are too stiff," he says, and hands the guitar to the Mandelas, and he's ready to shake a matchbox along with whatever samba they play. It almost always goes like this.

But sometimes Seu Nonô comes in, leans his guitar against the table, and tries to reinvent soccer. He declares that they should do away with the offside rule. Without it, there would be so many more goals, at least ten goals per match, and goals are the best part of soccer.

Fouls! How's it possible that every game has fifty, sixty fouls, and twenty of them are all against the same player, the star of the team, that rare breed, the star, who carries that lost art, the art of dribbling? So he wants to create a new rule: if a defender commits three fouls against the same player, he's benched, not banned, benched. Then after the tenth foul from all the players, the whole team is punished with a direct free kick in their penalty area. And the clock stops until the ball is back in the game. The ball is off the field, the clock stops, and only starts again when the ball touches a player's foot.

Pardal Wenchell likes to provoke Seu Nonô, and he gets too excited as he defends the referee and the four assistant referees in a booth, watching the game through a screen far away from the field. In difficult situations, the referee consults the video recording and the on-line referees have the final word. Seu Nonô, who'd never admit he agrees with Pardal, protests. Mistakes are human. No need to watch the video. No need to have four assistant refs in front of a screen. No need to have twenty assistant refs running around a field with a little flag. Just one referee, chance, luck, and the game. And Pardal Wenchell continues playing his own game: and what's wrong with the offside rule and the current regulations? You don't mess with a winning team. The Mandelas gaze with fondness at Pardal Wenchell, that fierce defender of tradition.

Deep down, no one knows why the Four Mandelas tolerate Seu Nonô, but they do, and have even given him dating advice. But Seu Nonô knows nothing about music or soccer, and much less about women, not even his own wife.

It was from the Four Mandelas' table, from that very spot, in the middle of the bar, that the order came down to treat Ruth with respect.

Ruth is white, blond, blue eyes. She knows how to dress well, speaks French, knows everything. People say she was beautiful at one point, but she's older now. In the good old days, Ruth was a lawyer, had a nice office downtown, many clients. She was married. Until she fell in love with a Black man. An average Black man, still young, a security guard at the commercial building where she rented an office. She left her husband to go live with this Black man.

She started to encourage him, she made him go back to school and he got ahead, he started working with her. Ruth didn't keep any of this a secret. But she started to lose clients and in two years' time she was in debt and in deep shit. No one invited Ruth to parties. Her husband was also a lawyer and all their friends and clients took his side. Ruth was out of luck.

But she was persistent. She asked for a divorce, married the Black man, and turned her life around. She took the civil service exam, and she was a good public servant. She worked in penitentiaries, with prisoner rehabilitation programs. And the Black man turned his life around too, he even got into a legal education program. The two of them danced with the samba school.

Until the day the Black man walked into a bank and a security guard thought he was a robber and shot him three times. He died on the spot. Ruth went mad. She sued the bank and the security company. The bank's lawyer was her ex-husband. At the time, Ruth was pregnant with the Black man's child. She lost the baby, then she came to the bar to watch life go by. A cheap drunk with her fits of anger and huge ordinary losses. She fell on her face, she broke her leg, she was all broken. She owes money in every bar and has no idea when she'll settle the bill. But she says she'll pay it all off, every cent, when she gets the settlement from the bank.

Today, like every Sunday, Nabor is there too, always standing like he's the odd man out, a party crasher. The vain thought he could be a fifth Mandela has crossed his mind once, but he knows they'll never respect him after his time as a jailer. That's why he savors a certain taste of revenge in his mouth when Vovô do Crime starts to rant against any and all types of tradition. But then the Old Ladies arrive for their hand-kissing session and the Mandelas remain impassive, untouchable. Then comes Lourinho to talk about his younger sister and the Mandelas absolve him. And more and more people arrive and Nabor gets up when Pardal Wenchell starts to speak the strange language, *Undzer Shtetl brent Sholem shalom Undzer Shtetl brent Sholem shalom,* and the Mandelas follow along: Mona Kamona Mona Kamona, and no one understands a thing, but it's always like that, unusual sounds, a beautiful sight.

MY DEAR

My Dear is turning eighty. At Assis's bar, he takes out his wallet and shows his date of birth on his ID. Everyone does the math: it's a lot of years. No one looks at his real name or sees his dark hair in the photo. They already know My Dear's face by heart. And they don't even notice his new shoes.

With his blue eyes misty with loneliness, My Dear begs to be seen the way he sees himself. But nobody wants to hear it. The sensitive ones drunkenly hug him. The practical ones buy him a glass of warm beer. Most go back to their conversations like they haven't been interrupted.

He replays the same scene at Kadhafi's bar, at Euclides's, at Luiz's, at Raimundo's, at Assis's again, at Maradona's. The white mustache over his toothless mouth goes limp and his eyes grow cloudier. Is this what he deserves: indifference? He's always called men, women, and children "my dear." He's always been polite. He doesn't owe anyone anything. Quite the opposite: he's lost track of how much money he's lent, how many rounds of drinks he's bought, how many ungrateful people he's fed.

But he doesn't give up easy. Lourinho, a big Black guy, and Periquito, the hunchback, are walking up Sampaio. "You have to hear this story, My Dear, but first you'll need to buy us some beers." They go into Kadhafi's bar and start telling it. The two have been friends since they were kids. They had just run into each other on a crowded bus when Lourinho called

Periquito a cripple and threatened to touch his hunchback to see if it would really bring him good luck, like he's always been told, everyone knows that touching a back is supposed to bring good luck. Periquito called Lourinho a dirty Black and a gorilla and said he was going to take him back to the zoo because they must be looking for their missing gorilla, he'd get a reward for sure, because that was some dirty gorilla. So they started arguing on the bus. Passengers sitting on the right side were rooting for Periquito. Passengers on the left were rooting for Lourinho, and the people standing were against both. Then a Black man from the Black Consciousness Movement told the driver to stop at a police station to drop off Periquito, racism was a crime, then a security guard suddenly pulled out a gun and held it to Lourinho's head, saying that he was the one who started this mess. So Periquito told the guy to shove the gun somewhere, Periquito told the guy with a Black consciousness to suck his dick, Periquito's, and then he said that Lourinho was his brother, they grew up together, and it was true, they'd been raised together, and he told the driver to stop that damn bus, and they both got off, pissed, Lourinho had grabbed the guy's gun and was about to shoot him, you don't put metal to a man's head, if you do, you better shoot, and Periquito had to drag Lourinho away, and the bus finally took off, and now the two are at the bar telling this story.

My Dear doesn't find it amusing and is ready to show his wallet, to talk about his birthday, when Lourinho gets up. "Guile Xangô needs to hear this one! He's going to laugh his ass off! Only he gets this stuff!" And off they go, leaving My Dear to pay for the beer and the two glasses of cognac.

At Nelson's bar, My Dear sits on the stool next to the stranger in shorts and a T-shirt. The stranger nods at My Dear and looks at the drunks, smiles like a tame dog or a cuck, a tame cuck. The stranger opens his hand and starts counting his coins. He gets up, goes to the other end of the bar, finds a little place to sit between the drunks, and asks Nelson for something, though Nelson doesn't hear it. He waits while Nelson gets the mocotó from the pot, pours the cow's feet stew in a serving bowl, fishes out two little cockroaches that were floating in the liquid, throws them on the floor, takes the big bowl of mocotó to the drunks, opens the freezer, grabs a bottle of beer, opens the bottle, palms the cash from the drunks, does some math, all in his head, opens the cash register, does some more math, figures out how much change he needs, fishes out the change, hands them the change, and when Nelson finally turns around, a smile on his face, content with the quality of his service, only then does the tame cuck raise his hand to say again what Nelson couldn't hear.

Then Guile Xangô asks the cuck, "What do you smoke?" And the cuck answers, "Whatever."

Guile Xangô asks for a pack of Hollywoods. Nelsons grabs it and opens the freezer to get the bottle of Steinhäger because Guile Xangô always orders more than one thing at once. Nelson pours the Steinhäger and Guile Xangô tells him to pour another Steinhäger shot for the cuck too. Guile

Xangô hands the cuck the pack of Hollywoods and slides the Steinhäger toward him. The cuck has the pack of Hollywoods in his hand and he looks at Guile Xangô and the glass. Guile Xangô grabs the Steinhäger and puts it in the cuck's hand, clinks his own glass against the cuck's, and takes a sip. The cuck drinks too, he drinks it all in one go and leaves. But first he puts his hand on Guile Xangô's shoulder and says, "We need to talk." And he leaves. The drunks ask, "Who's the fag?"

"He's the new priest," Guile Xangô says.

The drunks recycle the garbage in their heads: taking out the cuck, taking out the tame dog, taking out the fag. My Dear makes the sign of the cross and feels like the world has turned upside down. He's about to order another beer when Lourinho and Periquito come back into the bar shouting and pull Guile Xangô away so they can tell their story again. My Dear spits on the sawdust floor, disgusted by their ass-kissing.

By eight in the evening, there's nobody walking down Maia anymore. It's cold. In the mostly empty bars, just a few stray drunks, no one talking loudly, no one laughing, it looks more like a wake, and a spinster's wake at that. But the Old Ladies are there, unshakeable. My Dear excuses himself, sits down next to them, and says, "Today is my birthday." He gets some icy nods. He doesn't understand, he's forgotten how he went around saying that back in the old days Black girls weren't allowed in his house, not even through the kitchen door. "Things were different then. On a night like this, this part of town was teeming with people and there'd still be more people on the way," Dedé says, continuing their conversation as if no one has joined them.

"Now Arlindo is a security guard somewhere near here, they even say he's a snitch, a traitor, I don't know if it's true, but he's an idiot, that I know, and I'd say it to his face. Arlindo had a bar and he and Creusa were married back then. Naldinho was his partner, he was married to Denise. Not the one living in that big house, so many Denises around here, another one. The two of them kept switching wives and when both women got pregnant, no one knew which one was the father. But that's not why the bar closed. It wasn't because of the buffoon either. The buffoon? That was crazy. At three in the morning, when Arlindo rolled down the doors, that was when stuff really started to happen. All kinds of stuff. All hell broke loose. Everyone naked. No one belonged to anyone and everyone belonged to everyone. That was the buffoon. Why buffoon? It has nothing to do with Arlindo being an idiot. Though there were plenty of buffoons to go around, ask Marquete! Marquete was handsome back then, his muscles toned, and he could fight off a whole army, well, fight, I mean, so to speak. People would line up to come in. One day the police arrived. Everyone running around, trying to get dressed. When they came in, there were women in pants, men in skirts, people wearing whatever they could get their hands on. They wanted to round everyone up and take them in, but they'd need two buses for that, or at least ten vans, and then, they chatted about this and that, chatted some more, and that was it. Everything has a price."

"What do you mean, the buffoon?" My Dear asks. "The buffoon is the buffoon, damn it!" Dedé says. "Oh! Don't you mean '*bas-fond*?' Like in that French movie," My Dear says. "That's it: buffoon! And listen here: did anyone ask you to come and join the conversation, you shithead?"

Now it's nine o'clock and My Dear is in Raimundo's bar, behind the counter, pouring himself a shot of cognac and talking about why he doesn't like Black people. He and Raimundo have the same light blue eyes, they understand each other, but Raimundo isn't listening, he's watching the TV. Marcelo Cachaça too. He's always at Raimundo's bar, staring at the TV in a catatonic Zen trance. He only looks away when someone asks for the checkerboard and challenges him to a match. He stays in his trance and plays: he doesn't miss a single move. He's invincible. If they hand him a glass of beer, he drinks it. If they give him a cigarette, he smokes it. If they ask him to speak, he speaks. And he can talk forever. About anything: his best story is about how he was kidnapped by a flying saucer in rural Goiás and left in a bush by a landfill in Rio. He was admitted to a mental hospital at one point, lived on a farm somewhere, and ended up here. Now he lives at the back of a house on Santos Rodrigues, with Paulinho's mother paying for everything. His room is only a little bigger than a doghouse. There's food, clean clothes, and a comforter. And so he goes on living, between the plant and the ghost.

He has theories. HIV. He believes the virus is a very advanced form of life from space sent by a supercivilization to improve humanity. The virus is trying to get in touch with humans, to find harmony. For now, it still hasn't achieved that and that's why it's been causing so much harm. But when the right moment for symbiosis arrives, humans will change so much that people will look more like children or monkeys. He's sure that the people changed by the virus will be able to use more than seventy percent of their brain capacity; they'll be able to adapt to any environment (the bottom of the ocean, or Mars, or the void) without having to wear any type of space suit. They'll never get sick; they'll live to be two hundred years old and still look like kids.

Nobody really believes him because it's hard to understand what he says: DNA, aura, chakra, metabolism, abduction. But they put up with the ET stuff because of the checkers: how come he never loses a game? That's the first bit of proof that he isn't really crazy. The second: he's not so crazy he's eating his own shit. The third: he's not burning money.

And now Vavau comes in and shouts, "Raimundo, the board! Marcelinho, you better get ready because today's the day I'll beat you!" Raimundo puts the board on the table. Then he pops open a beer for Vavau, gets a Coke and a shot of cachaça for Marcelo, and he stands there, watching Vavau and Marcelo exchange black and white pieces. Behind the counter, My Dear watches the TV like it's a window to nowhere.

It's ten to midnight and My Dear is standing at the corner of Sampaio and Professor Quintino do Vale, looking at the beggars. There are about ten of them and no one's sleeping. They're piled on top of each other, drinking cachaça straight from the bottle, passing it from hand to hand. They laugh and sing. One of them runs along Quintino, playing with the street dogs. The beggar falls and the dogs roll on top of him, licking, growling, pretending to bite. Since there's no one else out there, My Dear lets the hurt and loneliness rise up to his throat and lets out a sob.

Now it's four in the morning and My Dear is sleeping at the back of Luiz's bar. Cezinha, the waiter, yells, "Out, out, out!" My Dear wakes up with soap suds inside his shoes. Cezinha rolls up the door and My Dear sees the empty street, just the cat woman feeding her children with tails and whiskers. It will soon be another day.

Did it hurt, my dear?

BETTER THAN ME

"The day I finally paid off this taxi was the happiest day of my life. I thought, 'Now I'm my own person, no one can boss me around, I can do as I please, it was like winning the lottery, though I never liked gambling, I got it with my sweat, my hard work, by going after it.' It was the happiest day of my life." Pedrão thinks of saying all this, but he knows no one is listening. And he's already regretting this ride, which isn't even a real ride, just some nonsense Vovô do Crime made up so he'd take Guile Xangô to Ceará Street, where all the whores are. And now he has to put up with the old man not letting anyone talk, as usual, Guile Xangô always finished off, My Dear nearly dead, Dafé who's dead already but doesn't know it yet, plus Nelson who will end up bankrupt from drinking so much just so he can put up with the drunks.

"No one believes in God. You come into Nelson's, get hammered, ask for the check, then you say, 'God will repay you.' Nelson will beat you up," Vovô do Crime says to Guile Xangô.

"No, not Guile Xangô, he has plenty of credit, and always pays, unlike some others," Nelson says.

"I believe in God," Dafé says.

"You know nothing," Vovô do Crime cuts in. "And I don't even know why you're here."

"You're a heretic," says My Dear.

"I am the Devil!" Vovô do Crime shouts.

"The Devil is just God when he's drunk," Guile Xangô says.

"Who said that?" Vovô do Crime asks, laughing.

"Good one. But I bet you didn't come up with it. That's your problem. You don't think for yourself. You don't bother having your own ideas."

Pedrão thinks: "Someone has to be the driver, then there's someone else higher up driving the drivers." He doesn't think that the world is a taxi, but he knows he's become a slave to his car, that it's been having issues since the first month and if it weren't for Vavau, "I would've been in serious trouble. Not even a spare tire!"

"Do you know what the most popular kind of sex in the world is?" Vovô do Crime asks and immediately answers, "Jerking off!" And to Guile Xangô, "You have a lot of experience. Every intellectual does. And you especially. A man who can't deal with life as it comes must like to jerk off a lot. Everything stinks, everything is shit, but no, oh no, the dumbass intellectual can always finds a way to close his eyes and live in the future. You especially, a priest, a pastor to boot, someone who only believes in a world beyond this fucking world, a better world, but fuck that better world! And what is this, this business of believing in life after life, a world after the world? Jerk-off!"

"Your problem is that you only believe in yourself, you're the center of the world," Guile Xangô says. "Then it's easy. You think with your belly button and can't see the real world."

"I think more with my dick!" shouts Vovô do Crime.

"Life is a woman, a woman to stick it in. And today we're going to be taking a trip to that woman. Down with jerking off! *Arriba la putería!*"

Pedrão thinks about his gay son, and he suffers. Even a dirty, dead kid like Dafé was better, a real man at least. He parks near Ceará Street. He goes with the group and wonders if this really is life and if it's worth getting it on with these women. "Better to screw at home, much safer." They're all sitting at a little bar shouting at each other because of the loud music. Vovô do Crime looks like a child on his first trip to the zoo, and he's pushing it, touching, kissing, ordering beer with Guile Xangô's money, as usual. And he shouts a poem by Augusto dos Anjos:

Kissed by pale drunk maenads,
His Hyrcanian arteries pulsing,
He smells the abstemious carnations,
And by night, he will come, dizzy with addiction,
In the dark bazaar of prostitution
The aphrodisiac spit of females.

But it's My Dear's show. He's treated like a regular, all pampered by the girls, "Come put a baby in me, My Dear," that filthy bastard! Dafé takes a brunette who looks underage and disappears with her. "That's a real man. Dead, but a man." Nelson only relaxes when he sees that Guile Xangô has been taken care of, and he's enjoying his chat with an old whore, the two of them talking about whores' unions, rights, retirement, and no pussy in sight, Vovô do Crime is right about this part, Guile Xangô is all talk and no pussy.

Pedrão lets his eyes wander and can't decide if it's better to pick a spot near there or to fight for a spot somewhere on Avenida Atlântica, Riachuelo, or Severo Augusto, in Glória, and laughs at himself. "My profession is no different from theirs, I'm also fighting for customers," he says in Guile Xangô's ear, and is happy to hear his laugh, the first of the night, and he's proud to have scored one in his favor. "I also need to work," he says loudly, and Guile Xangô puts three times the price of the ride in his hand.

Now Pedrão is out working the night, hunting, and he thinks out loud about the old Vila Mimosa, and he wishes Guile Xangô was there by his side, listening: My first time wasn't at Vila Mimosa, Guile Xangô, it was actually with a cousin, keeping it in the family is always better. I know a lot of fuckers who say there are plenty of whores there, but that's just talk, most of them have mothers still walking the streets. One day I took the most beautiful woman I'd ever seen to Vila Mimosa. Talkative. She was leaving a career as a model to become an actress. Someone had granted her a small role in a soap opera as a gift. She'd play a prostitute, and the part would last half a dozen episodes. The prostitute would get killed and my friend would quietly leave the soap opera, with no one noticing or caring much. She wanted to blow it out of the water, do such a great job that viewers would force the showrunners to call her back, to extend her part from five to a hundred episodes, she said. That's why she decided to go full method (research, she explained to me). Vila Mimosa was as decrepit as it'd always been. Only now there was a new situation: the city of Rio de Janeiro needed a new helipad and a big parking lot, and they would build it right there, on top of the sinful body of Vila Mimosa. The orders came from Piranhão, the city hall building, right next door. I ended up becoming a guide for the actress. We spent two weeks living with hookers, pimps, madams, and the like. They didn't like her at first. The whores saw her as dangerous competition. And, to tell you the truth, she'd have been a hit in that butcher shop. I even pictured, like a good son of a bitch, the poor, toothless men standing in a long line stretching through the alleys, while I stood by her door, collecting money from the customers. Me, a pimp! It would indeed be unfair competition. But she soon started making friends, and didn't let go of the tape recorder, listening to their testimonies, feeling it all out, and, as a gesture of acceptance, the whores let her hide behind the plywood and cardboard partitions listening to the sounds and whimpers of commercial love. Commercial love! Did you like that, Guile Xangô? To many of the whores, she had a gift for it, no need to come all the way to Vila Mimosa to study it, she could join the profession just fine, as long as she did it far away from them. What I do know is that, during those two weeks, after I drove the future actress back to her home in Santa Teresa, I kept waiting for her to invite me in and . . .

Two men and a woman hail the cab, get in and name a street in Alto Leblon. The men are both gay, all excited talking about New York this and New York that. The woman is pretty, and she says the city has been traumatized after 9/11 and it'll take it some time to get back to normal. They talk about New York with the same love in your voice when you talk about Maia, Guile Xangô, except that New York has class and Maia, give me a break! The woman works at a travel agency and says they'll be forced to close down because of the restrictions from the American authorities. The two gay men work for an elite modeling agency (who says there are no coincidences, Guile Xangô!) and they swear everything has been fine for them. Pedrão thinks about his son. After he kicked the boy out of the house, his wife wasted away, and the love ended, they separated, and he started another family. He thinks he's lucky he has three daughters now, though he didn't want to think too much about it because women could also, never mind.

"A rich gay is different, he's gay, he has class, he's different from the homos," Pedrão thinks, watching in the rearview mirror as the two men and the woman enter a luxury building.

Yes, I was there to see the end of Vila Mimosa, Guile Xangô. Obviously the city needed a helipad, though most people don't really even know what that is. Cidade Nova was destroyed and Vila Mimosa went down with it. The Machado Coelho building used to stand there; it turned to dust in just five seconds, the first building ever within Rio's limits to be imploded, did you know that? The destroyed building and city became the theme of that year's samba school parade. More than a thousand people applauded the spectacle of the collapse. And many people cried; they'd lost their home and memories, they would have to go live in Baixada Fluminense, in Campo Grande, in the middle of nowhere. When the city is made new again, the poor move out, the trash is removed. Goodbye, Vila Mimosa, a place free of whores. A cloud of dust went up. In just a few seconds all you could see were two thousand five hundred tons of rubble next to the two poles and three signs still standing. At times like these, there's always something that resists. One annoying thing about these live implosions is that there's no replay. You wait two hours to see it and in five seconds it's all over. In fact, this is what's happening in every city. This is what's happening to me. This minute is passing and there's no replay. I myself am imploding right now, we're all imploding all the time, but I can't even observe it properly. In any case, the city always rebuilds itself and it'll always remain new. The whores will always find another corner to do their work. It's passed, but it doesn't matter; right now a new life is being fashioned out of the rubble of our own implosions. I know, Guile Xangô, I can think too, and I learned through life.

The actress? I took her to the spas and saunas in the Zona Sul, then we went around the nightclubs and sidewalks, all the places with respectable façades. We did an internship by a building down in Cinelândia full of offices dedicated to the commerce of love. Children who sold sweets on the corners also earned some extra money by selling their thin and hungry bodies. We became such good friends that there would've been a way. I didn't fuck her. Yes, laugh all you want, I like to hear your laugh, Guile Xangô. And she did a good job. But it was by chance. The star of the soap opera suffered an attack of amnesia, fell off her horse, had part of her face burned by a product used by a makeup artist filling in for someone else, was run over by her boyfriend in a mall parking lot—the stories were inconsistent—and my friend's part got bigger so she could fill in the gaps. Twenty episodes later, the star finally returned but had to compete with the rest of the cast for the heartthrob. My actress lost, but as a consolation prize, she won the heartthrob's brother. Pure glory. Today she is one of the greats.

I should say more? You think? About my son? Did I tell you about him? Well. I beat him up and kicked him out of the house. Not only was he a homo, he went and tried to confront me, said I was just some macho and worse things too, so I beat him up. My wife wasted away, she couldn't have any more children because of complications during that homo's birth. The only and last time I saw him after that was at her funeral. Handsome, strong, he obviously he worked out, he was well-dressed, already had his degree, well-traveled, was already pretty rich or nearly so. Well off. You couldn't tell from looking at him, seemed like a normal man. And standing at the edge of his mother's grave, the bastard hugs me and kisses me on the mouth. With his tongue! I didn't even know what to say, and that same day I crashed the taxi, it was stupid, I don't even want to think about it anymore.

Pedrão drives through the night and thinks he's having a lucky day. He doesn't want to tell Guile Xangô that he usually refuses to take Black passengers, at least late at night, we have to protect ourselves, Guile Xangô. It's seven in the morning by the time he gets to Vavau's parking lot, and Vavau is already off his rocker, his eyes red from sleep and booze, his nose running from all the powder, and his mind scrambled because of his homo dog.

Pedrão jumps out of the taxi and has the urge to say things like, "I've been around, I'm old enough to be your father," but that's not true, how old is Vavau? Thirties or so, forty, fine, "I have more experience than you, and you know what's worse than having a faggot dog, it's having a faggot son like Bástian, which is what he calls himself."

But he doesn't say any of that. Vavau has a short fuse, he's crazy, he'd scream something like, "This dog means more to me than a son and you know what? Mind your own damn business, get this car out of here and go fuck yourself while you're at it, okay?"

Pedrão gives the keys to Vavau and asks him to throw some water on the car. Vavau asks if he has any coke and Pedrão says he's taking it easy, but he can spare some change, and Vavau sniffs deeply and says he's going to make the clunker shine like a mirror. Pedrão crosses the street, goes into the bakery, and orders a drip coffee. He thinks about his first wife, the only one he ever loved, Sebastião's mother. Vavau's a much better guy than me, Guile Xangô.

YOU DID GOOD

Family is something else: when it's good, it's great; when it's bad, it's terrible. I'm a mother, and there are people here who'd hit their own mothers, I know a bitch who killed her own mother, killed her then died herself, and doesn't know it yet. There are a lot of people here who are still alive despite not knowing how to be alive, not knowing how to live, dead but still walking, breathing, fucking up.

I'm the daughter of an Arab couple, Turkish, my father and mother raised me as Brazilian, me and my eight siblings. The only thing they kept from their world was the food, kafta, baba ghanouj, sfiha, but honestly I don't like it, I've never taken my grandchildren to eat at Habib's, which they say is the largest fast-food chain in the Arab world, they much prefer McDonald's. Speaking of which, I've never been to Kadhafi's bar either, I like his children, Bin Bin, a sweet boy, and Mimi, who's been a bit lost, teaching belly dancing to sluts who know more about it than her, and Kadhafi letting it all happen, his paunch growing behind the counter, though he's only really there when it's time to count the money, the rest of the day he's sitting at the card table and getting drunk and saying that the Palestinians will throw the Jews into the sea, the blabbermouth, that's why they kicked him out of the Sahara (not the desert, of course, the Society of Habitual Friends of the Adjacencies of Rua da Alfândega), they didn't want any religious fanatics there. Never, Kadhafi has never been my brother, I know he's been telling everyone this lie, it's just like him.

Life is a game and I like to play. The losers around here like to say that the slot machine is a woman. "She's a woman, the slut, you never know when she's in a good mood, she gives and takes away, she lifts you up just so she can take you down, she'll keep lying to you and you'll keep liking it, you'll keep liking it until you're addicted to it." That's what they say, the losers. There are a lot of slot machine losers right here. People who look at those who are still playing the game with contempt, resentment, jealousy. People who've already lost their house, their wife, car, motorcycle, their job, everything to the machine. They got tricked so many times they're broken and now they sit there, drunk, waiting for the others to fall on their faces, to fall out of bed.

Zé Maria is the clown of lost hope. He's already lost everything, but he's still in the game. He wears a suit and a bow tie to play the slot machine. He prays, goes down on his knees, he begs. He cries. It's pretty pathetic. There are people who'd pay just to see Zé Maria perform his act in front of the machine. It became a circus. Sheer clowning.

I also like the music from the machines, especially the ones with video. I can spend the whole night watching and listening after I get tired of playing. "I'm tired of looking into eyes that can't see me." I don't like this song, I don't know who sings it, but this thing of "I'm tired of looking into eyes that can't see me" sticks with me like the truth, like a child. And I think "We Are the World" is a kind of prayer,

I asked Guile Xangô to translate it, then I asked one of those sellers of phrases and prayers to make me one, he put it together and it's up there on my bedroom wall. I taught Sleepy a prayer against the evil eye. I learned it from my grandmother, who learned from her grandmother. It starts like this:

You are fire
I am water
You set me on fire
And I extinguish you
At two I see you
At three I scare you.

But what I really like is plants. I left a pigtail plant at home and my dog ate it and destroyed the entire flowerbed. I took a little piece of the chewed-up stem, buried it, and made another pigtail plant. Then I moved to Copacabana. It looked beautiful, its leaves already this big, then I came to Estácio, I got here and they threw a white powder all over my plants, the pigtail plant started to wither, but before it died out I pulled out a little stump, planted it again, I gave it to Lana to raise and it survived, so I took a cutting and brought it back here again, it's now a thing of beauty.

I did the same thing with the female Ming aralia tree I had, because there are also male Ming aralias out there. The stems were four times as thick as my fingers. Then they sprinkled dust on it, it was that bitch Darlene, she did so many bad things to people that her only son who still lived with her died of AIDS. For me, plants are light.

But even more than games, plants, machines, music, I like children. I was walking up the hill when the cops trapped half a dozen kids in the alley, Klebinho and Danilo and some others. I shouted, “Hey, assholes, put down your weapons, they're children, can't you see? Are you going to murder kids now?” And one of the cops said, “Sorry, *tia*, my bad, you guys, get the hell out of here.”

“You did good, Sandrinha, you did good,” Mirtes says as she lights a whole pack of candles on the first Friday of the year down at the Capuchinhos church.

NABOR

People don't die. They are enchanted.
—João Guimarães Rosa

The tree grew in the middle of the house and was now coming out through the doors and windows on the second floor. Nabor stopped to look once again, with his usual astonishment, concentrating on the strong roots, and thought of composing a samba about that phenomenon. He'd been thinking about it for over three years, but nothing ever came of it. Nothing came to him, not the words, not the melody. Confusing images from the twenty years he'd spent in prison popped up, but that tree wasn't trapped, quite the opposite, it had grown freely in the house and taken over everything. Now it climbed out the doors and windows, and soon it would make its way through the roof. He wanted to have that tree's strength and resolve, but there were seventy years weighing down his shoulders.

A couple of tourists came up to him and started speaking a strange language. They were old, but looked good for their age, their eyes were light blue, their teeth were perfect, their skin was the color of milk. Now *these* people can really call themselves white, he laughed to himself. He understood they wanted a photo of themselves with the tree in the background. After the tourists' explanations, Nabor pointed the camera at their smiling faces and clicked. At another point in his life, he'd have tricked them both, taken their money, their backpacks, their sneakers, their camera. He could be running away with the camera by now, but his legs were heavy like lead, and he thought it'd be too embarrassing to get caught as an elderly thief.

He felt like they were making fun of him when they asked, with hand gestures, for him to stand in front of the tree. But the woman stood beside him, put her arm around his shoulder and shouted something to her husband. His eyes watered, and at the same time her warm touch prevented him from asking the tourists for spare change. Since they were now friends, he started saying this area used to be the old Mangue whore district, and some forty years ago he had three whores working for him day and night, but he lost his train of thought, and just asked them to be careful, they could get mugged here or worse. Taxi, he repeated, take a taxi and get out of here, he said. The couple laughed, thanked him, and left. The woman didn't look half bad, Nabor thought, her perfume lingering all the way down to the city hall.

One of his eight daughters, the youngest and smartest one, worked there, he couldn't remember if she was on the seventh or tenth floor, at some organization linked to the Black Consciousness Movement. He'd have to get to reception, show his ID, stick a visitor's badge to his chest, take the elevator, look for his daughter's office, walk into the room, and, if she was there, brace himself for five minutes of lecturing and complaining about neglect and dishonesty. "You say you need it for meds, but I told you I could get the meds for free and you don't want that, you want cash for booze, if not for something worse," she would say. "And I'm too young to have a child your age, and on top of that a rude, moody child, always up to no good, you better quit behaving like that." And then she would give him some change, saying it was the last time, "Who do you think I am, some millionaire?"

He thought about the visitor's badge, the elevator, the scolding, and decided it was better to go ask for money from Guile Xangô, a friend who never denied him anything. On the contrary. Nabor found himself sitting at Adega Xerez in front of a plate of steak frites and a cold beer, as Guile Xangô asked him for stories from the old days, about famous singers playing music surrounded by whores, cops, and crooks sharing a table, sleazy *malandros*, senators, soccer players, a classy event, high society stuff, the crème de la crème of bad behavior. Later Guile Xangô would ask me to talk about my time in prison, on Ilha Grande, and how he found out that becoming a cook was the best way to survive there, and how that gave him a skill for when he got out, he ended up working in the kitchen at the Copacabana Palace hotel. But then he spilled some of his beer as Vovô do Crime came in, shouting to the entire bar, "Big Nabor! Listen up! This one here has more than ten dead people under his belt, that's why he walks with that limp! Ten bodies weigh a ton!" He had to talk to Guile Xangô alone.

He walked to the Estácio metro station thinking that Vovô do Crime was a big bastard, he didn't know why Guile Xangô put up with that son of a bitch. He sat on a cement bench to catch his breath, one day he would stab Vovô do Crime, not to kill, just to see the fear on the shitter's face. And he almost had a heart attack when Beleco put the barrel of his pistol to his head.

"Stay sharp, Nabor, come on. If you were anyone else, you'd be done." Beleco put away his pistol and sat next to Nabor, offering a cigarette. Beleco is fourteen years old, looks like he's ten, and has a body count of three. Every now and then he goes crazy and acts up.

"I don't want to talk to you, Beleco," he said, refusing the cigarette. Beleco blew smoke in old Nabor's face and started talking about immunity. "There's no such thing as being immune, Beleco, not even a bulletproof vest can protect anyone. When the time comes, it's here before you even know it." But Beleco doesn't want to hear it. "But it's fine, *tio*, don't worry, it's fine, they shot at me and then *woohoo*! I shot right back at them."

Beleco is looking at Nabor, waiting for the old man to laugh. Beleco tries again, "Then they're like *rat-a-tat-boom* at me and I *rat-a-tat-boom* back, and I kick their ass in the end." Nabor stares at Beleco and decides not to tell him how all the brave men fell, how Pará, Manaus, Micuçu, Dentinho would eventually fall too, all of them already past their expiration dates. It's upsetting talking to a child who doesn't have long to live, a dead kid who's only still there by accident.

Nabor lets the film images flicker to life. That violent boy from the São Carlos bar went out, left the Black girl at home, and was caught by the cops and handcuffed to two others, and the three of them were thrown off the top of a cliff. Four were put in garbage bags, thrown into the trash cans on São Roberto. Six or seven were burned in tires. The smell of burnt human flesh filling the houses and streets, and the drunks in Raimundo's bar telling stories. And him thinking the problem is that this new generation no longer kisses their elders' hands. Everything more and more out of control, their minds no longer in charge of their arms, each of their arms like a head, each of their legs like a head too, and then suddenly their left hands don't know any more what their right hands are doing. The result: brothers are born as enemies and wars bleed everything out. The tracer bullets, the lack of leadership, the smell of burning flesh. "Why are you looking at me like that, like I'm worthless?" Beleco threatens, his eyes watering. "It's nothing like that, Beleco, leave this old man alone, go hang with your gang."

"You having a hard time?" Beleco pulls out a wad of bills and sticks half of them into Nabor's hands, who considers refusing the money but then swallows his pride. "Careful out there, Beleco."

"You take care too, old man." Beleco holds up his thumb and forefinger, "*Rat-a-tat-boom*!"

"*Rat-a-tat-boom* right back at you."

How weird it feels to be carrying cash! Life feels lighter, his feet nimble. He barely even notices that he's running, ready to surprise everyone, to buy a round for Guile Xangô and Vovô do Crime. He's running straight to Nelson's bar and he's happy when he turns onto Sampaio Ferraz and realizes that it's a market day. The woman who repairs pots and pans must be there and Nabor thinks he might finally be able to invite her for a drink, something might even happen between us, it would be nice to end the night with her in a room at the Halley, I'm sure she'd be down for it, she's always flirting with me, and then he grabs a few bills from the wad of cash and puts them in his left pocket, hides the rest in his underwear, and decides to surprise Guile Xangô some other day, because if Vovô do Crime finds out that he's loaded right now he wouldn't leave him alone.

Sampaio Ferraz is teeming with people. "Poor Seu Nonô," Lana clings to Nabor as she sobs and drags him into the crowd, telling him what he already knows, that Seu Nonô is eighty and plays cards all day, doesn't drink, doesn't smoke, doesn't eat meat, just makes fun of all the drunks, complains about young people, says he still fucks once a day. Not Dona Vilma, his wife, who's fifty and fucks everyone but Seu Nonô. "Seu Nonô is hilarious, who would've guessed he would do that," Ruth says. Nabor remembers the day Seu Nonô came out of the barbershop with a fresh new haircut saying, "It's time!" no one knew for what, then he fell onto the sidewalk. People laughed, but he just lay there. Pedrão took Seu Nonô to the hospital and Nabor prayed for him not to die on the street, not like that.

Then Nabor sees more than thirty tents set up on the street and shuffles on the wet ground covered in blood, though when he looks closer, he sees it's the sticky juice of oranges, watermelons, tomatoes, and maybe only a bit of blood. A small crowd surrounds Seu Nonô's old car and he's sitting at the wheel in complete shock. He's run over half the market. He stopped the car only after four people were dead and half a dozen injured, started sobbing. A police officer holding a gun shouts at the crowd that wants to lynch Seu Nonô. "Poor Seu Nonô," says Míriam, throwing herself into Vovô do Crime's arms. More cops arrive and manage to get Seu Nonô out of there, while people throw eggs and vegetables and scream.

Nabor walks around the edges of the disaster's commotion, getting flashbacks from the prison massacre, and his stomach hurts. He hears screaming and sees a guy holding a knife and gets ready to run, but it's just a piece of wood from the tentpole and not a sharp blade. He sees the car in the middle of the market and remembers the time Nonô humiliated him and thinks this is well-deserved. He sees Seu Nonô's face again, behind the windshield, he sees the prison warden, cowering, surrounded by the rioters. He tries to feel sorry for the old man because he must be shitting his pants right now, but he can't.

Nabor meets Guile Xangô and Vovô do Crime at Luiz's bar. "Nonô is much better than you, killed half a dozen in just one go," Vovô do Crime says to Nabor. "And he's not even going to going to prison because he can just plead insanity." And he continues chatting with Guile Xangô like nothing happened, as if someone hadn't plowed into the crowd at the market, as if the dead and injured hadn't been driven away in ambulances. "An atomic bomb on the metro line,"

Vovô do Crime says. Nabor doesn't need to pay attention, he's heard this plan countless times before. The idea was to hold the whole city hostage. To place a bomb in a metro station in Zona Sul and threaten to blow everything up. All the residents of Zona Sul stampeding to Petrópolis or even farther out of town. They wouldn't be able to carry anything with them, just the clothes on their backs. They'd also take over the radio and TV stations and use them to give their orders. Nabor thinks Vovô do Crime should go back to the asylum he escaped from. He was the head of the asylum. "Insane!" Nabor shouts.

The pan repair lady comes in, sits down, and starts telling the story again, every unnecessary detail described at length, Seu Nonô's tragedy. Vovô do Crime pretends to listen attentively, drags the chair closer to her, and starts to comfort the woman, one of his hands on her breasts, the other on her thigh. Nabor lets his anger bubble up, maybe today would be a good day to stab Vovô. Then he feels immensely tired; the world has changed. Today he woke up to the roosters crowing at dawn: "Help! Help!" And others shouting back, "Help! Help!" There's nothing else for him to wait for.

THE COMADRES

Dedé complains about her boss, the bitch wanted her to work late because she was throwing a party for a friend coming back from London. Leila talks about her current patient, a violent old lady who likes to pinch people, she's like a mischievous child, but at least she'll die fresh and clean, a great privilege. Lucinha can't stand working at the bar anymore, especially for that stingy hick from Paraíba who likes to yell at her, but what can she do? Brechó is happy as a manicurist, the salon is doing well, and she has a good clientele. Núbia is looking for someone to help her at the cart where she sells corn on the cob in Largo de São Francisco, outside the college.

They've been living together for more than ten years, they love each other, they hate each other, they put up with each other. They fight and make up. They are good at drinking. They get off work and drink from Friday night until Sunday afternoon, nonstop, opening and closing the bars. In those ten years, they've changed men, jobs, everything, but they're still drinking, always together. And they pride themselves on drinking beer and nothing but beer. And they're even prouder that they don't need a man, that they don't need any bum to save them, they can pay their own bills, they have good credit, and have never stolen from anyone.

It's eight o'clock on a Friday night, and Dedé is the first one to arrive and sit at the sidewalk table outside Assis's bar. Soon Brechó and Lucinha join her, Leila shows up apologizing for her lateness, but you're late only if you arrive after Núbia, always the last to show up. Finally. Núbia is there, jumping up and down, waving at everyone, full of kindliness no one wants or even notices. The group is complete. In the long night that will follow, men and women will stop by, have a drink with them, chat for a bit, but the group will stay together there until the end, the Comadres.

Assis sees that the whole group is present and brings the first two bottles of beer. Dedé fills their glasses, they toast one another, "May we all be widows," and the journey begins. With each sip, they shed their individuality and take on a shared personality. But not yet, they're no lightweights.

If regret could kill, Leila thinks, I'd already be at my own memorial. Why, why, why? It was hard to explain. The first mistake was agreeing to share a room with Dedé. When she lived alone she had a hard time paying the rent, the phone bill, the building fees, and sometimes she even went hungry, but only for two, three days, never more than that. The second mistake was letting Dedé start to take care of her. It was her house, her life. Now, living with Dedé, she had more money, she could even occasionally splurge, but was it worth it? When she had been alone, she was more herself. She did more. Now she was Dedé's friend. Even her friends were now Dedé's friends. There were times when she answered the phone five times in one morning and every single time it was someone asking to speak with Dedé, all her former friends. She'd become Dedé's secretary in her own house. None of them can tell that Dedé is a phony? That she talks shit about everyone behind their backs? That she's a snake? A Judas? And Leila's sleeping on the pull-out couch in the living room while Dedé is in the bedroom fucking Rafa. Moaning loudly, screaming, howling. Can't Rafa see it's all an act?

"Socorro! Socorro!" The Comadres laugh as they watch Guile Xangô standing at the door, a pool cue in his hand, shouting at the short red-haired old woman across the street. Socorro crosses the street and lets him hug her tightly. Only Guile Xangô would talk to her like this, making a scene, and she doesn't like it. She doesn't know how a man like that, intelligent and distinguished, can hang with that crowd. An angel, a prince. Guile Xangô out here, because he is Guile Xangô among the wolves, or the Shepherd of the Wolves. Socorro withdraws from his arms, greets that whore Dedé with a nod, always with the other sluts, and rushes to get into the house. Now from the window, Socorro sees Guile Xangô down there sitting among the sluts, drinking and smoking, surrounded by whores and thieves. Throwing his life away, wasting his kindness and education, because he was a well-mannered man, the most well-mannered in all of Maia.

"I think you're kind of into this man," her daughter says.

"Me? I'm way too old for that. Besides, he's not my cup of tea. I just feel sorry for him."

"Talk to him a bit, who knows if he's not looking to do some charity?" Socorro lets go of her daughter's arm, and she walks away laughing. From below, he sees her and shouts again, "Socorro! Socorro!" She waves back, and he can't see how red her face is.

The Comadres can barely understand what Guile Xangô is saying, his speech has always been a bit incomprehensible, but they follow his gestures, his eyes, and they think it would be fun to hook up with him, to see if he's also a gentleman in the sheets, not their own sheets, the ones at the Halley, but his friends are already calling from the inside, and it's weird that he's only warm, all huggy and kissy, with the stuck-up old ladies who call him Guile Xangô. Or is he into something else? Guile Xangô comes out saying that the next round is on him, and the Comadres say thanks.

They keep drinking, getting hammered, getting numb, the wall is going up. But there they are, the biker kids going up and down Maia, and only Dedé thinks that all these bikes are probably stolen and that none of these kids will live long.

But Brechó is thinking that too, when she sees Dafé doing those stupid stunts to show off, and a hatred rises in her for that kid who got her nephew Beleco in trouble. "This Dafé kid came to the Paulo de Frontin gas station, I'd already cleaned out the cash register, but I wanted to get a tub of ice cream, and then the men showed up, things got out of hand, and Dafé had to run away, hear me out, I'm a minor."

Just yesterday, when she was going out to visit Beleco, walking to the metro station, staring with contempt at the two women distributing evangelical pamphlets, magazines, and newspapers to try to convert people, Brechó had thought life was good. She took a pamphlet, dismissed that talk of Jesus the Savior. This is what she believes: she believes that if you get down on your knees, lift your eyes to the skies, ask with genuine faith, a pure heart, everything will happen for you. She believes in positive thinking, angels, gnomes. She doesn't envy anyone. She doesn't have a single bad thought. But she hasn't been thinking straight lately. She watches TV but doesn't see anything, she talks but doesn't hear what she says. She knows some ten psalms by heart, she loves the twenty-third. And the thirty-fifth. She believes in miracles. She crosses the Red Sea: on this side, a wall of lies and crimes; on the other, a wall of massacres and scandals. You can only follow the road that has opened in front of you, divine, white with salt. She wasn't in Sodom, she wasn't in Gomorrah, she left before the destruction. She won't be there at the end of the world when they tally up the dead bodies because she'll have left two days before on vacation. She's a saint. But Beleco is in prison, a boy who needs another chance, and Dafé is playing around Maia, idolized because he exchanged shots with the police and came out alive.

The wall is going up. It's not a wall yet, it's something lighter, like a fog, and through the fog she can still see the most beautiful thing in Maia walking into Assis's bar amid a lustful silence. She's a real blond, green eyes, toned body, but no, her body's also real, her own, she says. She always wears short, tight clothes. In the morning, she takes her young son to day care, then comes back, stands there, by the bar, outside the building where she lives, talking, letting herself be ogled. No man approaches her, they just let a look of desire slide over her tanned legs, her small breasts, her round, hard ass. She wants to be an actress or model, but she doesn't lift a finger to make it happen. She is a cinephile, she has tons of movies at home, she's always complaining about her loneliness, but she'd rather be alone, living just for her son, who's her whole world. At the end of each month, she wears the same long blue dress to receive the old man. The driver opens the door of the imported car, and the old man, tall, a bit foreign, a bit like he owns the world, walks into the building. Half an hour later the old man leaves, the driver opens the door for him, and the fancy car glides away, a sophisticated machine. She wears the long blue dress for the rest of the day, and everyone can see she isn't being herself. The old man is her father. When the blond was married, soon after her honeymoon, she got into a fight with her husband, and he hit her. The old man came to confront him, and her husband said she was his wife now. He was young, a jiu-jitsu fighter (they'd met at the gym), and he shouted and punched her father hoping he'd go away. The old man emptied the magazine of his automatic in him. He died in his wife's arms. She was pregnant. She went crazy for a few months after this incident, was admitted into a clinic, and only left when it was time to deliver the baby at another clinic. It was a natural birth, and it seems she was cured when she saw the baby. When her father dies, the first thing she'll do is change her son's name, name him after her late husband, then get her hands on her father's inheritance (the old man is rich and she's an only child, her mother died when she was five years old, he'd raised her by himself with a lot of nannies, and she'd promised she would never get married—"Never, Daddy"—but you don't really know what you're saying when you're fourteen), when she gets ahold of the inheritance, she'll finally start living her own life.

The Comadres are filming Guile Xangô opening the car door for the blond so she'll show her silky legs and black panties. Dedé looks at her own table, fixes her gaze on Leila's sour face and a chill passes along her spine when her friend meets her gaze with eyes full of tears and hatred. Dedé gets up and says, "Pee." On the way to the bathroom, she thinks Leila is sick. She drinks, lives, and gets dressed in the morning on the salary she makes watching people die. She is trained as a nurse, but caring for patients at home is better than working in a hospital, she says. The old woman she takes care of, for example, has three rich daughters, and this illness eating away at her is a horrible thing to watch. The woman is just skin and bones, barely has a voice left, only her big eyes still tie her to this world, because she can't even eat properly anymore. But her eyes are still there, alive, blue, intelligent. She never sleeps. She just watches, watches everything all the time and doesn't say a word, doesn't complain, in fact she's pretty easy. The diapers are disposable, and she smells the same as everyone else. She's good with her medication. She even likes swallowing her pills. And watching. But Leila is drinking more and more. Every day she has off she spends drinking. And never fucking. There are tons of men after her, but she doesn't care for them. She doesn't even realize that she's becoming just like her patients.

Dedé comes around and kisses Leila on the neck. "Get off me, what the hell is this, I like men!" And they all look upset, staring at Núbia, who crosses her arms, closed off. It was because of the first and last man she'd had sex with. He was twenty-three and she was thirteen, he got her good. By the time she was eighteen she had three children and they got married. He was always a good husband. He brought home every bit of money he had, never let them go without anything. Until he lost his job and, in just three months, they were flat broke. She had to start working in people's homes. He started drinking. He hit her the first time because she got home late one night. She was at the boss's daughter's birthday celebration but he didn't believe her. He hit her other times, and she thought maybe he was jealous. Then he started hitting her for no reason. She ran away with the kids three times, but she had no extended family to run to, she stayed at her neighbors' house and always came back. The kids needed a father. She filed a police report, but the police chief said that there wouldn't be a cell big enough if he arrested every husband who hit his wife. She better behave, she better accept it. She tried to tell him that she hadn't done anything to deserve it, that he'd gotten used to living at her expense and that something terrible would happen any day. She came back there at least four more times and every time the police chief screamed and kicked her out, he had better stuff to do. She came back a fifth time, covered in blood. I told you something terrible was going to happen. He's there in the kitchen, dead. When she got out of jail, she didn't have children anymore, she'd lost her boys to the world. She started working as a cleaner. Then she met Gisele, and they started living together. They managed to save money and buy a cart to sell corn on the cob. Gisele was a sweetheart. But she was a different person when she was drunk. She knew that Gisele went after men from time to time, but she tolerated it, she was in love with her, she was afraid of losing her, and she always came back in the end. Now, just a moment ago, Gisele had sat there, in front of her, drunk, naked, with that contemptuous laugh, saying, "You're raggedy, you look terrible," shouting that what she really needed was a thick cock, shouting things that were unbearable to hear, things she couldn't stand when she had a knife in her hand.

"Let's go to Luiz's," Lucinha says. "It's weird here." They ask for the bill, split the cost, and walk together to Luiz's bar. On the corner of Sampaio, they run into Xuxa walking Karina and Björk. The Comadres cluck at Xuxa, the poodles bark back, and the Comadres also cluck at the dogs, and Xuxa hurries away, pretending they weren't talking to her. Later, around midnight, Xuxa will appear again, all dolled up to sit at Luiz's bar. She'll sit at one of the tables outside. A car will stop, she'll get in, then come back again. It'll go like this until morning, the playboys keeping her on a tight leash. She doesn't charge them anything. She enjoys it. All the sex workers hate Xuxa, though there's something about her that makes it hard for anyone to dislike the bitch. Apparently, she is good at everything she does, and she does everything. But she's so insecure, not charging them is her way of showing her superiority. The Comadres wait with growing impatience for the first creases to appear in her cakey makeup, and then they cackle.

Through the fog, Toninho walks into Luiz's bar and the Comadres, giddy and jostling against him, stain his white clothes and laugh. He'd washed those clothes in the mansion's laundry sink, while the women complained he was too slow and meticulous. He hung the clothes on the line, waited for them to dry, took them down, ironed them on his single bed with three wooden legs and three stacked bricks where the fourth should be. He also washed his white sneakers, painted his toenails and fingernails with clear nail polish, applied balm to his thick lips, put a pair of earrings in his small ears (two faux silver hoops), combed his hair and tied it with a white bandana. He picked a table and put his bag on it. He goes to the counter and orders a chicken drumstick and a Coke. He takes the money out of a little pouch (the bills rolled up together with the coins) and pays. Then he grabs the plate with the chicken drumstick and puts it next to the bag. He goes back inside one more time and grabs the Coke and the glass and puts them next to the plate. Then he goes back inside again, this time to get the change, counts the money and puts it in the little purse. He sits at the table. He moves the bag to the chair on his right and looks at the drumstick, the Coke, the glass. He gets up and asks for a fork and knife. Now he's sitting down, delicately eating the chicken leg with a knife and fork, and drinking Coca-Cola in small, careful sips. He's done well in the past, nowadays not so much. Hasn't dated anyone in two years. He was fired from the salon two months ago and he doesn't know why. He doesn't drink, doesn't smoke, doesn't make a fuss. He doesn't associate with bad people. He likes finesse; he eats his drumsticks with a knife and fork. He was once a pretty boy. He has class, but no one really cares about class, everyone prefers youth. His elders, who only like handsome, muscular boys, deride his white clothes, his delicate gestures, his table manners, his poise, his fragility. The Comadres know he can't always afford food and that at the end of the month he won't have enough money for rent or a cheap love motel.

Now, at four in the morning, the Comadres are fully behind a solid wall and laughing and laughing from inside the thick fog. At five o'clock Luiz starts splashing soapy water on the last customers so they'll leave. The Comadres go to Nelson's, then to Chiquinho's on top of the hill, and at ten in the morning they walk back down São Carlos to Luiz's. They're so drunk they can't see straight anymore.

They stop by Dedé's to take a shower, end up taking a nap, and then go back to drinking. Saturday night, they go to Lima to dance pagode, it looks like they're being paraded on floats at Carnaval, people clap and they picture themselves on the TV screen, they imagine that somewhere in rural Minas, in Fortaleza, deep into the state of Rio, their relatives are watching, the whole family there to see the Comadres, while they also watch each other, from their parents' couch, without ever having left, and the dead are also there, their grandparents, everyone, and the children they never had are beautiful, and the children who died are happy, and the whole city is watching the wonderful Comadres.

They have visions, flashes of reality: Brechó sees Dafé dying across the street; Núbia sees Gisele begging on the streets and hands her a coin; Leila sees an old man thanking her for his own death; Lucinha feels the gun in her hand and shudders; Dedé sees fat and bossy Mirtes crossing Maia and she kneels at her feet and bangs her head, though she didn't want to, Mirtes' laughter nearly wakes her up, but it's laughter that comes from another level and she bangs her head with pleasure. And life is good, there's no shouting about the dust, or about their shoddy work, just gratitude and universal love. But they're realists, and between one step and the next, between one drink and the next, between one trip to the bathroom and the next, they can already feel the cold touch of the shackles from Monday's crippling hangover, but they keep going.

On Sunday morning, leaving Lima, they come into Luiz's bar one more time and bow down to the Mandelas. Until Sunday afternoon stretches out over everything like a huge dirty sheet.

THE CLUMSY ONES

Mestre Amilton believes theater can change the world. "All the world's a stage, and we're all merely players," he says. His group, called the Clumsy Ones, is made up of everyone from kids and teens to retirees and well-behaved lunatics. In their presentations, the group focuses on both acting and the audience. They perform at the skate park, near the metro station, or up the hill on São Carlos, or right in the middle of the farmers market, if the market is on that day. Guile Xangô watches and films the Clumsy Ones in action, promising Mestre Amilton he'll "boost his guerrilla theater" while Vovô do Crime makes fun of the actors and the spectators. Here is a snippet of a scene:

LITTLE LIFE: Lúcio, a playboy with the soul of an artist, decided it was a good idea to adopt Geninho. The two of them became thick as thieves, like Lennon-McCartney, Jagger-Richards, Harley-Davidson, Batman-Robin, Verlaine-Rimbaud. And me in the middle. Lúcio got Geninho off the streets and out of poverty. They soon became fixtures in all the popular places. They did multimedia installations, threw bacchanalian orgies, and recorded a rock album in English. Lúcio never figured out that Geninho's greatest talent was failing. Like the quote from Sartre, "In poetry the person who loses is the one who wins. And the real poet chooses losing to the point of dying so he can win. He is certain of the total failure of the human enterprise and finds a way to fail in his own life, in order to bear witness, through his individual failure, to human failure in general." After Geninho's first episode, poor Lúcio, he was like a hysterical Juliet. He was shaking so much, so intensely, he couldn't even drive his own car. I was the one who had to take Geninho to the hospital. There were other suicide attempts disguised as overdoses. Lúcio tried to leave with Geninho and his heart stopped, he nearly passed on to the other side. Lúcio's parents saw there was only one way out of this: to kill Geninho.

HITMAN: So they hired me. And here I am.

GENINHO: You've been following me all day and night, on the street, at the bar, at parties, at orgies. You haven't given me a moment's peace. I thought you'd be the death of me, the death of everything I love. And now you're here, inside my dream. Welcome. Let's resolve this death thing once and for all. I've unsheathed my sword.

HITMAN: You're scared. You're weak. You flirt with death, but you can't let go of your shitty little life. If it were up to me, I would not be this ridiculous death, this sword fight, a romantic death fit for a king's musketeer. If it were up to me, I would be an outlaw death, direct, with a sharp knife. A favela death, with a sudden burst of gunfire and your body burning among the tires, your ashes spraying the rooftops. A suicide bomber's death, shards of your love pit stuck to the walls. But you chose a swordfight, a ridiculous and old-fashioned duel.

GENINHO: Who hired you?

HITMAN: I was hired to kill you.

GENINHO: I got it, Lúcio's father is a touchy guy.

HITMAN: But there's nothing like a mother's love.

GENINHO: This is getting tiresome. I hate the monotony of repetitive scenes and past lives.

HITMAN: Parents and children are monotonous. Daily life too. And what's life like without theater?

GENINHO: Sure, theater is life with a bit more rehearsing. Enough of this nonsense.

HITMAN: I was actually enjoying it.

GENINHO: Enough. Kill me already! I'm just a living being and you're a murderer for hire.

HITMAN: But I can only kill you gently.

GENINHO: Come on! Get on with it! I'd rather die than be bored at this point.

HITMAN: And I told mother courage, "I'll do the job. And it'll be clean."

GENINHO: Then do it! Do the job!

HITMAN: Then she said, "If you kill the guy, you'll kill my son too. If he dies, my son will kill himself right there in front of me."

GENINHO: Yeah . . . You can't know for sure what anyone would do.

MATADOR: And mother courage said something else, "You have to make sure nothing will happen to him . . . that . . . pervert. If anything happens to him, my son will say it was his father's doing or that I allowed it to happen."

GENINHO: Then do it. That's your final kiss. Come on, let's go! Kiss me on the mouth!

HITMAN: Yeah, but if I kill you, I'll be doing you a favor.

GENINHO: So what? I've already been murdered. Dying again is just a technicality.

HITMAN: Well, you'll have to face it. You're going to have to live life to the last drop.

GENINHO: But I came here to see the blood. I didn't come to see heaven.

HITMAN: All you know about is shit, you coward. You've never even seen blood.

GENINHO: I once saw two crazy boys shoving each other, crying, learning lessons in murder.

HITMAN: Shut up! You're a wimp.

THE HITMAN HITS GENINHO WITH A ROSE. GENINHO FALLS. THE KILLER LAUGHS AND STARTS COVERING GENINHO WITH FLOWERS. LITTLE LIFE COMES IN WITH A TASER AND TASES THE HITMAN. THE HITMAN FALLS.

LITTLE LIFE (*kicking the Hitman's body*): And that's for the "shitty little life!"

PARÁ AND MANAUS

Pará is always nursing this wound. He was five years old when his father beat up his mother then fucked her and then told her to go make him something to eat. She went to the kitchen, made the food, woke him up, he ate, went back to sleep, and started to convulse. His mother got into the pirogue with him, rowed to her sister's house, and disappeared. They only found his father's body three days later because of the smell, but everyone said he died from a snake bite. That's what he says, Pará.

In his first week at his aunt's house, Pará kept crying for his mother. So his uncle and cousin took him to the river. At some point, his uncle threw Pará in the water and Pará screamed, shouted that they were trying to kill him. They went back home as Pará cried and shivered. His grandmother, his mother's mother, started keeping him in her arms. The next day, she again took Pará to the river, got in the water with him to play with the dolphins. Then they left and walked through the forest. They picked herbs, flowers, seeds. At home, his grandmother continued playing with Pará until nightfall. The flower petals and seeds turned into stars, roads, boats, and flying carpets. Grandma became Pará's true mother. That's what he says.

Pará eventually learned how to swim, but he didn't stay there, between the forest and the big river. He followed his mother to the big city. He ended up becoming a mechanic and an excellent driver. He doesn't say how he learned, only that boat engines and car engines all sound the same, and he liked grease and oil better than water. Winning over Pará was easy: just call him Ayrton Senna. It was even easier to piss him off. "Go, Michael Schumacher!" When the crooks wanted some cash from the bank, Pará was always their choice. It was easy. He did it more for the adventure than for the money.

It's the middle of the night. Pará is driving down the main section of the Rio-Niterói bridge at two hundred kilometers per hour with some ten police cars after him. He feels like he's going to make it but then a tire suddenly bursts (a gunshot?). The men can't believe what they're seeing: Pará still manages to keep control of the vehicle and keeps going.

Then he realizes that he won't make it after all: a row of police cars ahead. Pará's ass is against the wall. But he keeps going and crashes into the railing. The door opens and spits out his passenger over the railing, down below, into the water.

Pará gets out of the car. The men already know what he's going to do. And he's doing it wrong. He crosses the road and jumps over the railing on the other side of the bridge. If he had jumped from the right side, where he was before, he would've fallen into the water, and he could've gotten to Caju and disappeared. But he jumped onto dry land, among the containers and cranes. Now he's down there all mangled.

The worst part is that the car was clean, an Italian super machine a playboy had asked Pará to warm up for him. No one understood why he'd done what he did.

Everyone's there just listening to Manaus's nonsense. The party had already gone sour when he ran into the house, covered in oil from head to boots, shouting, "I need a shower, damn it," and locked himself in the bathroom for an hour. Then he came out shouting, "Food, I want food," and then after the fifth bite, "Turn that damn music off," and after the next bite, cutting through the silence, "Pará lost," and he threw his plate, glass, and bottle, everything up in the air.

Now everyone is there, two in the morning on this miserable Saturday, listening to Manaus's nonsense, seeing tears run down his face, seeing him comb his long hair with his fingers, and no one believing a word. And what goes through the men's heads is: Manaus did Pará in, he did, he drowned him, so to speak, he's now sleeping with the fishes, and he did it because Pará was the only one who would confront him, he didn't cower at the sight of the pretend big boss, he laughed at Manaus's platform boots, he looked down at him when he spoke, laughing, but never being outright disrespectful, giving him advice, treating Manaus as if he were his son, though they were the same age, maybe give or take two years. Pará was smart, had a good head, more of a boss than the boss.

And to the women: Manaus smeared Pará's reputation, he was jealous of Pará because we liked dancing with him, sleeping with him, and he'd already put three babies in us, and there was one more on the way, six months in Lana's belly already, and Lana was thinking, "This one is coming to avenge his father, when the time comes, maybe not now, or tomorrow, one day, or if they don't do right by me and my son, and my man, betrayed like this."

Manaus senses that there's a sharp sadness in the air and starts laughing and telling his stories about up north, where he and his "brother" came from. "Pará is my brother, always will be." And he goes on saying how they sold monkeys, fish, frogs, and plants to the gringo researchers studying their home, "It was good money," until they were arrested and met Altamirando in jail, Altamira for short, and they helped him catch someone by the name of Bartolomeu Gaúcho, who was always causing trouble with farmers and loggers there. They kidnapped this Gaúcho guy, broke two of his bones, shot him in the head twelve times and threw everything by the Santarém-Cuiabá highway.

Then they did away with another guy from the same group, someone by the name of Felício, one bullet in the mouth, just one because the guy talked too much and was always causing trouble with the rubber tappers, wanting to try and put an end to the fires, stop the construction of the Belo Monte hydroelectric plant (who likes living in the dark?), and put an end to the mahogany trade, which was bringing in a lot of money, "A beautiful thing to see the river full of tall tree trunks, each one worth more than a car, dollar prices."

They were surfing the waves of the pororoca when they got caught with seven hundred and seventy kilos of explosive gel, a thousand bottles of gunpowder, two hundred and twenty detonators, and two hundred and fifty meters of detonating cord. They'd been following the loot since it left the

Port of Manaus on a tour boat to Tefé. Then they loaded everything onto another boat running the Tefé-Japurá circuit. The final destination was Limoeiro, on the Japurá River, on the Colombian border. But then the federal dogs wiretapped them and charged them both with "smuggling, possession of false documents to defraud, and endangering the welfare and property of others," big fucking deal. And the cops made an even bigger deal that the entire load was stored in boxes of food, candy and cookies, inside a plastic bag in the boat's hold, without any protection. "One spark and everyone was going to hell. Boom!"

No one laughs (everyone groans, "Maybe he's gone blind and thinks no one watches TV?"), nor do they have time to stop Lana from jumping on Manaus with a knife in her hand, slicing his shoulder open, though she wanted the throat, then the faster ones manage to grab Lana and drag all her anger to the next room. Then they have to convince Manaus not to whack her. What's going through the men's heads: You got this close, Lana, but you need to get it done right around here.

Locked in her room, Lana fears deep down that her life and her son's are hanging by a thread. She doesn't know whether to go to sleep or keep watch, but she has visions. She sees Pará jump off the Rio-Niterói bridge, from way up high, and fall into the oil-stained water, without making a sound. He hides in the shadow of a huge concrete pillar, dodging the lights coming after him. Far away, other lights, the still lights of the tall buildings, and the flickering lights of the big neon signs. Pará sees the blurry outline of the huge rusty ships floating in the bay like garbage, the dead ships. He decides to swim to one of them, the nearest one. A speedboat leaves the Navy base, on Mocanguê Island, with its siren on. And the lights, coming from above the bridge, continue to track Pará, but now they're going in the opposite direction. He reaches the ship and is astonished by its height. He swims to the bow and feels the outside of the boat with his hands until he finds the anchor chain. The speedboat lights up the bridge pillars, but Pará is here, going up the anchor chain, climbing onto the ship like a wet rat.

Pará walks up from the hold, goes into the engine room, gropes his way around, gets lost, finds himself, gets lost again, until he gets to a corridor lit up by a yellow light and starts opening doors. In the third one, he comes face to face with a mapinguari, covered in fur like a huge red monkey, attacking and devouring a hunter, starting from the head. The monster fixes its only eye on Pará, and its gigantic mouth, which goes all the way down to its belly, lets out a laugh and a burp. Pará closes the door and runs down the corridor, pursued by an old woman in black, with her hair covering her face, whistling like a terrified owl.

Then Pará manages to open the right door and comes into the room where Lana is sleeping, and he starts taking off his fish skin, getting naked, becoming more and more like a man so he can sleep in peace next to the woman mothering his son, and there they stay, the three of them, snuggled up inside the giant water lily.

K-9S

It was an absolute explosion. Nelson had decided to renovate the bar, paint the greasy walls a new color, and make it a little nicer. The stopgap workers (Léo and Monstrinho) managed to unearth the old bar counter, polished by the elbows of generations of drunks, from the swampy ground with sledgehammers, and a huge and fat-assed clan of rats scurried out of their clandestine hole in broad daylight. Thousands of screeching rats and their babies ran up Sampaio Ferraz, every man for himself, a stream of rats everywhere you looked.

Amarelinho, Edmundo, Targa, and Caveirinha were the first ones to try and save themselves, running up the street among the shaking and jumping legs of terrified women at the bar. All the businesses in the area closed their doors as if fleeing flash robbery. But when the four dogs saw patrons attacking Mickeys and Minnies with their feet, pool cues, broomsticks, and rocks, they found the courage to go back in and join in attacking the rats. In the commotion, they barked and whimpered, got hit by brooms and stones, and were almost shot at by an enthusiastic patron, could they not tell a rat from a dog? Targa, the bravest of the bunch, managed to corner a rat against the bookie's stand, then carried the trophy between her teeth to place by Nelson's feet. Upset by the devastating news that his business was now a public health hazard, Nelson kicked her, and the brave soldier let go of her trophy by the ungrateful man's feet and went to whine in front of the macumba cats, her humiliation heightened by the looks of contempt from the eight felines lying among saint figurines and seven-day candles, perfectly still and not turning a hair, not even lifting a claw, those cats who should have been the first to chase the long-tailed pests.

Still upset by Nelson's kick and with a gray taste of rat in her mouth, Targa thinks that humans can't even follow the most basic principles of canine love. Who truly loves animals? Who has enough time to take care of an animal? Who has room for a new friend in their lives? Who has the money to pay for everything an animal needs? To buy an animal's basic necessities like kibble, food and water dishes, toys for chewing and playing? Not one person on that street. It was a shame the witchy lady of the macumba house only liked cats, she stuffed them with so much food they were all overweight, motionless like plants, like the retired old men who played checkers and cards and sunbathed on the benches in the square by the metro station.

She didn't deserve to get kicked. She was part of a long lineage. After all, the world had more than six hundred million dogs, and Targa was the most beautiful of them all, the freest. Of course, there were more rats than dogs, billions of rats, minus one now. She didn't hate them, and in fact some men were nothing more than rats, but she didn't know what she thought or felt anymore, so she started to bark at the macumbeiro cats.

Amarelinho and Edmundo didn't feel as successful in the war against the rats. They knew they were cowardly. Caveirinha didn't even try, he didn't have time to go around playing anymore, he was old, just waiting for a bone feast. He was past his prime, like many a two-legged idiot. His calendar wasn't the same as a human's. At three months old he was already five years old, at one year old he was already fifteen, but more mature than most human kids in that area, who were always calling each other dogs and bitches, dancing to such loud music it sounded like it was made for the deaf. At two years old he was already almost twenty-four, at ten he was already fifty-two, and from then on he stopped counting, maybe he was fourteen, which made him seventy-two years old and entitled to sunbathe with the mangy old men outside the metro. If he made it to twenty, he'd reach the beautiful age of a hundred and one, and then, for sure, he wouldn't even be good enough to serve as a flea shelter.

All three of them knew they were not bred to hunt rats. They belonged to the Canidae family, which included about thirty-seven species of wolves, jackals, foxes, wild and domestic dogs. They were all carnivores and had specific hunting skills, armed with teeth to kill prey, chew meat, gnaw bones, and when necessary, to fight among themselves in their little groups, called a pack.

Canines walked on the tips of their toes. They had five of these "toes" on their front paws and four on their hind paws. Domestic dogs may have a fifth toe on their hind paws, though it's often removed, especially in purebred dogs. Caveirinha knew how to count, but the others didn't know that, and who cares? Science had not yet given a definitive answer to the question of how domestic dogs came to be. From a wolf, a jackal, a cross between a wolf and a jackal. From a coyote. Not so much from hyenas. There were fifty-thousand-year-old cave paintings found in Spanish caves that show dogs next to men hunting deer, bison, wild boar, and reindeer.

Edmundo hated Caveirinha's encyclopedic speeches, he was born with a silver spoon in his mouth and still couldn't let go of the juicy bone of his happy childhood, not even after years living in the gutter. But now, after hearing all this nonsense, Edmundo had enjoyed thinking that he might have had ancestors in ancient Rome, that they went into arenas fierce and proud, wearing iron collars with sharp blades like the ones from barbers and Paraíba outlaws, they fought against tigers and lions, they tore ancient Christians to pieces, the relatives of today's Christians shouting in the streets with that black book in their hands.

Amarelinho was all about peace and love, he'd never be a fight dog, not yesterday and much less today. His ancestors were certainly companion dogs, part of royalty. They were immortalized in paintings by the great masters, they were the subject of verses by poets and walked glorious stages in dramatic and passionate performances by playwrights. If it weren't for his ancestors, dogs wouldn't be found today on T-shirts, toys, greeting cards, movies, TV shows, commercials. He was proud to carry on the tradition and live his life as an artist.

Targa joined the K-9s and the four of them watched Xuxa walk by with her purebred pack. They hated purebreds. And they remembered the day Ruth took them to get vaccinated.

It wasn't the first time, and they were surprised by all the fuss. The needle prick didn't hurt that much. They paid the cats no mind, some of them brought in carriers or wrapped in towels, all desperate. Instead, they paid attention to their peers. The public vaccination clinic was set up in the church square and they were the only ones there not wearing a collar or a muzzle. They arrived like kings, but it was obvious some of the other patients there enjoyed much nicer lives.

They saw Poodles, supposedly the most intelligent breed, often used in shows and circus performances to do funny things and juggle, the idiots. The two Filas Brasileiros, great at breaking up fights and attacking criminals armed with things like broken bottles, their loose and thick skin making them more resistant to injuries, always ready to face anything, cross rivers, break through barbed wire, a row of cops.

A Rottweiler, that one you definitely didn't want to bite you, their bite force is the equivalent of two tons and, on their heels, they can reach up to a meter and a half high. A couple of Dalmatians, all proud because their relatives were in that movie, *One Hundred and One Dalmatians*, all running away from the crazy millionaire who wanted them for a fur coat, which wasn't a bad idea. But the K-9s had already seen many of them abandoned on the streets and they showed no gift whatsoever for surviving on asphalt.

A Doberman, another expert jumper, good at dodging kicks, shots, and knives, a real watchdog that can guard farms or industrial land. A Siberian Husky, originally from really far away, one of those that doesn't know how to behave indoors, furniture can't dodge their bites, nor shoes, or anything, they lose more hair than a well-trod carpet, and they don't know how to bark, but they howl beautifully, especially in the early hours of the morning to wake up the neighbors. They should be pulling a sled in the snow instead of sitting here in this heat.

And another cop, a German Shepherd, who at least makes up for it by also being a guide for the blind. A Pekingese couple, with that swaying gait, their bulging eyes, protruding farther than their flat snouts, growling bravely but never daring to bite anyone. Five or so pit bulls, the crazy ones, massacre professionals, proper fighters, four-legged fighting cocks, the terror of all children and old ladies. A masked Yorkshire, its face lost in its fur. A hideous Bulldog, indecisive, not sure if it was a dog or a bullfighter. About five Chihuahuas, a miniature dog, a toy dog.

A terrier, carbon copy of the actress who says she doesn't own the dog, the two are both mother and daughter at once. She and the dog met long before, in another life, in ancient Egypt, when the dog was a princess, and the actress was also part of the aristocracy. The two communicate in a humanimal language and also talk to trees, insects, and other creatures. They even talk to fish. Great things.

Targa just didn't tell the K-9s that the father of her future puppies was also there in line for vaccines. But she wouldn't be able to keep the secret for much longer.

She didn't like being in heat. Staying in that state for two weeks was completely inconvenient for someone of her social class. But who can fight their own hormones?

If she had a home, her owner would find her an experienced male and then her puppies would have a good future. She would be taken to a vet and then to a first-class hotel. But not her. She lived out on the streets and had to accept what the street gave her. Though she was lucky. She got to choose the father of her children herself.

Now she was on day fifty or sixty of her pregnancy, she wasn't sure, and she needed to find the right place. She chose the back of Caldo & Cana, Ruth's little bar. The only annoying thing was that Ruth's cat, Maga, was also pregnant. She thought Ruth might have favorites, but no, Ruth was a nice person.

Targa looked at Maga coming and going, wrapping herself around her owner's legs, and confusedly tried to picture how Ruth's life had changed. She remembered her dirty, smelly and sour, defending herself from beggars with a pocketknife or a broken bottle, sleeping under awnings, in Vavau's parking lot, at the square, and they were sisters, the two of them, sharing the same fate, sleeping in each other's arms through the cold nights, giving each other their warmth. Now Ruth was different, smelling of soap and fried pastel, always behind a counter, a little like the macumba lady, only much younger, and when Maga had kittens, she'd have a house full of cats just like the macumba lady.

She didn't understand, but who cared? Ruth lined the backyard with towels and newspapers. Ruth touched Targa's belly and felt the puppies move. Her teats were already dripping in anticipation. Targa looked uncomfortable, she couldn't find a comfortable position to lie down and sleep, and she was breathing fast like she was in pain, licking and looking at her vulva, refusing food, searching for her "nest." The contractions were visible in the muscles of her back, a downward movement. She hadn't realized it would be so hard. But she was comforted by Ruth's presence.

Edmundo couldn't take it anymore. The drunks with swollen feet sat there, their eyes glued to the TV sets, watching the civil defense firefighters, the army soldiers, the biologists, the oceanographers, the fishermen, the journalists, the reporters, the curious, all trying to free the humpback whale, ten meters long and weighing approximately ten tons of ignorance, unable to sniff out the path from Antarctica to Abrolhos, in Bahia, and now stranded on the Fort Imbuhy beach with its snout, fins, tail, and body covered in barnacles. Three days of that monstrous spectacle and they still hadn't tired of it.

A fire brigade boat, a Petrobras tugboat, and a fishing trawler also got stranded, or almost. On the seventh rescue attempt, the rope from the net that ensnared the whale from snout to giant tail came loose, and it ended up hitting two firefighters, one of them hurting his leg, the other breaking his arm.

Leo and Monstrinho hugged as they cried, Nabor buried his head in his chest and Vovô do Crime started talking loudly, "small men, incompetent, small men," "complete asses," and the reporter started saying that the whale had died after countless rescue attempts, its body would be taken by a Petrobras tugboat to the port dock, and then the monstrous dead creature would be towed to a truck and taken to a garbage dump, after being autopsied by the biologists who were unable to save it.

And Vovô started saying that life is beautiful, but every now and then you get stuck, there are always people working to pull your ten tons of sand off the beach, a hundred firemen show up, but they know much more about drownings and fires, a trawler shows up and the trawler also gets stuck, a tugboat almost gets stranded too and can't tow anything, there are a thousand curious bystanders hoping the tide doesn't go out, but it does, and you're left there shaking your tail in the sand, there's nothing else to do when you swim and swim and die at the beach, at people's feet, at life, you're ten tons of anger, of laughter, and you can't do anything but shit mountains at times like these, and all you can say is fuck it who gives a shit it's okay that's it tomorrow there's more and maybe worse—and he started shouting, "You're all beached, you dumbasses, beached," and Monstrinho clings to Vovô neck saying, "It's true, it's true," and Vovô pushes Monstrinho away, "Stop drooling on my new shirt."

Edmundo wants to howl with joy, but he feels the old sting on the neck from the gunshot he got from the man on the motorcycle, it's rising up and he knows that if it reaches his head it will turn into a headache, and he'll have seven hellish days ahead of him.

Amarelinho gets Edmundo and Caveirinha to visit Targa. They start walking, smelling the millions of familiar smells, looking for a new scent, spraying posts and tires with their pee. The good smells and the bad smells, the victorious and the failed ones, the living and the dead, the white and the black, the short and the long, the shallow and the deep, the daytime and the nighttime, the human and the inhuman smells. Caveirinha can no longer tell the difference between smells and sounds, and since he can only see a blur, he believes that men are followed by other shadows born from their thoughts or from their past lives, in addition to the shadows light casts on their bodies, and he cannot explain whether these shadows are angels or souls. Edmundo doesn't want to chat and is on the verge of falling into that stage where even his own tail is his enemy.

Two men pass on a motorcycle and Amarelinho, against his will, despite what happened to Edmundo, runs to bite the heel of one of them. He runs for it, the taste of leather and grease between his teeth, but the boot slips away and comes down on his back with the familiar pain, sometimes from a broom or a club, and he sits on the sidewalk, breathless, his tongue hanging out, regretting that he always lets himself get carried away by that childish impulse to chase tires and heels.

The smell of boots, the taste of shoe polish, the pain of the black kick of the boot, all of these remind him of Salgueirão, the crazy sergeant. As he catches his breath, Amarelinho returns to that night when Salgueirão left the military police hospital, down the hill from São Carlos, took a police bus and started to collect all the criminals off Maia and Sampaio, Targa thought he was going to make soap out of them, and Caveirinha had to growl that it wasn't true, that it was all a way for Salgueirão to sniff out smells, lots of them, and for free.

The first puppy came out of her, still wrapped in the amniotic sac. Like she'd been doing this her whole life, Targa tore the sac with her teeth and pulled it down. She cut the umbilical cord and licked the puppy. The other five arrived one after the other, all greeted with licks of joy and nervousness. When the labor was over, Targa calmed down, her breathing returned to normal, the contractions stopped, and five mouths were attacking her, hungry for fresh life.

Now Ruth is cleaning everything, wiping Targa's body with a towel, offering a bowl of ground beef and dog food. All the puppies are still attached to her full breasts, the greedy babies. Exhausted and happy, she's finally able to sleep a little.

Amarelinho and Caveirinha sniffed the babies, but Targa didn't want anyone to touch her puppies. Edmundo showed up alone and was beside himself when he saw that none of the puppies looked like him. He felt betrayed, kept hanging around, and when Ruth's wasn't paying attention, he attacked the feline, who was pregnant and slow and couldn't get away. Ruth delivered the kittens, managed to save only two of them, and didn't know what else to do. Until Targa showed up, took the kittens, and adopted them both as if they were her own. It became an attraction at Caldo & Cana, with customers eating there just to see to see the spectacle, both dogs and cats suckling on an attentive and focused Targa, half knowing and half not knowing that what she was doing was more than human.

SIBYL MAYA CARPE DIEM

He's the man, the clown. He might have run away from a circus, an insane asylum, or a wedding. From a zoo, the board of a big company, or a flying saucer he lost on a tourist trip to planet Earth he and the aliens had decided to take just to see what hell was like. Maybe the most likely scenario is that he absconded from a wedding and now is here licking his wounds. His name: Guile Xangô.

He has several nicknames too, Professor, Pastor, Doctor, Poet, Nutcase, Life, Janjo (Janjo!), Xaxango. A very beautiful, distinguished and very angry lady once shouted in the middle of the farmers market, "Life, you are Life," but he is Guile Xangô.

He performs little tricks for children, pulling a coin out of his nose, putting the piece of change into the kids' hands, and waiting for it to get warm, but he himself is the actual trick. His eyes turn green or blue. Sometimes he's tall and thin, going from elegant to cadaverous; other times he's fat, heavy, almost rotund. He moves back and forth between healthy and ill overnight or from day to night. He likes the beach. He gets some sun and suddenly looks Black. Even his hair grows thicker. He can be white and Black, like the boys in the movement.

When he turns Black, he's happy to sing, play samba, say nonsense words in English, a big old party. When he is white, he is something else. He has fits of passion and gets dizzy, an idiotic smile plastered on his face as he gives those speeches that make you either sleepy or pitying, speeches about a certain Sibyl, and especially about someone named Maya. Stuff like: "We are divine, we are inebriated with being, we are great. But why do we live in this shit? The answer is Maya, the veil that covers our true nature and the nature of this world. A veil, a fog."

And like: "Maya's world is a movie screen. But without a screen, no movie can be projected. We are a movie without a screen we can be projected on. That's why we're living through this horror movie." (And he dances!)

Sad to see, hard to hear. Rumors began to circulate among the women that Maya was a rich hottie who'd abandoned him, cheated on him, or that he'd abandoned her, or that he'd killed her, and so on. Among those closest to him, it was said that Maya was the street Maia de Lacerda, and that he was in love with the street, with its spirit. That is, no one calls him crazy for nothing.

In short: on workdays, he has this thing of not letting anyone else speak and then he becomes more and more incoherent, people just float on the surface of his words and gestures.

The only one who can make sense of what he's saying is Vovô do Crime, another card-carrying lunatic. The two of them argue all the time, like God and the Devil, shouting then sitting in uncomfortable silence, hugging then giving each other the finger.

Scene: he compares Sisyphus to Job. No one knows who they are, except for Vovô do Crime, who listens to everything with a look of disdain on his face. He continues, "Sisyphus is condemned to roll a boulder up a hill for eternity then watch it roll back down, only to push the boulder back up again, etc. Job, tempted by God, in a bet with the Devil, suffers horribly, but in the end he's rescued. Sisyphus's life is Human Life, this life of Maya (always the one!). Job's is Life Beyond Humanity, the Other Life. We're all men from the house of clay. All our arguments and reasons are made of dust. All our crumbling is the work of clay." Etc. And Vovô do Crime, "I'm sure you were a priest somewhere and got excommunicated!"

When he turns Black, he likes to say he's the master of ceremonies of the Maya's Children Samba School and that the world is just a warehouse lit up by the allegories in his head. Go figure!

Guile Xangô always has money, and people who have money here can talk to themselves as much as they'd like, as long as they pay for everyone's beer and save some for their other little vices. But that isn't the whole truth. He also listens and, surprisingly, understands almost everything. He's a good guy, shrewd in his own way.

It pisses off Vovô do Crime that he's so generous, but everyone knows he says that only in self-defense: he wants exclusivity. "You give money to anyone who asks. Start an NGO already or use it to fuck women. It's cheap to have children here and at least you could say you got some pleasure out of it. Doing good or doing evil is the same thing here, and when you die no one will know the difference," Vovô do Crime fires off.

But there's also literal fire. He was among the bums at Nelson's bar watching the Brazilian rocket explode on live TV from the launch center in Maranhão. Tears streamed down his face. Vovô Crime kept joking, "You live in a country where people are starving, then you decide to take a trip to the stars. That's what happens." And he shouted at Vovô do Crime, "What if it was your bomb? Would it be better off if it was your bomb? Thank goodness it wasn't. But if it were your bomb, it wouldn't have exploded! You're a failure too!" Few people understood what he was saying, but everyone enjoyed seeing Vovô do Crime getting yelled at.

And every now and then he goes crazy. Something happened. He showed up one night from God knows where, completely blind. They thought he'd fallen into himself, and inside him there was a well, and at the bottom of it he was saying, "I want to die."

He was still in one piece. He could walk in a straight line. He was laughing and still understanding things, being nice to people. But then, in the middle of speaking, he would close his eyes and say, "I want to die." Until at some point Mirtes heard about his condition and sent the nurses to drag that I-want-to-die man to her house, even if it was by force, as long as it didn't hurt him. That was late Saturday, early Sunday.

By that Sunday afternoon, he was back in the same state, hanging around the bars, saying, "I want to die." He said, "The boys asked and Sibyl answered, 'I want to die.'" He also talked about some Carpedim, Carpediene, Carpegim.

Something had happened. All the rumors said a certain Sibyl was at the heart of it. People also said he was going crazy, though that didn't quite hold water; everyone knew he'd been crazy for a long time. Many people thought he'd snapped out of his madness and begun to see reality then grew desperate; he fell into a reality well. It had to be desperation or something worse. It must have been that Sibyl.

Who among us has never seen a crazy man talking on a pay phone for three hours straight? Maybe that Sibyl caught him with that Carpediene and kicked him out.

The stuff he likes to say, which only Vovô do Crime understands, he goes on saying, "Existing, nothingness, time and other animals are here to satisfy our hunger. It's two in the morning and the waiter hasn't collected the plates of bones from the tables. The napkins are bright white, the ashtrays are overflowing. The empty bottles are praying for rain and the empty glasses waiting for water. The cemeteries are overflowing, and the rivers are busy carrying the dead on their backs, but the boats are also dead, stranded in the middle of an impossible escape."

Then he left and went to Raimundo's house and walked among Raimundo's fruit trees, banana, mango, guava. And he kept saying things, "Technology has been killing off generations, nothing lasts more than a year anymore, soon it suffers an attack of obsolescence, this senile sun that ages everything with vertigo's sick clarity."

Women tried to take the madman to bed and pussy-whip him, but he kept raving about nonsense in the middle of it.

"Is thinking about a desert just thinking about nothing? But the desert isn't sterile, and a lab isn't a desert either, immune to contagion, even an image can have a thought, even at the very center of what can't be seen there's the shadow of a hidden presence." The women didn't get anywhere, and he went back to Luiz's bar.

Sitting on Dedé's cushy lap, he continues, "There's a hidden presence behind our existence and underneath that too, the world is a veil. The face is a mask. The rest is Maya. And let no one be silent, no one, no one let the silence get in, no one."

Vovô do Crime follows the madman's delirium like a dog. They'd arrived together but now the madman wouldn't let anyone take care of him, but even so, all Vovô do Crime could do was make him sit at a table here, another table there. When he calms down a little, he stands at the pay phone making collect calls to the aforementioned Sibyl.

Olivia thinks about taking him to the hospital, but everyone's against the idea; they'll end up committing the crazy man. Or calling Mirtes again and asking her to medicate him with some injection. Or taking him to the Bezerra de Menezes Spiritist Center and asking if they can heal him there. The saint of a man has been out of commission for three days. Olivia takes him home, bathes him, feeds him, cuts his hair, puts him to bed, but the man is possessed, sleeping with his eyes open and wanting to leave. She gives him some new clothes and lets him go. Thank goodness Vovô do Crime is there at the gate to follow the insomniac down the hill. Olivia cries when she sees him gesticulating wildly and saying things no one understands: "Those who can't think outside themselves fall into the void, onto the other side, but without their faces, they dive behind the mask, and drown. I am the weed, no one chews me, no one cooks me! Cities must be destroyed. Ruins and weeds among the ruins. Mountains become plains and on the plains the wind licks statues of salt. A river and, on the right bank, the desert. On the left bank, a boat takes us to the previous century. The survivors are now angels and pigs. The angels form elite troops above good and evil, desire without need, need without desire. I think against myself. I think like a mountain. I agree with another and guard the crossroads. Remember the murdered generations. There were millions and none of them managed to climb out of life toward their own voice. That's why I think like a mountain. Millions couldn't turn their scream into language. They were buried in silence, millions."

The street artist sets up his circus on São Roberto. The madman stops to watch and calms down a bit. Then he whispers things in Vovô do Crime's ear, "Make a circle with knives. Go dive into the circle of knives. It's a birth, a delivery. The baby is going to come into the world, but first he'll have to overcome the toothed vagina. A prophet is going to come into the world, but first the whale needs to vomit him out."

But it's just a circle of knives. The crowd around them waits and watches. The artist keeps delaying his jump. And he says in Vovô do Crime's ear, "That's how it goes, a suicide from the top floor. Between the flexing of the muscles and the jump, the crowd mulls over their own reasons for jumping. Each and every one of them is attached to a gesture. They would boo the suicide. But they ask this man to jump between the knives anyway. They are puppets, puppets of that small gesture between life and death. They're all on the tightrope of the moment. Now they're all trapped within a circle of knives."

Vovô do Crime wants to shout to the crowd everything that's been whispered in his ear: "They're all stuck on the tightrope of the moment, their muscles tense, and if you touch those tense muscles, it all becomes music. They're suspended. The crowd is in a state of levitation, on autopilot. It just takes a center, a stage, a spotlight, and everyone forgets what they are, they become part of the herd. Humanity will take a long time to get free. We need to think like a mountain."

The mountain man leaves and doesn't wait for the street artist to jump. Vovô do Crime stays for a moment longer and finally sees the artist jump into the circle. A perfect jump, but easy, smooth, disappointing. Vovô do Crime looks around and sees Guile Xangô's ghost turn the corner of Maia and Sampaio, and he's gone for weeks.

YOU NEED TO MEET YOUR MOTHER-IN-LAW

The pagode stopped playing in the living room and Bob Marley came on at full blast. In the bedroom, Bastian was deciding whether to wear brand-name clothes or cheap stuff. He didn't want to go, this Saturday was a beautiful blue ocean, why throw away a good day? But Xande didn't want to hear it. "You're going to meet your mother-in-law today."

Xande had been insisting on it for almost two months. He nearly had a heart attack the first time Xande said it. Were they married? Was this serious? He told his friends, regretted it, and it became a joke. "And your mother-in-law? Have you met her yet?" No, he always found a way to delay the visit. This was good enough. A little longer getting ready and he'd end up ruining it.

He decided on cheap, worn-out jeans, a T-shirt, sneakers. He'd met Xande in a bar in Lapa and realized right away he was kind of trashy, but he'd been too turned on. In the taxi back, he'd started to sweat, looking at Aterro like it was the last time. Something definitive and terrible was going to happen to him; he wouldn't see morning. He walked into the building and there was no sign of the doorman: it'd be a perfect crime, no witnesses. Inside his apartment, he thought about calling someone, letting them know he was in danger, but he was already inside the cage, with the beast there with him, saying, "I don't think I'll ever be able to have a place like this," taking off his clothes, laughing.

He woke up to pagode on full blast. He was alive. He stumbled his way into the living room and saw the Black man, sitting naked among his CDs. He stood there looking until the Black man turned to him and shouted over the music, "You have great taste," and laughed. Bastian laughed too and started thinking of a way to send the (what was his name?) Black guy away. But the guy was already walking toward him. He only managed to get rid of him on Monday morning. That was Xande.

On Thursday he started looking for Xande, though he wouldn't admit it. On Friday, Xande called (he didn't remember giving him his phone number) and they met at the same bar in Lapa. It was raining and it was nice to go home. He didn't ask him to leave and he stayed again.

The fear was still there. He checked the clothes, CDs, DVDs, jewelry, but everything was there, in its place. Then he started to worry about his neighbors. A Black person in the building? Two men living together? He was already bracing himself for a scandal. Would he fight for him or let him get kicked out? Should he ask for his keys back? People are racist and homophobic (explain to him what that means) and I think it's better if we meet on neutral ground (motels, etc.).

There was no need. There he was playing capoeira with the kids on the playground. There he was changing the tire of the blond in apartment 505. The doorbell rang. It was the building manager.

"Is Xande there?"

"He's sleeping."

"When he wakes up, will you ask him to stop by my apartment?"

"What happened?"

"He said he'd check the leak in my bathroom."

The day the boy in apartment 701 came in person to deliver an invite to his birthday party, Bastian threw a tantrum.

"You're ruining my reputation!"

"The invitation is for me, sweetheart, but your name's here too, you can come if you want."

"Do you think I should? I've lived here for five years, and I've never been invited to anything."

"You could help with the rehearsals."

"Which rehearsals?"

"For the play."

"What play?"

"For Leandro's birthday."

"Who's Leandro?"

"Leandro. I'm not sure yet if I'll play the Cowardly Lion or the Tin Man."

"Which Leandro? What Lion? What . . . "

"Forget it."

If he didn't show up for two days, Bastian would be questioned in the elevator, stopped in the lobby. When he was home, on holidays or weekends, the phone wouldn't stop ringing: children wanting to remind him about the capoeira lessons; the women wanting help with their plumbing or VCR; the men about the soccer or volleyball match on the beach. In six months, he was just Xande's friend. Behind his back, for sure, his wife, his bitch.

Every now and then, it was he, Bastian, who was ready to make a scene. He even tried. "What's going on, sweetie? Relax. Throw on some nice clothes and let's go for a walk." He tried again. He got drunk and started throwing all the capoeira, soccer games, and plumbing repairs in his face ("You're always fixing that blond's plumbing!"). Xande jumped on him and suddenly he was on the ground, his head buzzing and his voice coming from far away, "Don't do that again, man. If I hit you, I'll hurt you all over, you'll blow all your savings at the Pitanguy plastic surgery center. And I'll get out of here. And that won't be good, for either of us. Now get up, I'll give you a bath and then put you to bed. And stop acting like I smashed your face. It was just a slap on the ear." And he went on to say that a man has to learn to defend himself. His way of asking for forgiveness for the slap. "You have to learn to throw a punch and to get punched. You can't go around expecting to always be the one landing the hits. You can't only expect to get hit. It's basic self-defense." That must have been what he repeated to the kids in his classes at the playground. Until the day some parent asked him to show them his diploma as a teacher of hitting and getting hit. And it wasn't hard to imagine that he would end up throwing parents into the fighting circle too, laughing, "You're born already knowing this."

Bastian couldn't even say to his face, "You're a parasite, you live off me, you a pimp, a gigolo!" At bars, he insisted on splitting the check. He wanted Xande to depend on him. Could money and a credit card be a stronger leash than . . . love?

He started to shower him with gifts, always clothes. Xande put a stop to that. He preferred CDs. But the best gift was teaching him how to use the computer. They would go to the theater, the movies. Until Xande came up with an idea. "You have to meet your mother-in-law."

Now they're walking up Maia, to a warm reception, "Look who's still alive!" Bastian starts sweating and shaking at being introduced to the five drunk women, wasted but still standing, as "my main squeeze!" He thinks he might've heard wrong, but that's exactly what Xande says, "This is Bai, my main squeeze." His hands are sweaty and half an hour later they're also sore from the long, tight handshakes, his back is sore from all the friendly slaps or blows of false excitement. They go from bar to bar, and Xande drinks at all of them, dances, sings. A young man jumps off his motorcycle and throws himself on top of Xande, the two fight, roll around on the floor, get up, continue holding each other, until Xande, with tears in his eyes, introduces him, "This is Rafa, my brother, my little brother from another mother," and this Rafa cries on Bastian's shoulder like a child. The news must have spread quickly and women start pouring in, curious to check out Xande's "main squeeze," and at least two of them bring children with them who clearly resemble Xande. But there are no demands or embarrassments; that noise is all pure joy. An old man with white hair gives an endless cynical speech about love. A pagode group appears out of nowhere. Bastian decides to get drunk, since the sedative he'd taken that morning wasn't doing anything.

It was already getting dark when he climbed Travessa Carneiro, slipping on the cobblestones, out of breath, and stumbled on a deafening party. Xande introduced him to a fat, imposing woman, who welcomes him with a wide smile of astonishment. He walks around the party and is immediately part of the group, surrounded by too many compliments and stories, a man squeezed between the waves of affection, amid all the smudged makeup melting off the faces, sending bunches of kisses and hugs through the hazy certainty of a safety net, immersed in the joyful unconsciousness of a sleepwalking trapeze artist.

At some point, the fat woman grabs Bastian by the waist, and they lock themselves in a small room with an oratory, saint figurines, huge burning candles, incense, cats. The woman kneels down with great difficulty and asks Bastian to do the same. The woman prays, whispers something he doesn't understand and Bastian falls asleep, he's almost dreaming but still awake enough to hear, in a last glimpse of lucidity, the giant woman mother earth say, "My son was the devil, I suffered so much trying to get him off that bad path, I couldn't do it, I never thought he'd straighten up, thank you for what you did for him, for saving my son's life, only God knows that this was the best gift I received today."

SINGING BIRDS

It's the Sunday of the championship final and everyone at Luiz's bar is glued to the TV screen. In other bars in the city, the kiosks up in the hills, in the tenements and in the apartments, there's a shared focus. "Everyone's remote-controlled," Vovô do Crime spits out, upset he has to share the spotlight. Guile Xangô agrees and starts pulling phrases out of his archive of television terminology: "Take the TV out of Brazil and Brazil disappears;" "There's no difference between what's on the television and in society after a while;" "It all depends on who is manipulating it." "Everyone's remote-controlled," Vovô says again, and walks down the empty street, a bottle of vodka in hand, the Sunday afternoon covering the houses and trees with a heavy blanket of silence.

Guile Xangô walks by his side thinking about the collective unconscious, the remote control, the panoptic society. We don't need guards for security reasons. Control is within individuals themselves, deeper inside them than a pacemaker, a prosthetic in their consciousness. They're all being held hostage, everyone remote-controlled. And he takes mental notes: commercialism, sports spectacle, mass doping, public spaces being reduced to a dream-control screen, space-time packaged in myth. A boatload of madmen sailing on a river of images. Outside the space and time of the video, each individual is like a fish out of water. Connected to their devices, viewers behave like fish caught in the TV's net. Fake reality shows. The Olympic Games of mediocrity. Remote-controlled, catatonic hostages of a mental siege.

Vovô pauses and asks him to be quiet, points at the top of the tree, whispers "thrush," and the two of them wait to hear the song. Meanwhile, Guile Xangô digs deeper into his TV terminology archive: "The television screen has become a sort of mythical reflection of Narcissus, a place of narcissistic exhibition," "a formidable instrument for maintaining symbolic order." A reflection of the banal, of the commonplace, of ready-made ideas, fast-thinkers ("thinkers who think faster than their own shadows . . .") who want "cultural fast food, pre-digested, pre-thought-out cultural nourishment. . . ."

"That ain't no fucking thrush," Vovô yells. A bird sings, *Bem-te-vi,* and, from another tree, comes the answer: *Bem-te-vi*, I see you too.

ETERNAL RETURN LINE

The Angolans from Estácio have left their post and are now gorging themselves on pastels and sugarcane juice at the Chinese café. They don't know that here, the birthplace of samba in Rio, tigers' footsteps have already echoed as they carry on their backs, barrels overflowing with white people's needs, heading for the bay, into the heart of darkness, the stench, the stench! Or that the masters, thinking about the idleness of their businesses, plotted to replace Black slavery with yellow slavery. Thousands of Chinese men working the farms, building the railroads, and those who didn't die of yellow fever became fish and shrimp mongers, the target of gypsies' stones. Two exiles: the Blacks losing themselves to homesickness for the motherland; Asians losing themselves to opium. They survived. And what the imperial class had feared didn't come to pass: the country didn't become African or Oriental. It's still yearning for its future.

Now, in this cybernetic century, they're still riding the same tiger. The Angolans fled civil war and colonial misery to come to Brazil and serve as drug mules or soldiers, is the word on the street. The Chinese work just as hard for the Chinese mafia, the rumors say. But today the Angolans are just hanging out at the Chinese café.

They came out today because someone discovered a glitch, some kind of issue in the system, and they're all there, huddling around the pay phone by the Estácio metro station as if it's very cold, as if they're at the South or North Pole and the pay phone is a fire, it's a Saturday night in Luanda. Or a minefield (but without the mines), or someone's prosthetic leg after one of their legs was destroyed in an explosion.

They came here to make steaming bowls of mukunza, to buy clothes like the characters' in the Globo soap operas so they can send them to their relatives who'll sell them in their shanty towns. They're young and beautiful, they want to make money and time, to avoid mandatory military service, since they wouldn't want anyone over the age of thirty in their uniforms, the age they'll be when they return. They're just passing through. They don't want to be confused with the Blacks here, who don't like them. They crossed the Kalunga, the huge sea, as illegal immigrants and were never enslaved, they were never taken from the roots on slave ships. They're out here, the fellow malungos, the only passengers on the only weekly flight on Transportes Aéreos Angolanos between Luanda and Rio.

The pay phone is a baobab tree and they're lions in the sun. They're talking about the living to the dead and about the dead to the living, about an unreal country like something out of a soap opera. They believe they can escape the ground they walk on, and they make calls, they connect. They don't realize they're losing what they are and what they've been, dissolving in the mirror, disappearing, vanishing, disconnecting. They're there, huddling around a glitch in the system.

The malungos from Kalunga stand around the pay phone, under the sky in Estácio filled with low-flying planes, heading for the Santos Dumont airport, but they only know the Tom Jobim airport, whose halls they go through every Sunday, waiting for new arrivals, dollars, messages, requests. If they ever return to Angola, in ten or fifteen years, they'll return as foreigners, wearing another character's clothes, gestures, speech. You leave as one person and return as another, the opposite of whoever's made the crossing. For now, words cross the Atlantic like a capsule of pollen, a spirit, a bird of fire. And the pay phone is a baobab tree without any roots, or with roots made of sound, aerial roots, impulse drums, and they sing in Kimbundu, Umbundu, Kikongo.

Until the company fixes the glitch and they return to their tenement, the solitude of forty-four people in a room, only Sundays at the airport. And when they cut down the baobab, they'll no longer stand there outside the café, kimzuba-ing and mazomba-ing, killing time, under the gaze of the Chinese man who wipes the marble counter, oblivious to the tsetse of the flies and the parade of German cockroaches.

The Angolans close their eyes when the bleached-haired funk carioca singer claps his hands, spins around, and raps, "Hey, Maria, close the drawer, get the cash, let's go up the hill, I want to make out with you at the favela, put my ping in your pong," and the little Chinese girl with dyed red hair lets out a glamorous, mocking laugh and tells him straight up, "What do you want, dumbass? Are you stupid? Are you slow! Get the fuck out of here! Go see if I pay you any mind! You know what? Go fuck yourself, asshole!"

All the Chinese people there offer a polite smile, and the Angolans can't understand if this is a game or a fight. If you asked the two older Italian brothers at the newsstand, they'd say that that if you don't get out of this damned country soon, it'll get you, fill you with promises it won't keep, steal your youth, put you down with no mercy and then bury you with no forgiveness, naked, your hands covering your crotch, without your nest egg, that fucking slut, that big old slut, that beautiful whore—in this parable, she is the bitch and you are the cuck!

JOSEPHINE POPERETTA

Vovô do Crime is an opera fan. He had ambitions of becoming a tenor, singing at the Municipal Theater of Rio de Janeiro, but he couldn't even make it as a regular at the Amarelinho bar near the theater. He was kicked out after an incident with the check. "I'm not a tourist! They're charging me for a vodka caipirinha in dollars! I won't pay! I won't pay!"

But nothing keeps him from dreaming, and dreaming big. On that cold morning, Vovô do Crime hands Guile Xangô a thick stack of papers with food stains (ketchup, beans, rice grains, breadcrumbs, butter) and ring marks left behind by drinking glasses.

"You have to read it," Vovô do Crime yells. "If this really is samba's birthplace, I present to you the redemption of music. Take it and read it."

Guile decides to put off reading it for a few years. He leafs through the paperwork: the first ten pages are covered in typewritten words, followed by almost an entire ream of blank sheets.

"I'll read it," he promises. "I'll read it and then we'll talk."

"Just don't lose it. This is my only copy."

"I won't lose it."

"If you lose it, I'll kill you."

"You won't have to kill anyone."

"Are you going to read it?

"I will."

"When?"

"Not now."

"When?"

"I'll give it back next week."

"Next week."

"Yeah."

"If you lose it . . . "

". . . I'll kill you."

"No, I will kill you."

"Deal."

"And remember: this place, the whole city, the whole country—no parables or allegories—would be the perfect habitat for the mice and cat burglars of the world, and horror would reign."

"I'll remember."

It read:

Introduction

In "Josephine the Singer, or The Mouse Folk," Franz Kafka launches an attack on music through the perspective of his mouse-narrator. The piece's goal is to reconstruct the soundtrack of her existence through an electroacoustic intervention. Or in other words: to give a voice to Josephine and the soundscape to the mouse folk's world.

According to the mouse-narrator, Josephine is a little opera diva who wants to save her kind through singing. According to Günther Anders's *Kafka, Pro and*

Contra, the story of the singing mouse is a reference to the Jewish people; Kafka changes the names, he never uses the word Jew in the piece, but tips off the reader that among the mice without a history, without a past, who can't create art and therefore live in an unreflective tradition, in a nomadic condition, Moses's disciples hide, creatures who would write without thinking, who would write the way mice would squeak, who produce long critiques of the Torah without stopping to offer an alternative or propose new writings. In Josephine the little mouse there was yet another metamorphosis of Kafka himself, troubled by his literature and the loss of his own voice at the end of his life.

This project aims to focus solely on the music, and through the music itself reflect on questions such as: artist/audience, success/failure, celebrity/anonymity. It is a closed circuit.

Jorge Luis Borges writes in his essay "Timeless Writing," "I discovered Franz Kafka's work in 1917 and now I admit I was unworthy of his work at the time. . . . I read right past the revelation and didn't even see it. . . . Later his books found me again and I realized my insensitivity and my unforgivable mistake."

This particular work is a "pop operetta," a "poperetta" in Josephine's defense and against the mouse-narrator's attack. Not coming to Josephine's defense would be an unforgivable mistake. . . .

Josephine needs to be given a voice. It's essential that we bear witness to the revelation of her futile singing.

Josephine Poperetta's Libretto

Josephine—Mezzo soprano
Narrator—Bass
Chorus of fans
Chorus of the apathetic
Chorus of bodyguards

Opening

Mouse folk. Background noises. Whistling.
Squeaking.

Narrator—Our singer is called Josephine.
Those who have never heard her don't know yet the power of singing.
There is no one
Her singing can't enrapture.
This is proof of her worth:
Our people do not appreciate music.
Quiet is our favorite music.
Our greatest virtue
Is a certain practical cunning.
Our people aren't interested
In the nostalgia for happiness
That music creates.

We are entirely anti-musical. Static is our tactic,
We have no aesthetics.
Only Josephine is the exception to this rule. She is
Black,
Black and Greek, she is a mouse.
She is the only one
And with her disappearance
Music will also disappear.

Hisses and squeaks gradually turn into melody.

Chorus of fans—Get up and sing,
You living in the dust.
Get up and sing.

Narrator—The bodies are burning
In the dumpster, among the tires,
And the ashes falling on the alleys
Amidst screams of despair.
Enough of hard work.
Pleasure is not a guilt.
Doing nothing is not a crime.
Why is every gesture of love walled off
Like cats in heat and dogs on a leash?

Chorus of bodyguards—There is a hot breeze
blowing from the poles
And up the thawing current

Comes the winged flu, the morningless fever.
Our people drag themselves from day to night,
From a short life to a certain death.
On the edge of night, from life to death.

Chorus of fans—The truth is that no one
understands each other.
Let's break this silence,
This silence,
Let's populate this silence.

Chorus of the apathetic—Silence!
Let the world sleep,
It isn't time to wake up.
Silence!
Leave everything just as it is!
Leave the world just as it is!
Silence!

Chorus of fans—Ashes fall on the alleys
Like the gray hair of old people,
Like the gray hair of children,
They fall like life and death.

Chorus of the apathetic—Silence!
Silence!
We want to hear
The silence!

Chorus of fans—There is no silence.
Only the breeze and disease.

Narrator—We have a certain idea of what singing is,
And it is clear that Josephine's singing
Does not match that idea.
Is it singing?
Isn't it just a squeak?
We all know:
Squeaking is our people's great art.
Art?
A natural talent.
A vital expression.
We all squeak,
This is not new,
It is part of who we are,
But no one believes that squeaking
Is an art.

Chorus of fans—It's a part of who we are,
It's new.
It's the new art
Of our people.

Josefina wakes up.

Chorus of bodyguards—Come all.
Come all the people.

This life,
Your life,
Our life,
Can change.
Long live the diva.
Long live the divine
Diva Josephine.

Josephine's voice is heard.

Josephine—Wake up,
Wake up.
No one sleeps anymore.

The light escapes,
The nightly struggle
begins.
In the attic,
In the cellar,
In the sewer,
The dark struggle
For a face,
For a taste.
Without hope,
Without fear and without tears
In this world of terror,
Get up,
You living in the dust,
And sing."

CHRIST IN ROSEBUD

Guile Xangô dreamed that he was Pastor Jonas Brandão and shouted, "Hallelujah." And his entire flock shouted back, "Hallelujah!"

Jonas Brandão opened his eyes and was afraid of what he saw: tears streaming down the huge faces of his followers. Tears of blood running down his people's Black faces. He saw sharp yellow canines, empty eye sockets, hairy faces. Paws beneath their skirts and claws on the ends of their arms.

He needed to get some rest. How many years had it been since he'd taken a vacation? It'd been fifteen years since he experienced that revelation. "You must not make idols. Don't erect any statues or pictures, and don't sink any carved stone into your land to bow down to, for I am the Lord your God." He needed to get some rest.

He locked himself in his office. Was he being abandoned? He loosened his tie, kicked off his shoes, and lay down in the armchair. He tried hard not to fall asleep, but he knew it was all in vain. With his eyes open or closed, there he was, desperately trudging through the deep snow, and the snow was the soft sand of a desert, and huge white worms leaped after him, while in the distance a dark fortress stood against a violent sky. He would never get there, and if he did walk into the fortress, he would walk this nightmare through reeking rooms, shrieking dungeons, and creatures in ragged, ghostly agony. A sun burning like lava spilled from the sky as he entered the village at the head of a twelve-man army. Women and children huddled in the small square while he ordered the massacre. Then the army went down the wide river singing an old song about having sympathy for the devil.

"I'm going to serve the food," a voice said.

Jonas Brandão tried to wake up. Each day it became harder and harder to arise from his waking nightmares; he raised both hands to lift the lid of his casket and kept his eyes closed as they got used to the light of reality. He opened his eyes slowly, afraid he was just passing onto another form of lethargy, as he was now. Still leaning back, he saw Natália, the assistant, sit in the tall chair and cross her legs with serene elegance. She wasn't wearing underwear, and he could see the red hair that adorned the mystical rose down in her secret garden. He closed his eyes and recited, "The Lord said to me, 'Go and buy yourself a linen belt and put it around your loins, but do not put it in water.'"

"The food is delicious," a voice said.

Jonas saw Pastor Josué spread the cloth over the table. Then, place a plate on the tablecloth and a knife and fork next to the plate. With a spoon, Pastor Josué arranged the food on the plate—rice, beans, meat, farofa, two eggs, and French fries—and smiled at his handiwork. At the other end of the table, Bishop Romildo emptied the bag of money and started counting the tithes from their disciples.

"I'm not hungry," Jonas Brandão said.

"But you need to eat," Pastor Josué said. "We have two more services."

"There won't be any more services today."

"No?"

"No."

"I'm confused."

"I'm shutting down the temple."

"We can't do that," Bishop Romildo protested. "It's the most profitable one."

"I'm shutting it down anyway. It's already decided. Until the curse ends."

He closed his eyes. "You must not make idols." Behind his closed eyelids, he saw Pastor Josué attack the plate of food with gluttony and exchange a treacherous look with Bishop Romildo.

"We'll take a break," Jonas Brandão said.

"But this was your idea: to shut down the cinema, get rid of the stars, tear down all the idols," Bishop Romildo said.

"It's just a break," Jonas said.

"But we've already closed down all the movie theaters. The city doesn't have a film club, a video store, nothing anymore. The images are gone, all the idolaters have been converted," Bishop Romildo said. "We've won. We're the only voice now."

"That's not true," Jonas said. "Listen."

Everyone listened. The silence started to weigh everything down like a fog. Walking through the fog, Jonas Brandão heard the black footsteps of wolves and the red footsteps of assassins. Then he started to run. He didn't believe he'd be able to jump from one building to another, but he jumped anyway and realized that he hadn't been abandoned;

two wings carried his body through the cold night air. He didn't have time to make sense of what he was feeling. He was attacked by a cloud of dizzying birds ricocheting against his body like stray bullets.

"Get him!" Bishop Romildo shouted.

"He got me!" Pastor Josué moaned, "He got me!"

"Let go of that knife!" Bishop Romildo demanded. "And you, Natália, get going, call security! And a doctor!"

"What he needs is an exorcist, and he's needed one for a long time," Natália said, unhurried.

Jonas managed to escape the killer birds and in his last attempt, at wits' end, he landed on the tower of the haunted castle. He took a deep breath. It took him some time to accept his metamorphosis as he felt the wind blowing through his feathers, and he thought that it was a good thing. Out of nowhere, another bird landed next to him and told him that the real Christ was in Rosebud, trapped by a magic word. And it flew away.

Jonas Brandão tried to ask, "Who was the root of wisdom revealed to? Who can discern the devil's devices?" He screamed, but all he heard was a hoarse little chirp, nothing more. He tried to fly.

"He bit me, he bit me! He's turned into a vampire," Natália said.

"He needs a straitjacket," said Pastor Josué.

"Come now. He just needs some rest. He works too much and doesn't want to take any time off from God," Bishop Romildo said to the nurse who was preparing the injection.

“I can’t take him! Give me a hand. Hold his arms,” Pastor Josué said.

“He kicked me!” Natália said.

“Hold him tight, it’ll only be a second and then he’s out,” the nurse said.

Jonas Brandão flapped his wings, but he couldn’t move. His consciousness turned into a white screen, and he plunged into darkness.

LOURINHO'S YOUNGEST SISTER

My younger sister, thinking she was hot shit, thinking she was hot, and she was, a hell of a body, always reading artist magazines, painting her nails, earbuds in, singing, doing it all at the same time, full of herself, always wagging her tongue, always picking on me: drunkard, pothead, you're not even worth the air you breathe, the food you shit! She was poison, born a little diva, she wanted a big party for her fifteenth birthday, and she got it, a party at the club, the school gym wasn't good enough for her, it had to be at the club. And she only dated white men. She'd save herself for marriage, have two children, a boy and a girl, but only after she turned twenty-eight. Before that, she was going to enjoy her life, study, go to college, work, build her own future. Always talking without thinking, hurting people, the little queen, full of shit, and I didn't like her, our personalities didn't match. I left home because of her, I threw a plate of pasta at her horns, and I missed. I'd been discharged from the army, I couldn't find a job, and she said, "You don't deserve the food you shit!" I threw the plate at her, but I missed, and then I left home and stayed for two weeks at my aunt's house in Baixada. Then I came back home, but we didn't talk anymore.

It happened when we were sitting there, in the living room, watching the soap opera. My father, my mother, my two single brothers, there were eight of us in total, seven brothers and one sister. She was the only sister, the only woman, and also the youngest, and she took advantage of that, because besides the fact that she was the youngest, my parents had tried really hard to have her. That was after Sheila had died following her birth. They'd tried and tried and tried, until she came, and then they finally stopped trying, they should have stopped earlier, if you ask me. So we were sitting there and, suddenly, she walked in, bleeding, naked, frozen, with one hand covering her breasts and the other between her legs, bleeding, looking without seeing us, crazy. My father stood up and fell, he had a fit and ended up on the floor, drooling, his body shaking like he was being electrocuted. My father loved my sister, his favorite. My mother started screaming and my brothers jumped to their feet to help my mother. I stayed where I was, helpless, and then she walked toward me. She sat on my lap, put her head on my shoulder, put her thumb in her mouth, and started crying softly, telling me what had happened, and sobbing, without taking her thumb out of her mouth, telling me everything.

We lived in a housing complex, up on the fifth floor. At first regular families lived there, then it was more of a slum, with a drug dealer and everything. Rê and Roni lived down in block four, they were brothers, Tavinho in block six, and Bexiga, I don't even know where, but he never left the complex. The four of them ambushed her between blocks five and six, took her to the soccer field behind block seven, made a mess of things and left the wreckage for Bexiga. They ran away and Bexiga didn't do a thing, he just gave her his shirt, but she didn't put it on, or she lost it on the way and went upstairs. No one said anything, no one did anything. It's insane, unbelievable, Rê and Roni ran a junkyard, it belonged to their father, Seu Roberto, and now it belonged to them since Seu Roberto had a stroke and got paralyzed on his right side. And Tavinho was a great mechanic, he could assemble and disassemble any car. We grew up together, Rê, Roni, and Tavinho. Bexiga was a nobody and limped on one leg, a let-me-kick-it type of limb. Rê's problem was drinking, two beers in and he was already making trouble. Roni really liked to smoke and was scared shitless of Rê, who was always getting him in trouble, and Tavinho's problem was that he was a cocksucker, though he always hid it. Acting all macho, he fucked all the women, but he really would much rather fuck Roni. They did that to her.

I took my sister to the bathroom and turned on the shower. Then the neighbor, who I was hooking up with, her husband was . . . I didn't know what he did or who he was, all I knew was that he couldn't handle her, Marta, and Marta said, "Let me do it," and she pushed me out of the bathroom, but my sister held on to me, she didn't want me to leave, so I went, "*Ssh, ssssh,* it's okay, I'm here," I put her under the water, Marta also got in and the three of us stayed there under the water, until Marta put her arms around my sister, and the two of them stood there, and I left and closed the door.

My mother was fanning my father, who was lying on the couch, and then she started yelling at me because I was dripping on the carpet. My two brothers had gone to see Seu

Macedo, the neighbor who had a car and was always taking sick people and pregnant women everywhere. But then the day Seu Macedo had a heart attack, no one came to his aid. Seu Macedo wasn't home yet, and my brothers walked up the five flights of stairs just to tell us that Mr. Macedo wasn't there, and then they went back down another five flights of stairs to call the hospital from the pay phone. No one had cell phones back then. My brothers, I won't even bother telling you, and my mother, yelling that I was ruining her carpet.

So I went into the bedroom, grabbed my father's piece, a .38 my mother liked to hide in a cardboard trunk full of family photos, strapped it to my waist, walked down the five flights of stairs and headed, instinctively, straight to the pitch. The soccer field was packed, with a pagode playing, everyone was making fun of me, laughing at me, I was drenched, and Rê was there, leaning against the counter at Dona Zilda's bar, he started laughing when he saw me, laughing and scratching his balls. Roni moved closer to Rê, and Tavinho wanted to leave but he stayed, he grabbed the beer bottle and filled their glasses, his back turned to me. Then Bexiga grabbed one of the glasses and it fell to the floor but didn't break, and he didn't pick it up either, the glass lying there.

Rê said I looked like a dumbass, then took his hand out of his bag, stuck a finger to his forehead and said, "I know; you're here to even the score, because of Denise." Denise is my sister's name. "Denise must have said something, you know how it is . . . she liked it, she liked it . . . didn't she like it, guys?" Roni: "I don't know what you're talking about."

Tavinho: "I think you're talking too much shit," and Rê: "What the fuck, you guys scared of this dumbass?," and to me, "She let her guard down and I fucked her, I fucked her and called my friends, and if you want to drink with us and chill, that's fine, I'm buying, but if you want trouble, that's up to you, my friend," and he stood there laughing, I don't even know.

Rê had blue eyes, but he had a blond fro. He had beef with the fact that Roni had straight Indian hair. Seu Roberto was blond and blue-eyed, but his wife was Black. People even say that Seu Roberto had the stroke because Rê hit his mother and Seu Roberto tried to stop him, but then Rê punched Mr. Roberto too. Rê was a big guy, he lifted weights, took supplements, but he let himself go and got fat, bloated pig. Roni had always been thin, a stick figure. Tavinho was also blond, his hair down to his shoulder, and from behind he looked like a girl.

And then Rê said, "What are you looking at, *negão*?" And all I could see was his hand scratching his balls, scratching his balls with such commitment, his hairy hand scratching his balls, and Rê said, "I think this negão wants some too." And he took his hand off his balls and grabbed the glass full of beer and drank it all in one gulp. He saw that I noticed that his hand was shaking, and he was shaking because I already had my shiny weapon in my hand. So I dug my finger in, right in his horns, I wanted to hit him in the balls, but I shot him in his horns. Then Roni grabbed Rê and I pulled the trigger on him. Tavinho raised his beer bottle to hit me, and

I smoked him too, and then Bexiga tried to run, and I struck him too, and then I went over to where Rê was lying and this time I aimed better and shot him right between his legs, but he was already dead. But Roni was still struggling, so I stuck the barrel right in his mouth and pressed, then I started walking away, away, away. The soccer field had suddenly gotten very empty and then I felt a bang in my head, and I was being punched on all sides, and if the guys hadn't arrived right then they'd have finished it off.

Tavinho was the only one who escaped, swearing until the end that none of them had done anything, that it wasn't them. There were no witnesses, so it was his word against my sister's. And to screw things up even more, I told the judge I'd do it all over again, that if they hadn't arrested me, I would have killed Tavinho right there, in front of everyone. Then the judge said I was a cold-blooded killer, a danger to society, that she was going to give me the maximum sentence, and I said I'd get her too and make her pay, and then I was real screwed.

No one in my family visited me, except for my sister, until I asked her not to come anymore. She really was a beautiful woman, and after her visits, everyone made fun of me, and I would lose it, and they would make fun of me even more. Then she stopped coming, but she always found a way to send me things. I'd been in there for some five years when she showed up with a very polite Black guy, her husband, and the asshole hugged me and said he was going to do this and that, I didn't believe any of it, and I wasn't happy about my sister either.

While I was inside, I discovered I could do whatever I wanted with my hands. The social workers were obsessed with everything I made, and I even got a painting teacher. Things got even better when they changed directors, Dr. Pedro came, and suddenly I was working at a fancy house, cleaning the pool, fixing the floors, eating the maid's meals, taking care of the dog. I became a free prisoner and ended up working security for an important guy who reviewed my case, and after nearly ten years in prison I was out on the streets, parole letter in hand, and a clean record.

In a way I was still in jail with what I'd done, but there wasn't a single bit of remorse. My sister had a son, but her marriage was over: her husband could never get the whole thing out of his head. I told her she shouldn't have told anyone, but then she said to me, "Then I wouldn't be your sister." And my father: "I should've been the one doing what you did," and I told him, "You never had the balls for that," and he looked down at his feet, and my mother held onto him, the two of them alone, two old people, their kids raising families, everyone in the shitter, the dumbasses.

One day I saw Tavinho sitting in a wheelchair, selling candy downtown. "You don't know how happy I am to see you," I told him, and he started screaming so loud a crowd gathered.

ONE FOR ALL

It was like I was Vovô do Crime, Guile Xangô, Vavau, Beleco, Pardal Wenchell, all in one, all in me, Pedrão, and I was all of them, but I was still just me by myself, having fun, and I even thought about that movie about the musketeers, one for all, all for one, and everyone, Vovô do Crime, Guile Xangô, Vavau, Beleco, Pardal Wenchell, they were all dead, and I was the only one alive, One for All, All for One, me, Pedrão.

I parked my taxi outside one of the departure gates at the Galeão airport and waited there, lighting a cigarette with the tip of another, I who don't even smoke, thinking about God and wishing I had some vodka, I who don't even like vodka, and foolish nonsense kicking around in my head, sticking out my tongue to taste blood, thinking about killing someone, but holding back. I got out of the car, walked down the taxi ranks, and there was no one to talk to, all the taxis were empty. I walked through the airport lobby, everything deserted, no one at the counters, no one in the stores, no voices on the loudspeakers announcing arrivals or departures. I arrived at the runway, all the planes were as still as sharks out of water. I looked up at the sky and understood: there was an immense cloud of vultures, blacker than the blackest of clouds, swirling over Galeão, no way for a plane to take off or land. "Stop being so dumb," a voice said inside my head. "Don't you see the city is dead, you idiot?" It was Vovô, but it could've been Beleco or Vavau. "Cities also die!" I hung up, I'd rather not answer.

I walked back, hearing my footsteps through the deserted airport, and I stopped, kind of stunned, when I saw the seven tourists squeezed into my taxi. I wondered how they'd managed to fit in such a small space. I sat behind the wheel, more out of habit, more out of inescapable duty than anything else, and I couldn't hear my voice asking where they wanted to go. I couldn't hear or understand what they were saying either, and I focused on their clear eyes, some of them looking nearly blind because they were so blue, and their mouths moved without a sound like fish in a tank. I didn't let myself get scared with this feeling that they were ghosts, or worse, exterminating angels.

I left Galeão, took the Red Line expressway, and we ended up stuck in a huge traffic jam. The heat was unbearable, a stinky greenhouse of a dead city, and since I had nothing to do, I started paying attention to what the tourists were saying, and at some point, I realized that they were singing in unison—*Lo! Death has reared himself a throne In a strange city lying alone / Far down within the dim West, / Where the good and the bad and the worst and the best / Have gone to their eternal rest*—and I couldn't understand a word and they continued—*The viol, the violet, and the vine*—it really did sound like music, or a prayer, and they raised their hoarse voices a little louder—*While from a proud tower in the town / Death looks gigantically down.*[1] I wanted to laugh

1 Lines from Edgar Allan Poe's "The City in the Sea."

out loud and tell them to stop that nonsense, but my voice wouldn't come out.

I jumped out of the taxi, bothered by the heat, the stench, the hubbub of voices, the stillness of the engines and tires in front of me, preventing me from going anywhere. All the cars were empty, almost all with their keys in the ignition: it was like the drivers had abandoned their cars in the middle of a shooting. Or like all the drivers and passengers had been kidnapped. Or like all men, women, and children had suddenly turned into vultures in a colossal metamorphosis and were now swirling up there, a thousand, more than a hundred thousand, millions of them, black as the blackest of rain clouds.

I started to run between the cars. The tourists or ghosts or angels walked behind me on their immense legs, and didn't need to hurry. They said their foreign words—*Tandis que d'une fière tour de la ville, la Mort plonge, gigantesque, le regard—der Tod taucht, gigantisch, den Blick—la morte osserva—Mientras desde una torre orgullosa en el pueblo*—and their gray words hovered in the heavy air like the Japanese paper lanterns of my childhood.

I don't know how we ended up at Central Station, after we drove past the bus station. It's possible I was so desperate in the face of this immense paralysis that, like a child, part of me wanted to see the buses coming from faraway cities, trains leaving for the suburbs, but there too, emptiness had taken over everything.—*Time-eaten towers that tremble not!*—*Une clarté sortie de la mer livide inonde les tours en silence*—the ghost angels echoed in my ears. I decided to walk to the bay to see if the boats, ships, and trawlers were also motionless in waters of glass and silence.—*À l'entour, par le soulèvement du vent oubliées—auf Mauern wie in Babylon—sotto il cielo le acque di malinconia si trovano—avec résignation gisent sous les cieux les mélancoliques eaux*—the ghost angels chattered around me.

With a terrible feeling of guilt, I remembered my wife and daughters, and I shook just thinking about what might have happened to them. I tried to go home, my heart was telling me to go home, my legs wouldn't obey me. "Come on, come on," I begged, "come on, come on," I begged myself, and then I heard loud and clear inside my head (though it sounded like it was coming from the radio in my taxi) Guile Xangô telling me to take the tourists to the Christ the Redeemer, I'd be able to crack this mystery up there, this strike of all the senses, this stealing of time, this solitude on the streets, on the avenues, up the towers of churches and shopping malls, this cemetery-like silence. Up there I would find all the explanations for the social tsunami generated by the civil war between men and their tactics, what started the cosmic war between the demons of good and the angels of evil. I heard laughing and booing, and above the laughing and booing, Guile Xangô's operatic voice saying, "Fear, hope, repetition. Freedom! Free! Free! Nothing is free. Late have I loved you, beauty so old and so new, late have I loved you.[2] Who is God? I asked the earth and it answered, 'I am not.' And everything in it answered

2 Guile Xangô's words come from St. Augustine of Hippo's *Confessions.*

the same thing. I questioned the sea, the cliffs and their living, breathing reptiles and they answered, 'We are not your God; seek Him above us,'" and more laughing and more booing, and I realized, with great sadness but no surprise, that Guile Xangô had gone completely mad, my poor friend couldn't find the patience or the courage to bear the death of his beloved city, the end of the world.

And I said to myself, "I'm not going, I'm not taking any tourists to see Christ. I have a family at home, and this isn't the time to be anybody's guide."

I tried to sneak away but then the ghost angel tourists grabbed me by the arms—*Hell, rising from a thousand thrones, shall do it reverence*—lifted me up in the air and carried me to the entrance of the metro station—*l'Enfer, se levant de mille trones, lui rendra hommage.*[3] I couldn't figure out what they wanted, I assumed that everyone who didn't manage to get wings to fly up and escape were dragged down, and I started to kick, to bite, even though I knew that there was no point in resisting and that I'd certainly (with a certainty that wasn't mine but that belonged to all the damned) be killed like a dog. I screamed. I screamed in shame. I screamed in despair. I screamed in terror. I screamed until I saw Beleco come down the metro stairs and shout ("Survivors! Long live the survivors!"), shooting a gun, and I saw Beleco waiting to be stopped by a bullet, it would be like hitting a wall, but there was no wall, and the kid went around the pillars, kept

3 French excerpt from Edgar Allan Poe's poem "The City in the Sea," in Mallarmé's translation.

shooting, I saw shadows fleeing, three of them very fast, two staggering, I heard moaning and noticed two German tourists crawling on the ground, he walked up to them, pulled out his Glock 28, shot each of them in the head, more economical that way, and then came pointing the gun at me, laughing, the little fag, his red tongue licking the blood running down the corners of his mouth, the vampire. I screamed, "Hells angels, hells angels, hells angels!"

And then I heard Pardal Wenchell's voice, "If you're going to do something stupid, you better do it right." They were all there: Ruth, Mirtes, Olívia, Dafé. "Let's walk along the train tracks," Pardal Wenchell said, standing a little ahead of Guile Xangô. He handed a pistol to one of the angels and asked him to stay in the middle of the group, and asked Beleco to come last. "Shoot anything that moves!" he shouted. The K-9s watched from the sidelines and, without anyone having to tell them what to do, they ran back and forth through the woods, sniffing and watching. Halfway up, Beleco pointed his Uzi Suzi at an angel officer and told him to close off the line.

We got up there as night fell. The K-9s led Pardal Wenchell to the restaurants, and despite the emptiness there, there was plenty of alcohol and cans of food. Everyone threw themselves on the empty chairs and on the tables. After the break, Ruth and the Comadres began to prepare a big dinner, and sent everyone, even the police officers, to gather firewood. Music was heard for the first time in days. Vavau and Ruth sang to entertain the officers. The night was going to be good. The wind was blowing.

The elevators and escalators weren't working. Beleco followed Guile Xangô up the old stone steps and he was so amazed by the statue's height, by that Jesus he'd only ever seen from far away and without paying much attention. How had they carried the statue up there?

I woke up with Christ flickering like a giant blurry firefly. It was Vavau messing with the wires and engines, trying to turn on Christ's lights. Vovô do Crime, drunk as always, nudged me with the toe of his smelly red sneaker and mumbled, "Come with me." I kicked his thin leg with my boot. It must have hurt, but he didn't even feel it, completely numb. I went after him, went around the statue's big base. "I'll show you what's inside the Trojan horse," Vovô do Crime said. He went in through a hole in the wall that seemed to lead to a basement, a lit flashlight in the pocket of his clown jacket that he never took off, and he started climbing the endless iron staircase. I went up after Vovô do Crime, as he kept talking and talking as usual, the climb endless, Vovô do Crime never lost his breath, talking and talking and I couldn't hear any of it, until finally, when my arms were hurting and my hands were skinned, we arrived at an iron platform. Vovô do Crime pointed the flashlight, I thought he was going to show me a horse, but it wasn't a horse, and Vovô do Crime let out that cutting laugh of his. "His heart is made of stone," he said and repeated it several times, laughing and saying, "His heart is made of stone," and I saw the heart, a heart of stone. "You get it now?" Vovô do Crime asked, as he climbed even higher, talking and talking, "You must not worship idols," "Golden calf," "Trojan horse," and he tried and tried to open a trapdoor, managing to open it with an angry cry, and he took a step back so I could look, and I pressed myself against his stinking body, I stuck my head out the trapdoor and saw the enormous arm of Christ, and higher up, Christ's enormous face, his chin, his mouth, his nose, his hair, all made of stone, and the moon like an enormous coin or a silver hat that the strong wind had blown off Christ's head, and the fog didn't let me see the city, I felt butterflies in my stomach, butterflies in my whole body, I was shaking, and I said, "Let me off this damn thing," and I went shoving Vovô do Crime, shaking and screaming, stepping on his hands and head, and him screaming in sheer terror. "Calm down, Pedro, calm down," and when I finally got down there, I tripped over Vovô do Crime's body, I hadn't even noticed that he'd fallen from up there and now lay there like a broken doll, groaning, gasping for air, "Did you see? Did you see?" gasping for air, until he stopped groaning, and I stayed there holding his hand until it was as cold as stone.

Then Beleco woke up as he was sleepwalking in the middle of a thick white fog, surrounded by dead people. He'd scraped and bruised himself throwing Vovô do Crime's body over the railing, unseen, like a cat burying its own shit, and he hadn't done anything, there was no need to hide the body. But there were no dead people, everyone was sleeping, everyone was sleeping soundly, even Pardal Wenchell and the K-9s and the Comadres and the Four Mandelas. And Beleco looked at Vovô Crime snoring to his left and Dafé smiling to his right and he curled up under his blanket.

Only Guile Xangô was still standing, motionless, like he hadn't slept a wink all night, a small statue standing there wrapped in a red blanket, with a giant statue dressed in mist watching over him.

The curtain fell and now they could see reality. Guile Xangô saw the mist dissipate and reveal a world of silence by the sea, an immense cemetery, a dead city, a metropolis turned into a necropolis. It wasn't the first time he'd stood there, he remembered an old dream, not that old of a dream, but now a real dream, as vivid as it'd been at first. And what everyone feared had happened. The city had fallen apart, destroyed itself. The green people had expected the cataclysm to come from nature. For years, they'd prophesied that temperatures would change, that the poles would melt, that the sea would rise and take over everything, that the city would turn into a huge artificial reef, fish swimming between buildings, sharks roaming the avenues, whales stranded on rooftops. But none of that had happened, and neither had the cyclones and hurricanes come to sweep everything away. Disaster came from where we all expected, from the great fury of men, but without the nuclear spectacle Vovô do Crime had imagined. It was not the end of world history, but a return to prehistory, and without any remorse. In the first moments, explosions and fires, looting and massacres. Then, among the ruins, groups struggling to survive or simply to protect their territories founded new and precarious quilombos, following in the footsteps of their enslaved antecedents. The average man, obsessed with crowds, began to attack, joining the horde.

Beleco got up and stood next to Guile Xangô, waiting for a miracle, the city back to normal, crowds filling the buildings and streets, traffic noises, the rumble of voices, but none of that happened. The fog started to rise and the first thing Beleco saw was a cemetery.

The sun started to pierce through the fog and vultures started to circle around and around, going up and down like acrobats. Pardal Wenchell pulled out his pistol, shot at a vulture but missed. Beleco laughed, fired his Uzi and took down two vultures. "You have to do it one by one," Pardal Wenchell said. Beleco pulled out a pistol and saw Guile Xangô coming down the stairs, the others following in a line behind him: Mirtes, Olívia, Rafa, Marcelo Cachaça, Meu Bem, Lourinho, João Amorim, all of them, the Comadres, the Mandelas, the K-9s. I signaled for Beleco to come with us, but he'd rather stay shoulder to shoulder with Pardal Wenchell waiting for the vultures to go back to their circular flight, elegant in their black gowns, their cassocks and togas, their wings curved in mourning and hunger, their beaks like tombs, curved, hooked, their nostrils already smelling the world's rot, and Beleco stretched out his arm, aimed at me, again, and pulled the trigger.

My wife woke me up in a panic with a slap, I was drenched in sweat, my girls were screaming and crying. I tried to get up, I tried to find myself again, but they threw themselves on top of me, hugging me as if they were shielding me from stray bullets, or from visions of the future, or from madness, and so I cried, I cried because I needed all the love in this world to get up and face reality, I cried and quietly swore that I needed to protect my women before the final disaster, before I lost control of the car on the curve of this world with no brakes.

I fell asleep again and dreamed that Vovô do Crime, Guile Xangô, Vavau, Beleco, and Pardal Wenchell had died on their way to a Mangueira rehearsal. They were (tightly packed and happy) in a jeep driven by a woman. That vehicle was cut off by an ambulance (the siren howled in pain like a run-over dog), zigzagged, flew over the railing and fell from the Rio-Niterói bridge, onto the deck of a ship loaded with chemicals, explosives, and the explosion hovered in the air like a white flower, very white, pale and poisonous. Half asleep, I thought, "This nightmare should have come before the other one." And who was the woman? Death? I need to tell Vavau about this, warn everyone, wake them up one by one, except Beleco, protect them one by one from all the danger.

AND THEN THERE WERE NONE

Guile Xangô says the TV crew burst into the lobby of the Fonte Nova country inn with their lights, cameras, microphones, and arrogance in tow, and the reporter didn't even say good morning good afternoon how are you, she just fired questions at them—are you the Baron, was it the Baron who found the slaughtered bodies in the chalet, did his employees do it, were your security guys a part of it, did you give the orders?

Maximiliano Álvares de Albuquerque, the Baron, told the reporter she was just a rude asshole and she and her crew should leave the hotel premises right then and there, the door was open, and she could see herself out. He told her he didn't get it, all that noise because of half a dozen bums, where he was from, back in his town, you were supposed to nip the evil in the bud; the last thief walked away on his own two feet, but without his hands, and they all lived peacefully in God's grace for more than fifty years.

The reporter insisted it looked like rain, and they hadn't gotten any rain there in a long time, how did it happen, when did it happen, why did it happen and if Mr. Baron wasn't the one who gave the orders, then why did he let it happen, as the owner and boss of the place? The Baron said he'd never get his hands dirty for so little, and the reporter once again pushed it, who killed the boys, and the Baron bristled at that, they weren't boys, they were thugs, and they had certainly killed themselves, criminals are capable of anything, better them than me. "And the law?" the reporter asked; "I am the law," the Baron answered; then the reporter: "And justice?"; and the Baron: "I am justice"; and the reporter: "So you would agree you took the law into your own hands"; and the Baron: "Justice is blind, it always has been, and I saw nothing, I know nothing, I saw nothing"; and the reporter: "But it's not mute, and I know it makes no difference to you, it's all the same, that's fine, you already said what I wanted to hear." And the Baron, trying not to jump on the woman's neck: "I didn't say anything, you're the one talking, and talking nonsense, am I being interviewed or on trial here?" And the reporter: "It's just an interview, and a very revealing one"; and the Baron: "You're making a tempest in a teapot"; and the reporter: "If we're talking water, a jug fills one drop at a time"; and the Baron, cocky: "And you're here to draw the water to propel your own mill"; and the reporter, shouting: "This interview is over, you dumb shark, we'll see you in court."

The Baron banged his cane on the tabletop, to the rhythm of the crew's stomping away. A trembling boy came in carrying a bottle of mineral water and a bunch of pills. The Baron: "Who asked for this? I want cognac, cognac, and tell them to get Zelão ready." And the boy: "But the doctor said you can't."

"And do I look like I give a fuck what the doctor says I can or can't do?" the Baron asked, throwing the cane at the boy, who luckily dodged it, caught it mid-air, then placed it on the table, out of reach. "You're a man now, Tavinho," the

Baron said, angry and surprised. "Do as I say, it's best for both of us."

The Baron was already on his second glass of cognac when Pedro Paladino came in with Gypsy. "You got in trouble with those TV people," Pedro Paladino said. "I gave you explicit orders to keep your mouth shut, to only speak in my presence."

"And who are you to give me orders, kid?" the Baron said. "You should be making sure no reporter comes snooping around here, but you didn't even do that, and look, I pay you very well to take care of this stuff."

"The boys dying certainly doesn't help, quite the opposite, it only complicates matters," Pedro Paladino said. "Those thugs have nothing to do with my land," the Baron said. "You may even think so, but listen to what I'm telling you, they're going to cut your head right off, they're going to end you," Pedro Paladino said. "That's not going to happen," the Baron said, getting up to pick up his cane. "And are you going to just sit there, Gypsy?"

"Times have changed," Gypsy answered. "Times have changed and all you do is fuck up, Gypsy," the Baron said. "Get out of here, get yourself cleaned up, take some time off."

"Dinosaurs," Pedro Paladino grumbled. "Speak up so we can hear you," the Baron said. "I was just thinking the current extinction of living species on our planet is a natural phenomenon, part of the evolutionary process, but still, though, because of human activity, species and ecosystems are now under more serious threat than ever before in history," Pedro Paladino said, taking a generous swig of his brandy. "Zelão is ready," Tavinho said. "You come with me," said the Baron to Pedro Paladino. "You are way too fat, with that beer belly, take this time to get some exercise and keep me up to date." "You do the paying, you give the orders, and I follow," Pedro Paladino said. "But careful there not to fall off your high horse."

From the top of his horse, the Baron listened to Pedro Paladino's chatter: the mortgages, lawsuits, injunctions, wills, land tenure regularization projects on government-owned land, titles, records, temporary constitutional permits, justifications for freezes or suspensions, ascendants and descendants, guardianship and curatorship, the new civil code, senility. "Translate this Greek for me," the Baron asked. "The federal government wants to give away your lands to the peasants," Pedro Paladino said, drinking cognac straight from the bottle. "The state wants to build a country club for public servants, the city wants it to build public housing, businessmen want to open a soccer school, and your biological children are trying as hard as they can to put you in a nursing home under claims of senility, among other less dignified claims, and then get as much as they can from the federal government or the state or the city or from the businessmen, if possible from all of them at once, not to mention your nephews and grandchildren who also want a piece of the pie, I mean, you're still quite the catch, my advice for you is to marry a twenty-year-old beauty, thirty at the most, a nice young woman, have some kids with her, if possible with my help, I'm ready to do that, I'm a man of good will, a fair man, and I believe you deserve a better family in what little future you got left in this cruel world."

"Are you done yet?" the Baron asked. "I'm done," Pedro Paladino said.

"So you got no news," the Baron said. "Now leave me alone and go find something better to do, cognac of this quality shouldn't be drunk straight from the bottle."

"Have a good trip, boss," Pedro Paladino said. "You should go see Machu Picchu, the ruins there are much better, I know, I know, there's no need to shout, you don't want to keep up with reality, I understand, go for it."

The Baron trotted across his imaginary domain. Nothing there was real now. There had been a farm with a big house, chandeliers, silverware, a harpsichord, three pianos, settees, vases, wicker love seats, portraits on the walls, memories of a grand past through the ages, a visit from Emperor Pedro II turning into a visit from the dictator Getúlio Vargas though probably neither of the two visits were real, just lies of prestige. A typical coffee farm, with a vegetable patch, orchards of jaboticaba, mango, guava, avocado, papaya, rose apple, tamarind, star fruit, jamelão, blackberry, and grumixama, a huge jataí tree, a splendid sapucaia tree. Pigs, horses, oxen, cows, goats, lots of goats, it was a large goat farm. The land spread out in orangey hills, plowable only at a high cost, yielding little, and only through animal traction.

The farm was a natural resting place for travelers. Once the hard times hit, expenses were high, the family began to charge a nightly fee, and the quiet resting place became more of an inn, then a boarding house, a bed and breakfast, a country lodge. They took advantage of the springs, the waterfalls, the abundant water, and the business grew. Swimming pools, saunas, tennis courts, soccer fields, fishing lakes, reservoirs, horses, game rooms, an airstrip.

None of that wealth was the result of his labor, his business acumen, or his entrepreneurial vision. The Baron enjoyed showing off his athletic prowess in the pools, giving tennis and horseback riding lessons to the most attractive guests, livening up parties, and sponsoring gambling adventures and gambling rooms. That was his glorious and reckless phase as a youthful shark. As time went by, he took on the role of cultural impresario and public relations officer. The arrivals were joyful and the departures melancholic, the shows unforgettable, life good. All his siblings, five brothers and four sisters, ended up marrying guests. The weddings were held in the main hall with much pomp and circumstance, wealthy best men, and powerful guests. His own wedding was by the main pool.

Births and deaths came and went, and life went on. Until the springs dried up, the waterfalls turned into ravines, and the demise of the country inn announced the end of the family. Fonte Nova fell into his lap, what was once the center of the world now barely on the outskirts. Weeds consumed the tennis courts, the soccer fields, the pools turned into sewage, and mold, decay, shadows, ghosts, silence, ruins took over everything else. No planes descended anymore from the empty skies. Now they wanted to sweep away his memories, but only over his dead body. He would die without leaving a trace. His name wouldn't linger on an avenue, a square, a school, a club, a housing complex, a poor neighborhood. He would fight until the end, until total oblivion.

He came trotting back to the hotel, wind blowing through the grass, flocks of nunbirds, vultures in the dead sky. He came across four workers still trying to salvage something from the termites of time, a futile task. The old Gypsy, a jack of all trades, was cleaning the only swimming pool still in working order. The water came in tank trucks so he could swim his daily laps; he was still proud of his physique; he would not give up without a fight. Gypsy raised his hand to wave, his body in a military posture, the gun at his waist, a loyal bodyguard. He should have been very far away by now, but he was still visible, as if nothing had happened, stubborn. He waved back and continued his trotting. He would talk to Gypsy later, when everything calmed down, but he already knew the answer to the question he'd ask, Gypsy was a man of his word and was basically all he had left for family. He shouldn't have shouted, "Get yourself cleaned up." At the end of the day, nothing had happened.

He handed Zelão over to Tavinho and went up to his room. It didn't take long for him to fall asleep. He had always been a good sleeper and couldn't remember how long it'd taken him to get used to being the only guest at his own hotel. "I need to get the Gypsy to clean the chalet," the Baron thought, "throw gasoline on it, set it on fire, fire cleans better than water." Sleep came as a form of redemption, set everything ablaze, from the city people would see the great fire.

He pushed it off for a week. "I won't go. He who owes nothing fears nothing." But the inconvenient police car parked by the hotel entrance, for days on end, pressured him to give in. "I'll ride my horse out of here," the Baron said. And off he went, riding Zelão, followed by Pedro Paladino's car. He dismounted outside the police station to be greeted by a small crowd shouting, "Murderer, murderer." He went on his way with his cane and his whip, declining police protection. "You don't need to protect me. I know how to defend myself from the plebs, you should protect them instead, these dirty bums."

The police chief welcomed Maximiliano Álvares de Albuquerque into her office with the curious look of someone studying a relic. "Sit down," she said, and he sat down with a schoolboy's awkwardness.

"Do you know Rogério Rodrigues dos Santos, former marine?"

"No, I don't know him."

"He's worked for you for thirty years."

"I don't have any employees by that name."

"And does the name Gypsy mean anything to you?"

"That's one of my employees."

"You didn't know that Rogério Rodrigues dos Santos and Gypsy are the same person?"

"I didn't."

"Are there any other details you don't know?"

"I don't pay much attention to the details, do you?"

"I ask the questions here."

"Gypsy's in jail?"

"I already told you I ask the questions here."

The police chief showed images of the young men's bodies, presenting the photos like they were playing cards, a game of poker. "I have nothing to do with these criminals," the Baron said. "They weren't criminals, Mr. Maximiliano, they were all honest workers, all four of them were working and studying, and they just made the mistake of thinking your property was vacant and spending the night in one of your chalets one long weekend."

"The world isn't going to end because of half a dozen Black boys," the Baron said. "How long has it been, Mr. Baron, if I may call you by your nickname, how long's it been since you've left your property?" "I've never left, I've always lived there," he said. "It's the whole world, my world, I don't need anything else." "Yes, you do, Mr. Baron," the police chief said. "You are not the law, you are not justice, you don't own the world, you need to answer for your actions."

After four hours of interrogation, the Baron wanted nothing to do with his horse anymore. He returned in Pedro Paladino's car and didn't react when the crowd met his dejected figure with more cries of murderer, murderer.

He settled into the old rocking chair and, from the hotel balcony, let his gaze wander off to the empty fields and shadows. "I don't want to get arrested," the Baron said. "It's Gypsy's turn, a chain is only as strong as its weakest link,"

Pedro Paladino said. "If I get arrested, I want you to make sure it's a house arrest," the Baron said. "You've always liked your comfort, Baron, that's fine," Pedro Paladino said. "But if they throw you out of here the whole world will fall apart, then it won't matter whether you rot in a nursing home or in jail."

Tavinho came in with a bottle of cognac and two glasses.

"I don't know if you noticed, Baron, but the dead boys were Black, the reporter who interviewed you is Black, the police chief is Black, I'm not one bit white either," Pedro Paladino said.

"Nonsense, my father's grandfather, my great-grandfather, the real Baron, was like I used to be, a happy man, a lover of life's pleasures, wine, cognac, gambling, women, he loved to sit in a circle of Black boys, to tell them stories, to take the reins of a horse carrying a bunch of little Black boys, and when the abolition of slavery was decreed, all the slaves decided to stay right here at this farm, they even thought abolition was a bad idea."

"That sounds beautiful, Baron," Pedro Paladino said. "But take it easy there, the world has changed, it's a different story now, we can't keep abolishing all Black people."

THE SIBYL NOTEBOOK

The anthropologist and her assistant spent a whole week searching for news of Guile Xangô, who'd shouted that everyone, everyone! should hide any clue of his presence in the area under investigation. "Operation Misdirection" was commanded by Vovô do Crime, who went above and beyond his mission and even stole some pages from the crazy hunter's personal notebook:

I wanted to walk up the São Carlos hill. But Palmira reminded me of that case with the boys from São Gonçalo, who were tortured and abused up there, shot in the hand, and then burned with cigarette butts. There was no way Palmira was going. I left him waiting for me at the Xerez wine bar and went up the hill by myself. I spoke to a woman, then two others joined in, we drank, talked, and they took me through the alleys and lanes. We got wasted and nothing happened. On the way back, I found Palmira outside the wine bar making out with a drunk who said she was Ten out of Ten, you are Ten too. I dragged Ten by the arm and we went into a bar owned by a guy called Nelson, we drank, then headed to Raimundo's bar, and we kept drinking. But no one said a word to me. It was like I was contagious. Ten just wanted to drink and bum around. I drank and kept trying to follow Guilherme's tracks.

Out. In. Going. Returning. I'm with Palmira having a beer at Nelson's bar down on Sampaio Ferraz. Then an old man with white hair is greeted by an enthusiastic drunken chorus, "Scoundrel!" He raises his right arm, places his left hand on his chest, and bows elegantly amid hoarse laughter and sincere applause. He gestures with his right hand, asking for more, and they give him more laughter and applause. Across the street, two boys in school uniforms shout in high-pitched voices, "Scoundrel!" From the windows of the building across the street, families lean out, see the white hair cascading over the shoulders of the bowing man, and laugh. A taxi stops and honks, "Scoundrel!" The people at the newspaper stand on the corner, the bookies outside the barber shop, the barbers, the salespeople in the shoe store, the customers and clerks at the café, the witch in the macumba house, they're all flies stuck in his great web.

The man stands in an alien-like pose, legs close together, hands pressed to his body. The sun shines on his handsome, furrowed face. His clear, intelligent eyes look in all directions: the emperor reviewing his troops. He takes a deep breath and his powerful opera voice explodes into a ceremonial silence, "SCOUNDREEELS!"

The scene comes to an end and the man orders the first cachaça shot of the day. He sits down next to me, and we start drinking. And he says, only to me, "That's how it should be said, in that voice, with that conviction, with all that splendor. But you can't even ask that of them. They'll never get it, the scoundrels." He becomes crazier and crazier, while I keep picking up the tab. His humor turns to sarcasm and he barely hides his contempt for his royal subjects. From what he tells me, between one shout and another, one laugh and another, he could afford not to drink cachaça and to maybe even have a house. But he preferred to live in a tenement (the tenement across from the Royal Inn), where he'd come in and wake everyone up with his shouting, "Scoundrels!" The stench of misery was unbearable. He would throw himself on the dirty bed and yell for his cat, "Corumbo! Corumbo! I'm home, Corumbo!" He'd hear the cat walking on the roof, passing through the hole between the wall and the ceiling and then jumping onto the bed. He'd talk to the cat until he fell asleep, "Scoundrel Corumbo!"

He believed he could talk to animals. He told endless stories about horses, birds, dogs, and cats. He was not only king of the peasants. He was also king of the animals. But not for long.

I talk to Rafa (that's the name he offered, when I asked). We're in a two-story house and the walls are covered with Che Guevara posters. Rafa is a cold guy, capable of anything. He has immunity. His father is (or was) some hot shot in the federal police and no one can get to him. And if they do, he shows that little card he never shows anyone and he's all set. No, he doesn't play with other men. He doesn't play with anyone. He plays even against himself.

The only woman Rafa loves in this world is his mother. He lives with her, but no one has ever seen this mother. People say she is bedridden, that an old maid takes care of her, but others say the old maid is actually his mother and Rafa is ashamed of her. That's the thing with Rafa: no one knows who he is.

Rafa's other obsession is his motorcycle. He always has his motorcycle with him. He wheelies his motorcycle. He fucks on his motorcycle. Nelson had a partner and the guy's name was Harley Davidson. Can you believe it? Well, Rafa went to confirm it, the guy showed him his ID, and it really said, "Harley Davidson." Rafa never went into Nelson's again. In fact, he never used to go in before. Rafa hates the poor people there.

Rafa is the father of one of Taís's children (or Lana's? Or Leila's? Or Dedé's?). No one could understand anything because the two hate each other and always just end up hitting each other. Rafa is king of all the women in the area, to him they're all whores and he doesn't live with whores, he only fucks them. He fucked Taís and put a child in her.

The strange thing is that after Harley Davidson ended his partnership with Nelson, he opened a pizzeria. Rafa gave him all his support, even putting in some money and two of his motorcycles. He didn't ask a single question beforehand.

One night he was there at the pizzeria to collect his share of the profits and the delivery guys and their bikes were nowhere to be found. Harley Davidson was desperate, the orders were pouring in, and he couldn't keep up with the deliveries, he needed more people on the road. Rafa got an address, packed the pizza on his motorcycle, and went to deliver it, the address was close by. He rang the doorbell and a woman answered. An old woman. She was bleeding and behind her a voice shouted. Rafa pushed the woman away, went inside, and saw a naked young man, sitting on the couch, watching TV. Rafa beat the guy up and threw him out the window, the woman screaming, "You killed my son. You killed my son." Then Rafa threw the woman out too. It was in the papers and everything. The apartment was on the fifth floor. Rafa is as cold as a motorcycle, as hot as death. (Cut that.)

I keep asking about Guilherme. "He lived here, that is, if that's true, but no one has seen him in at least two years. And his name here wasn't Guilherme, I'm sure. It was Gonçalo." "What do you mean Gonçalo?" "Gonçalo, but his nickname was Gongolo. And I think you better not ask any more questions because you won't like the answer."

The motorcycle speeds away from the shuttle stop up the hill to São Roberto and then down again before it comes to a halt. The bills keep changing hands. Rafa bets everything on Beleco and everyone keeps eyeing Beleco, but it's a sure thing.

And there's something else. Beleco is very much Rafa's. It's nothing kinky. Rafa has all the women, women of all races, ages, he's never had just one. Sometimes he goes a week without going back there, but never longer than a week. At the moment, he has three women with baby bumps, all his, and the joke around town is that they're all going to give birth on the same day. Rafa's thing with the girls is very well planned out. And Beleco. Beleco's perk is that he doesn't look like what he is. In his school uniform, he looks like a student. In his nicer clothes, he looks rich. Beleco already has more than ten dead people on his tally.

Rafa can be surprising. And he says: there's this rain, this strong wind that came from the poles and down the mountain slopes. There's this chill. And that empty road. It wasn't hard to reinvent myself, what I decided to be, all that had been a long time coming, preceded me even, inevitable like fate, the way love is colder than death. It's not exactly Russian roulette, but life begins to make sense, or to make no sense at all, when you lose twenty thousand dollars in two minutes and win one hundred thousand in the next ten minutes, the beggar and the prince wear the same clothes, hanging on by the same roll of the dice, in the middle of the same gunfight.

It's easy enough to get a hold of your life. After a five-minute lesson, a ten-year-old boy already knows how to pull the trigger and fire the projectile, firing thirty, forty, and sixty shots up to four thousand meters away. Bursts. Pops. Walls can't protect you and skin isn't enough armor. The body is much more vulnerable than any soul.

Life on two wheels: fortune and misfortune, body and spirit. Atacama. Titicaca. Machu Picchu. Santa Cruz de la Sierra. The towns, the cities, the deserts. The mountains, the lake, the extinct volcano, the empty road. The roar of the engine, the headlights cutting through the darkness, and you, a minotaur, going at two hundred twenty kilometers per hour like a shooting star.

I was getting my official drunk woman certificate and would soon be trained to sleep under bridges, canopies, and overpasses. A taxi stopped outside Raimundo's bar on Maia de Lacerda, and Palmira dragged me inside, covering her nose. I hadn't showered or taken my clothes off in a few days. We went back to the dump in Lapa, I showered and slept for twenty hours straight.

I felt like I didn't know anything there. There was no sign of Guilherme having passed through, not a single fingerprint. I felt rejected, as if they didn't want me to enter the life Guilherme had there. And I didn't have enough money to open as much as a window in that big wall of cynical silence.

Palmira stayed in that little den and didn't want to come with me. It was midnight, I was walking around Lapa, and life was good. The bars were full. She didn't want anything to do with the bars that night. "You got me hot! Cutie!" "Please, I'll be gentle, just the tip!" (Don't men ever change?) "I could be the president of your fan club." They go by smell, I think, following the pheromones like dogs. I stand on a street corner for five minutes and hear things that would make any mother tie her tubes. Outside a hotel, people came out of a taxi. Suitcases, kisses, "See you soon." I read on a sign: Paradiso. The name was promising. (Or maybe it was Tropicana or something like that, or neither.)

"Are you new around here?" a woman grabbed my arm.

She was dressed in all red, her dress well above the knees, so short it was almost to her neck. She wore large earrings and a worn-out blond wig, probably borrowed. Her face was smeared with makeup, the eyelashes on her right eye a little longer than those on her left. She was smiling and her false teeth were about to pop out of her mouth. Everything about her was fake. She was about thirty, but looked fifty.

"Are you new around here?" asked the woman in red. (I am.) "The competition is fierce here. The girls are no joke. Besides, you look very distinguished. You can tell right away you're different. Pretty, well-groomed, well-off. Brand new, barely worn, not very experienced. Brand new. You can tell right away you're of a different quality, a card from a different deck." "I just wanted to have a drink," I say, cowardly. "See what it's like."

"A tourist, are you? Wanting to be a tourist at my expense, are you? Advice doesn't come free, but I'll give you some: get the hell out! Get the hell out! Get out before things get too hot for you. You have a very pretty face; you don't need plastic surgery. Or do you?" (I didn't need any plastic surgery, I thought.) And I said, "But this is a public place," without much conviction. "That's where you're wrong," the woman in red said, lighting a cigarette. "Do you see this sidewalk? It's mine. It's my livelihood. It's where I get money for my food and rent, school supplies, medicine. It's mine. To stand on it, you have to ask me for permission. And I'm not going to give it to you. Get out of here! Get out of here! Get out of here! Get out of here!"

"You don't have the right to do that. I'm just passing through. And I'm going in there."

"I don't think you understood my philosophy." (I understood it perfectly.)

"You're making yourself too comfortable! You want to fight me on it, do you?"

The woman came toward me, showing me something small in her left hand between her thumb and forefinger. A razor blade. (I better learn karate, I thought.) "I'm going to wreck that pretty face of yours, you little bitch!"

Suddenly, the door to the Paradiso opened with a bang. Something rolled onto the sidewalk, barking. "Pimp! Thief! Murderer!" the thing barked. "Shut your filthy mouth!" a man ordered. The barking came from a thin woman, a girl, no older than fifteen. The man was short, stocky, like a weightlifter. "You son of a bitch! Scumbag!" The girl stood up and clawed at the man's face. Or she tried to. The man hit her with his open hand, and she fell. She felt soft like rubber. Then she jumped up. She took another hit. She fell again. "Asshole! You can only hit women smaller than you!" The weightlifter guy started kicking the girl. She curled up on the ground, protecting her face, and he kept kicking. It sounded like he was beating a drum.

The woman in red, who owned the sidewalk, screamed and threw herself on top of the weightlifter. She was elbowed and fell with a splatter on her sidewalk, and she remained there, her hands on her chest, her mouth open, gasping for air, like a fish out of water. On the other side of the street, curious bystanders watched the spectacle without blinking, without as much as lifting a finger. A car with two police officers, not even them, it passed by slowly, and was gone.

The weightlifter went into the Paradiso wiping his hands on a large white handkerchief. Other women and *travestis* rushed to help the girl, who was bleeding from her mouth and nose. The sidewalk owner, on all fours, looked for her purse, holding her fake breasts in one hand.

I went back into the hotel. "Do you know where Paradiso is, Palmira?"

"No."

"Then don't even try to find out."

I slept soundly, my heart also beating like a drum. I slept for three days in the tenement, in an empty room, and everyone there accepted me without even asking for an ID. I had rights, money. On the third day I saw the king of the animals finally fall.

I met Vavau and a bunch of insane people there. Nabor, Rute, Mirtes, a whale queen who reigned over the ocean, the Four Mandelas, the living four-volume encyclopedia of old-fashioned trickery and deceit. Vavau owned the parking lot next to the tenement, and he was the only one who challenged the Scoundrel. They were always fighting and making up.

Vavau's house was on the parking lot, just a narrow hallway divided by plastic curtains to the bedroom, the kitchen, and the bathroom. "Don't be scared, Dona Bela," Vavau said. I promised I wouldn't be. The three of us went into the kitchen and Vavau started making strange sounds near a hole in the wall. That lasted for about five minutes, while the Scoundrel called Vavau crazy and threatened to leave.

"Just wait."

Vavau continued what he was doing and then a huge rat stuck its head through the hole. Hissing sounds were replaced by whispered and unintelligible grunts. Then the rat revealed its entire body, huge, fat, with shiny gray fur. Vavau reached for it and started petting the rat, who accepted his love with evident pleasure. Then he stuck his hand into a pot and the rat ate from his hand. It ate until it was full. Vavau wiped his hand on a dirty cloth and resumed the petting session until the rat closed its eyes, curling itself around its long tail, and fell asleep.

We left without making a sound. On the sidewalk, Vavau whistled to himself and danced. The Scoundrel looked Vavau up and down and roared, "You know what? That was disgusting! That was disgusting!"

We went to Nelson's bar and the Scoundrel decided he should treat Vavau like an equal, worthy of a certain respect, but with some harsh restrictions. "Any king, even the king of rats, is a step above the scoundrels, and deserves a certain respect," Vovô do Crime said, devastated.

THE END

Pleasure to meet you. Emanuel Terra. (Vovô do Crime held his finger to his temple and circled it two or three times for the whole bar to see, his indifference to yet another madman on display.) This is the name I was given in this life. I have had other names, other bodies, other selves, other incarnations. I've been man and woman, I've died old and young, a few times I was barely born, I was aborted, but I always came back, and now I'm here, with you, having this pleasant chat, coming and going, existing almost, preparing myself for the end. I wish I'd been born a tree and today I would be a forest. I've never been born a tree. We are at the end.

I'm always saying this, I live to tell people this, I will die talking about this, I will be reborn talking about this, but no one believes it. We are at the end. I don't know when I got the message, if it was just spam sent to me randomly, it was an email sent to me without a sender but with an attachment, the message caught me like a virus, a worm, a Trojan horse. We are at the end.

The glaciers of the world are melting faster than ice cream in a microwave. Antarctica holds about ninety percent of all the ice on the planet, and if all that ice were to melt, the sea would rise so high that Christ the Redeemer would have to walk on water. Greenland is spilling into the Atlantic Ocean, polar bears are drowning. The Himalayas are nearly naked by now, though happy as a clam in high water. The Andes are also not in good shape. Has anyone seen that movie, *The Snows of Kilimanjaro*? Because now the snow is only in the movies, Kilimanjaro is more naked than a Zulu.

And let's not even talk about the icebergs. The icebergs are melting. People who like whiskey can get ready, because there won't be a single ice cube left. Only cowboys drink whiskey now. And the cowboys, who knows, have you seen that movie? *The End.*

We're at the end. Let me say that again: we're at the end. Do you know your individual contribution to global warming? Do you know how much trash you produce every day? Well, just imagine how much trash you've produced so far in your dirty lives. Do you know your dirty thoughts can fill a theater and contaminate the audience? That your dirty lives can poison the vital energy of planet Earth? I wanted to purify myself, to ask forgiveness from Gaia, Mother Earth, for this life of mine so full of trash, scum, garbage, detritus, debris, shit, but she will hit us with tornadoes and hurricanes, she will spit typhoons and cyclones in our faces, wash each one of us away with tsunamis, crush us between her fingers like we're fleas and ticks, shake millions of us off her quaky face like someone beating a carpet. We're at the end.

I wanted to live on light. Through photosynthesis, a process where light is absorbed. It's how plants produce food, an essential fuel for themselves, humans, and other animals. We are all prisoners of oxygen. We live in an oxygen balloon. We are tree parasites, sucking up their breaths. And ungrateful parasites at that. We are deforesting the world. Poisoning the rose. Murdering the plankton. Suicides living in suicidal cities. Serial killers among serial killers. We're at the end.

Deserts were once forests, and I don't even care about deserts, I'd send them all to the moon if I could, that's where they belong, the deserts, on the moon. And I don't like the sea either, and to hell with it if the sea swallows all the cities, if all cities are submerged, it's happened before, it's not even that special if it happens again. I also don't care if the seas become deserts. It's fine by me. We're at the end.

But I'd prefer if the trees invaded the cities, enveloped them in a suffocating embrace of roots, stems, leaves, branches, moss, petals, xylem, and phlegm. This has happened before. It will happen again. Look at that long line of buildings. They look like they will last forever, but no, they won't. A little seed will fall into a crack in the asphalt and thin tentacles will grow out of it. Another seed and another and another, sprouting their sinuous fingers, grabbing here and there, climbing up the walls, breaking the windows, taking over hallways, invading rooms, and searching and spreading, until they reach the rooftops and swell their strong trunks and powerful branches and gorge themselves on their own glory and drink more and more of the world's sunlight. And now what do you see? The city buried under the forest. Wood being stronger than marble, steel, all kinds of metals, plastic, plexiglass, cement, mortar, concrete, ceilings, floors, sockets, light fixtures. Roots crushing reinforced concrete. Goodbye, goodbye, the fragile plans of human engineering, goodbye. We're at the end.

I've never been born a tree. The other day I looked at myself in a shop window, people passing by, cursing into their cell phones, smoking, breathing, suffocating, and I saw. I ran to a restaurant, went into the bathroom, and I saw. I went back home, took my clothes off, looked at myself in the mirror on the wardrobe, touched my own skin, analyzed myself, searched my own body, and I saw. A little leaf. Green. I'm turning green.

You're at the end.

GRAND HOTEL

The homeless slept on Professor Higino Street with the dogs. A hotel can also lose its class and become a beggar on the street, in a way. Pernambuco cleaned the bottle neck and drank from it; he was going from manager to unemployed. He passed the bottle to Pardal Wenchell, the guard from the bus drivers' union. The two drank and watched the couple leaving the hotel. Pernambuco got up, but stayed next to Pardal Wenchell, thinking he should be at the reception. The boy was blond, he was getting a little fat, his face was round, his blue eyes were very clear, almost watery. She was Black, a pretty Black girl, with straightened hair, earrings and bracelets, big teeth, a handspan taller than him. He saw the men and took his arm off her. She looked at him, at the men, at the boy again. He must've turned red with embarrassment. He put his left arm around the little Black girl's shoulders, and she kissed him on the head. He lowered his arm to her waist. Pernambuco laughed at his awkwardness. Pardal Wenchell yawned mercilessly.

The boy got into the car parked on Professor Higino Avenue, the hotel garage was full of construction material that had never been used. The boy opened the door for the little Black girl. They said something, laughed, they were always laughing. The car stopped next to the two men and the boy stretched out his arm. "For a beer," the boy said awkwardly. He even blushed when signing the hotel form.

"You're leaving early today," Pernambuco said, pocketing the bill with his best smile. "Yeah, you're right," the boy said, looking at Pardal Wenchell out of the corner of his eye.

"Is there a problem?" Pernambuco asked.

"No, not at all," the boy said.

"The shower worked fine," the little Black girl said, her teeth big and white. "I think the cockroaches are on vacation."

"It's hard to get rid of them," Pernambuco said.

"Don't worry," the little Black girl leaned over the steering wheel. "The cockroach guests are pretty friendly."

"Leave them to me," Pernambuco said, and the car drove away, tentatively, and turned onto Sampaio Ferraz.

"What does he see in that servant?" Pardal Wenchell asked.

"She's not a servant," Pernambuco said.

"How do you know?"

"I just know."

"The boy has such a dumb face and he's also a coward."

"She's much smarter than him."

"Much smarter."

"They bring in books to read. They study together. Her handwriting is big and round. His is small and complicated."

"Nonsense. Servants don't study."

"I'm thinking the opposite: what does she see in him?"

"Money. They're all after money."

"I think they really like each other."

Pernambuco went back to the hotel, a long night ahead. He opened the door to the storeroom. On top of piles of dirty clothes, among buckets and brooms, Badu sleeps. Black, small, and fat. He woke up this lump of fat with kicks, he wanted to talk. What do you think, Badu? How do you get out of this shitty life, Badu? Are you ashamed of being Black, Badu? He closes the door.

He went behind the counter: files, records, a cockroach. Nights at the empty hotel felt like his insomnia had rooms, retreating thoughts, empty ponds. He was waiting for Saturday. Every day it got harder to wait for Saturday. He opened the drawer: Western novels, a Bible, a gun. He took out a bottle of Paraguayan whiskey. A glass, a smoke, a cigarette. He started to read. All wind, chasing the wind.

Morning came with the boss and the boss was followed by a new woman. They didn't go in right away. They kept walking up and down the sidewalk, smoking one cigarette after the next, the boss with his hands behind his back, listening, that was his style.

"Wake up, Badu, the boss is here."

"Fuck it. There's nothing to do. Is he going to pay the money he owes me?"

"Talk to him."

The woman went in first, used the floor as an ashtray, and looked at everything with her shitty face. ("Good morning, Severino," the boss said. "Good morning," Pernambuco said. "Good morning, boss," Badu stammered.) The woman shuffled through the papers, her face all made up, she looked like she owned a brothel. The boss looked over her shoulder and didn't say anything. Then they went upstairs, the woman with the papers under her arm. ("What's up, Badu, are you going to ask for a raise or what?" "Who's that bitch?" "It looks like she's the new owner." "I won't stay here another minute with her." "You don't have a say, Badu.") They came downstairs half an hour later, cheerful and smiling. ("See you later, Severino," the boss said.)

Pernambuco went into Nelson's bar and, as always, envied the stranger behind the counter. Raimundo de Jesus was his brother, but now his name was Nelson, he had a bar, women, a different life, a different name. "How're things at the hotel?" Nelson asked, placing a plate of tripe in front of his brother.

"Haunted," Pernambuco replied.

"They're going to tear it down."

"You know more than I do."

"That's what I heard, at least."

"You heard too much, Jesus."

"You're not all right," Nelson said.

"I get by," Pernambuco replied.

He asked for two bottles of cachaça and his brother wouldn't accept his money. He left the money on the counter and left. He didn't want his help, advice, or blabbering.

Badu was asleep. "Wake up." He went up the stairs and, before he'd reached the top, Badu was asleep again. He walked into his room and took his clothes off. From the window he could see the quarry and the houses perched on the edge of the cliff. Armed boys walked through the alleys. Other boys flew kites on rooftops, one of them also armed. In a few more days, a month or two, he would have to look for work. Maybe not, maybe he'd just do nothing and play dumb for a while. He turned on the TV and then muted it, turned up the radio, opened the bottle and continued drinking, the same binge that had already been going on for two years.

He woke up to the sound of motorcycles and roller skates on Maia de Lacerda. The night floated over the quarry, the houses on the edge of the cliff, a world that wasn't his. He could at least wake up in good company. Women always manage. His brother already had enough children for both of them. He didn't need children. He wasn't well.

He opened the door. "Badu." Badu's heavy footsteps came up the stairs.

"What's up, boss?" Badu said sleepily and sarcastically.

"Here, go get us something to eat."

"At the gas station?"

"Is there anywhere else, dumbass?"

He ate two sandwiches and lay down in the dark. That's why you came to the South, his brother kept complaining about his life. He could complain, he'd been a father since he was seventeen and he was only nine years older. But he was right. He'd worked hard, gone hungry in São Paulo, built skyscrapers in Rio, almost lost an arm to a hungry machine, helped raise his children, and buried his brother's first two wives. Three years ago, he'd gotten that mouth, why not kiss with it, wake up late, be lazy, bite with it?

It could be different, of course, but we're killers. You shall not kill, but we've killed a brother, for a brother, for a woman, we killed the Minister and the Pope, the soul turns red, bleeding in the streets, and the man tries to hold his guts back, screaming, "They got me Jesus, Jesus, they got me, Jesus." He tries to put his guts back inside, the stench, he should think before speaking, he should think before he does, but we kill for nothing, for a slap in the face. People around him: "Run away, you wretch." His brother: "I didn't ask you for anything, give yourself up, that's not why I brought you down South. Six years with my soul in the mud."

They would tear everything down, nothing would be left standing, but the quarry would be there forever, the armed boys throwing unarmed boys down into it, the smoke from charred bodies forming clouds of stench and death streaked by tracer bullets. He got dressed, while he drank and smoked. While he drank and smoked, he walked through the halls, checked the rooms, the dirty sheets, the towels yellowed to the last thread, the secret work of the termites deep in the wood frames of the beds, in the floorboards, the sinks squeaking, the showers giving their zaps like electric fish, nothing worked right, while he drank and smoked, feeling like he was in a jail cell, the walls damp from leaks, the mold stains, and he laughed: now he was a jailer. "Since they're going to knock it down anyway," he said to himself, "an accident might happen, a little gasoline, a cigarette."

He went down the stairs, his soul light. Badu was snoring in the lobby. "Have you been home yet?"

"You know, the woman said I can only come in the house when I bring money."

"It's like here," he laughed.

"See if that'll do the trick."

"I'll stay for today. But tomorrow I'll go."

"It's up to you."

He'd learned to be alone, he enjoyed not having company. He sat down and made himself as comfortable as possible, with his glass, his bottle, his Bible. He didn't want anything else. He envied the doormen in big buildings, he'd always wanted their velvety, silent nights, their empty early mornings.

Three couples came in. The girls walking sideways like crabs, the boys together, huddled together, supporting each other. The same old thing. They rented a room for two hours, one couple went in and the other two stood making out in the hallway, waiting. "This is a hotel, not a brothel," he said, and they stared at the tips of their worn-out shoes, their hands deep in their pockets. "Let me see what you got." They were ashamed of their own money, they apologized. "Next time, have the girls wash and iron the bills." They sprinted upstairs and cheered in the hallway like soccer players, the first child would tie a noose around their necks and then there would be no more money to be ashamed of.

That was all that was left of the clientele. Better than when the armed boys came to hang out or the bums and tramps off the street who came to fuck and sniff, more snort than fuck. He managed to throw them all out. The very misery of the hotel translated to the few strays they had as clients, a handful of nobodies. A little later, two more couples came in, brought together by a random encounter, and it seemed like the night was over.

"Good evening," said the boy. "The same room as usual."

Happy, a little too happy. The little Black girl was holding a bag and smiling.

"We're getting married tomorrow," the boy said out of nowhere. "Do you want to be our best man?"

Pernambuco looked at the little Black girl, wondering if they were making fun of him, and she nodded yes yes yes then no, smiling with her lips tightly pressed.

"You think about it and decide tomorrow," the boy said, more to himself. "You just go to the courthouse and sign the papers. It's in and out."

"We'll figure it out tomorrow," the little Black girl said. The boy threw the money on the counter, he could afford not to be ashamed of his own money.

"Keep the change. You'll be there, right?"

"Tomorrow, my dear, tomorrow."

"I want to know if he's coming."

The little Black girl made a sign. "I'll be there," Pernambuco said. "See you tomorrow, then."

The boy climbed the stairs with some difficulty. He stopped at the top and turned around, nearly losing his balance. "You'll be there tomorrow morning, won't you?"

"Yes."

"Scout's honor?"

"Scout's honor." He tried to come down to shake his

hand, but the little Black girl took him by the arm. She began to sing in a slurred voice.

"He's going to throw up, he's going to throw up, then forget about all of this, just a daddy's boy," Pernambuco said to himself. He took a swig, lit a cigarette, and continued reading. The little Black girl didn't drink, or she drank but kept her cool, she stayed in control. Normally the boy embarrassed himself, they'd fight about once a month, argue, and you didn't have to be a soothsayer to know who was at fault. Scout's honor. She had thick legs, a little chain around her ankle. One night she threatened to leave, and he came running after her, his pants in his hand, drooling. All Black women have asses like fat leafcutter ants, hers was round, not big or small, just right, no wonder he was drooling, the idiot. In the beginning she wore her hair short, she looked like a little boy.

The couples had left, they were in their forties, getting a little tired out, they were as flammable as green wood, burning slowly, without much desire. At half past one in the morning, he knocked on the door of the first three couples. They came downstairs, very sleepy, handed him the key, and opened the door to leave, and then he said they could stay until seven. They headed upstairs looking a little more alert.

The middle of the night was the best part of his day. He thought about that place where night lasted six months, it was cold there, he liked the cold, a dreamland. At three in the morning, he decided he was going to test Pardal Wenchell's patience. He took the second bottle, already half empty. Two cars stopped in the empty street, their headlights on, the doors opened, and the men got out. He counted six of them standing against the headlights. He shivered. He went back inside, stood behind the counter, his hand inside the drawer.

They had short hair and were healthy like athletes. The oldest was about fifty years old, but with the body of someone in their thirties, cold eyes and a thin, bitter mouth. Two of them jumped over the counter easily. The tallest one pushed Pernambuco and forced him to stand facing the wall. The other one, slightly shorter, read the files. "He's not here, Colonel." "Search everything." Four of them went up the stairs. A fifth one stayed close to Pernambuco. The one they called the Colonel opened the door and stood looking out at the night, his hands clasped behind his back.

There were knocks on the doors, voices, shouts. Two men came down with the little Black girl, naked, her hair standing on its end, terrified. As she passed the man with the bitter mouth, she tried to spit in his face, but her mouth must have been dry, nothing came out. He ran his hand over his face anyway and stared toward the stairs.

The boy came struggling down between the other two men. They had dressed him. The eyes of the man with the bitter mouth softened a little. "Asshole!" the boy shouted. "It's no use anymore! We're already married! You're a cuckold!" It was obvious he was lying. An engine started and one of the cars drove off. "Come on," said the older man. "Let me go, damn it!" The boy was crying, he couldn't resist anymore, "Let me go!" They left.

"Oh my God!" said Badu. "I'm going home." Pernambuco woke up, felt dirty. He took a long sip. He was shaking. "They can't do that."

"Don't get involved," said Badu, putting him in a chokehold. "Listen to what I'm saying, you better not get involved, it's what's best." Pernambuco dragged Badu out. "Help me out here," Badu shouted to the boys at the top of the stairs. Two of them came down, but Pernambuco managed to get away. There was gunfire. He ran toward the shots.

Pardal Wenchell was in the middle of the street surrounded by the beggars' dogs. "They stole the boy's car," Pardal Wenchell said, reloading his gun. "But I hit one of the sons of bitches."

GUILE XANGÔ ON THE STEPPES

At least once a month I get really depressed and stop wanting to go out to the bars, movies or museums, and I turn into a wolf. And the wolf goes out into the city, walking in the dark of night, not this ordinary night, but some other night, the night of night, and I walk in silence. The rain soaks my fur, the wind chills my spine, and the stars sketch out misfortune, while hunger passes through my body, voraciously invading my spirit, and absence threatens me with emptiness.

To defend itself, the wolf starts making plans: drink eat party watch time pass kill drink eat sleep wake up no dreaming pack a backpack go to São Paulo come back from São Paulo no dreaming.

And the wolf, with its ears pricked, tries to replace old songs with thoughts of defeat, I don't want to win, I give up easily, I want to die with some dignity, with a little pride, with some merit, I don't want to live, I just want to pass away willingly.

And then the words tumble into the wolf's mind. The life he chose isn't worth it, that's true, or barely, you never know, but, loose in the wind, he goes on living his life, this, exactly this same life that's directing me, this, not another parallel life or a similar one, not another one, this one that lifts me up and that I think isn't worth it, that's not worth leading, empty.

The wind is another wind, and the wolf goes without seeing anything, focused on being a wolf. You can ride two horses at the same time, galloping in sync: you're the centaur of all this. You can inhabit two worlds, bleed from two wounds. You walk the streets of duplicity and can only rest in duality. Remember: you're banned from unity; wholeness is no longer available to you.

And the wolf wants to stop this voice, but it can't, it wants to stop the voice that tells it things it doesn't want to hear and I'm tired of this too: leaving myself, fading away, waking up, entering myself again, returning to myself, carrying on with the life that I'm living as if nothing that happened had penetrated me. I'm already more cancer-ridden than alive, so close to death that I say that not even silence can soothe me.

Then the wolf wakes up from being a wolf and stops in front of a church and remembers all the churches and temples of all creeds and beliefs and sects and traps; whenever it passes by one of these constructions of stone and illusion its fur stands on end, its nose starts to bleed, it licks its snout and the taste of blood leaves its body calm and floating in a sea of certainty: if the wolf is hungry, it can still devour sheep and, if it disguises its agony, join a flock.

BIG BANG AND A HORIZON OF EVENTS

(They come here, visiting us like they're descending into hell, and then appear on TV or the radio, acting like good people, like fine people, the con artists. One of them ended up in the mansion, another one doing security for a farm, and they left a letter for no one. And even when the truth comes out, they lie.)

I was doing well. So well that I started to think I was immortal. In May, I got a role in a miniseries about the golden youth of Rio. They saw me on TV, and in August I joined the cast of a play that was a hit with both audiences and critics. In September, I recorded a CD with songs only in English, all mine, my own arrangements, me playing the guitar, and I was also the lead singer. In October, I moved from the outskirts to the city, to a nicer place on the south side of town. Until finally, in November, I was in a trendy bar when I saw the girl of my dreams, I looked at her, she looked at me, and I walked between the tables toward her while she came toward me between the tables too, laughing, beautiful, all mine, and I started falling, I started fading away, and she disappeared. It was my death.

I woke up a week later in the hospital and the doctors told me I had a rare disease, one of those cases that's one in one hundred million. It's not like a modern and transmissible disease, it's really rare. It feels like I'm getting a year older every month. And there's no point in going to the United States for treatment. There's no cure. It's just my luck.

At first, I fought like hell. I did everything I could to keep my routine. I wanted to sleep with all the girls I had on rotation. But the news had made its way out and all I got was distant answering machines, emails, cold affection.

So I clung to God. I sought solace in every religion. I talked to priests, pastors, rabbis, yogis, magicians, gurus, crooks. I went to spiritualist centers, the Candomblés, regressed, looked into past lives. But I got nowhere.

I immersed myself in literature. I read *The Magic Mountain*, *Doctor Faustus*, *In Search of Lost Time*, *Crime and Punishment*, *Lost Illusions*. It was no use.

I tried drugs and other artificial promises. Until I gave in, stayed at my mother's house for a while, and then came to this small farm I bought in this little town in the middle of nowhere. Every day is the last day of my life. The red summer moon floats above the church tower, a stone's throw from me, I can almost grab it. You can see the gray shadows of the moon's mountains and valleys, the pale expanse of its deserts of cosmic sand.

Early in the evening, the first artificial satellite appears, a small point of light, punctually hurried, moving high and mechanically against the eternal sky. Six or seven other satellites cross the almost eternal sky with small, fixed pinhead glows. In a near or distant future, far from here and from today, an orbital station may shine in the sky like a small city, an astral village floating over a future world.

A breeze that seems to come from a sea of the future or the past raises a sad dust, suspends a child's laughter in the air, makes dry leaves fall from trees the sparrows use as a summer night's lodging. And meanwhile, in this world, lab-made Galileos build bridges that one day will connect the man of clay to other distant heliotropic stars. In their temples, in this same world, Galileos of other doctrines preach that the moon will fall into the sea and gigantic waves will drown all creation, and that has happened before. The children of Satan and the children of God continue their endless fighting. But I know, more than ever, that nothing is up to us. We have never had any control over anything. Destiny itself lost its thread a long time ago. It is impossible to distinguish, here and now, the beginning from the end, the end from the beginning, the end from the beginning of the end from the beginning of the end.

The breeze blows stronger. Clouds cover the sky and the moon and the stars. It's the middle of the night and I cannot sleep. I walk through the night. They talk about me, they tell me things, they make up fears. I walk through the night while other people's collective sleep frees souls and shapes. The dogs can smell the new animal that will inherit the Earth and they bark a warning. It's always walked among us, this new animal. And it will be relentless like us. But we will not be alive to tell the story.

FISH TANK

"Are you coming to Araçatuba with me?"

"I'll only go with you if it's to Narilla."

Betoca and I have been sitting at this table for two thousand hours and I don't know how many bottles of beer we've had, but it's safer not to count the hours or the bottles, the endless nights, the words exchanged, the silences. We're here inside the fish tank that is Graça's bar, a new spot on Sampaio Ferraz, in the Estácio neighborhood, in the city of stray bullets, in the land of lost opportunities, on the planet of wars for peace.

The place used to be a typical Rio de Janeiro dive, but Graça bought the bar next door—which had been a shoe store, a lottery ticket place, and an Umbanda house—and set up a family restaurant that turns into a smoky, cozy pub after three in the afternoon. The old regulars, traditionalists resistant to any kind of change, called the new space "the love motel room," "VIP lounge," "the snob's den," and "the fish tank," which was the only name that really stuck.

Here in the dive bar, the young and much sought-after waitress smiles all pretty, a seaweed necklace around her neck, a small star shining on her forehead between her eyebrows. The speakers play overly sexual forró songs over goals being scored and news of political scandals on the TV. Slot machines contribute to the sounds and the players who search for the millionaire bonus in the monkeys, tigers, Tarzans, in the fruits, the numbers, as they scream, shout, curse, and tremble according to the tides of good and bad luck.

At the fish tank, all you have to do is close the glass door to attain a kind of underwater calm. A starfish (insatiable devourer of oysters and other mollusks) is nailed next to the clock that's stuck at twelve o'clock. The second hand ticks, and the hour and minute hands, which don't move, say that whoever comes in will die of idleness in the still water of time. All you have to do is pull back the curtain, look through the glass, and there's the sidewalk with the Portuguese stones that mimic the undulating, world-famous Copacabana boardwalk. The Captain, the king of thieves, is today the beggar lying under the awning across the street, drowning his sorrows and glory days in a bottle of cachaça. (The slot machine players are also stuck in their lane; they are the "victors" of a future that escapes every one of them and defeats everyone.)

"Are you coming to Araçatuba with me or not?"

Betoca exiled herself in Rio for love. If it'd been a matter of money, she would've stayed in São Paulo, but she ended up falling in love with a Rio angel, a crooked angel, a member of the same urban legion as the one who'd told the poet Drummond de Andrade to be a misfit in life. Then she tried to imprison the angel in Araçatuba, they bought a house, lived there for a few years, and they were happy, but during the summer the angel would flap his wings to the beaches of Rio, and then that became summer, spring, fall, winter. That was when Betoca packed her bags, got on a bus, and came to clip her angel's wings before he turned into nothing but a memory or a desire to kill and die. The house remained there in Araçatuba, the furniture covered with dusty cloths, the books voraciously read by moths, the records stuck in a musty silence, the ghosts of happy moments dragging chains through the rooms and moaning in loneliness in the yard now overgrown with weeds and lacking so much as the shadow of a dog. (The house in Araçatuba is also a fish tank, the fish of memory floating in suffocating absence.)

Here in this other fish tank, I hear Betoca's voice. Her green eyes, her white hands, her small body, her thin gait, everything about her is evocative. And everything about her is reminiscent. Voice, eyes, hands, her entire body summons memories. Her childhood in Araçatuba, her father in the back of a truck selling grain and cattle and everything in the towns outside São Paulo. Her father, José Antônio, Tonho, who switched names with his brother Antônio José, Pepe. The Japanese friend who, after a drunken spell in Itu, put his friend Tonho on a plane so he could spend a weekend in Buenos Aires, the city where he was born, and then go to Montevideo, where his brother Pepe was born.

She remembers her father's death and the Centaur's arrival. He showed up in Araçatuba, out of nowhere, bringing gifts for the widow, and he was always drunk, inebriated, always losing his balance, he could barely walk on his own two feet. Her widowed mother let him sleep in the living room, the bathroom, the barn, but the children never even knew his real name, his true intentions, they never saw this visitor sleep for real, only precariously on top of the horse, half awake, saying good morning or goodbye, the Centaur.

The Italian mother's old age, the sadness of her last two years. The lioness mamma who didn't let the family fall apart after their patriarch's death. The brave fox mamma who managed to smoke for twenty years in secret, without her children ever knowing. And when Betoca became her mother and then her mother's husband. ("When she became senile, my mother would call me by my father's name: 'Have you eaten, Antônio? Your plate's on the stove. Just heat it up. Do you want me to heat it up?' 'It's very cold, Antônio, I'll get your coat.' 'It's raining, don't forget your umbrella, Antônio.' I was always crying in that house.")

But she especially remembers her grandfather, her father's father. "*Me voy a Narilla. Me voy para Narilla,*" he would repeat over and over in Spanish, his eyes filled with tears, his hands shaking. He wanted to die in the village where he was born. After more than sixty years in Brazil, he dreamed of making the two ends of life meet, of any life at all. He came with the first waves of immigrants from Spain, rebelled against the coffee farmers' exploitation, got a ticket to Buenos Aires, then went to Montevideo, and ended up coming back to São Paulo. "Me voy para Narilla" became a kind of a password, a code for anguish, for despair, for longing for a lost paradise. ("Me voy para Narilla "was his last breath, in illness, loneliness, death.)

There's childhood, powerful and overwhelming, with the smell of jackfruit, the texture of watermelon. Children burying their faces in the watermelon, sticking their fingers between the segments of the jackfruit, the slime, the joyful hunger, the mess. And the snake. The uncles running through the bushes and bringing a dead snake swinging on a piece of wood. "The snake bit you and now it's dead, the poor thing." As an adult, Betoca remembers being barred from going to the movies because she looked like a child. The mayor shouting, "Go, Blond Devil, go, go!" when she played on her school's soccer team. And her brothers, sisters, aunts, uncles, neighbors, and friends, all delirious, watching and listening to Caetano sing for the "Araçatuba crowd" in the packed stadium; this is one of her brightest memories. The darker memories were in the many years she spent working as a bank teller in the city of São Paulo, which hurt and felt like a kidnapping, embezzlement, a bad check. (But today she's also not happy working as the manager of a beauty salon in Copacabana. "As a bank teller, I was a virtual millionaire and today I have no pride in being a poorly paid worker in the human vanity industry.")

Every now and then Betoca tries to fence off words with pens and napkins. For her, writing is like putting loose chickens in their coop. "Today I wanted to die . . . But then I thought: yesterday I wanted to live. What the hell? What's the difference? How is it that living is also killing me little by little?"

"Friendship is the mother of love. Is respect the father? Because no love survives without respect and friendship. It can be fraternal, maternal, paternal, hellish. It's love."

"Jesus is a Pisces and God is a Cancer."

"No one should think they're fooling anyone by pretending to be kind. To be is what's important, that's it. Being who you are: that's your strength, your calling card, your ID. Don't go beyond the light of that lighthouse."

Of course, Betoca has more current, waking dreams too: paying off her debts, being happy, taming her angel, walking alongside Maria Bethânia along the streets of Santo Amaro da Purificação, going back to Araçatuba.

"You'll like Araçatuba," Betoca says.

"I'll only go with you if it's to Narilla," I say. "I googled it when I was at the internet café and saw that the city is pre-Roman. The Arabs called Narilla Narixa, Naricha, or Narija. In the tenth century, women there worked with silk, such fine production that it became known throughout the Mediterranean. We can stroll through the Cuevas, named after the prehistorical cathedral and declared a National Historic-Artistic Monument. Pray at the Church of Our Lady of Wonders and pay penance at the Chapel of Anguish."

"What do you have against Araçatuba?" Betoca bristles. "Do you think it's just for us country folk? You're totally wrong. There's even an airport there."

"In the indigenous vocabulary, Araçatuba means 'Land of the Araçás,' marking the two hundred and eighty-first kilometer on the railway route. It's also known as 'the fat cattle town,' and it also has cotton and peanuts. It was founded on December 2, 1908, and became a municipality in 1921. The airport is called Dario Guarita State Airport and it's ten kilometers from the city center," I repeat.

"That doesn't mean anything at all! Do something real, come on! The internet doesn't smell of rain, sun, people on the street, noise, children leaving school. Are you coming to Araçatuba with me or not?"

"I'll go with you if it's to Narilla."

"What Narilla, dude! We'll never have enough money to go to Narilla."

"Miracles happen."

"We don't need a miracle to go to Araçatuba."

"Given how hard life is right now, in deep debt to Graça, rent already overdue, phone line cut off, credit card blocked, nothing from our paycheck left, we'd need a miracle even to go to Araçatuba for a week."

Betoca shuts her eyes and dives deep into herself. She exiles herself on a little island. An exile planted in her soul by the Spanish and Italian immigrants that came before her and which is now the exile of a São Paulo native in Rio, an exile within an exile within another exile.

"Open your eyes and tell me that story."

"What story, Gui?"

"The one that makes me laugh."

Betoca opens her eyes and smiles. When she smiles, it's like a child jumps out of her. She sings, "Appearances deceive both those who hate and those who love."

And she begins to talk about how her older brother convinced her and her younger brothers to swallow a live fish, telling them it was the only way to learn, according to two old Indians (an old crowned Indian and an old Kaingang

Indian, shamans of the tribes that once lived in those lands and that had since fled to the forest), an infallible, terrifying and tremendous way to learn how to swim in the river, to swim faster, farther, deeper, to swim more like fish.

Betoca tilted her head back, looked at the immense blue sky, an infinite sea suspended up high, opened her mouth and, possessed by a feeling as big as the sky, her heart doing somersaults like a cowboy, she swallowed the fish with shivers of pity, faith, and hope. But she never learned how to swim.

(And now here we are, at Graça's bar, being swallowed by time, inside a fish tank.)

THE TWO SOLDIERS

João Amorim is sitting with Rafa in the back of the Xerez wine bar.

"Rubem Braga wrote that the war in Italy was nothing but dust, mud, and snow. But he was just a war correspondent. I was in the infantry. My war was nothing but dust, mud, snow, and blood," João Amorim says, using his fork and knife to make geometric mounds of food, then shoving them in his mouth and chewing on them like an old, tired ox. "I think if we had fought against the *scugnizzi* we would've lost. The scugnizzi were the punk kids of Naples. You ask the Italians, 'Who kicked the Nazis out of Naples?' 'The scugnizzi did,' people would answer."

"Some Germans surrendered to my platoon. They were tired of war. Two of them, the older ones, had fought in Stalingrad. The other two were very young, teenagers. They said the Brazilians were barbarians and our Black soldiers were cannibals. They must've felt the same way about Black Americans. But neither we nor the Americans were as good soldiers as the Germans," João says. Then he says, "You're worrying me."

"I'm fine," says Rafa.

"So stop acting like a cornered rat."

"I'm not."

"Did they try to kill you?"

"They did, but then I did them all in. Only two of them are still alive."

"Gotta keep your eyes peeled, then," João says. "We called their German machine gun Lurdinha. We spent a lot of time digging, like moles, like armadillos. Shelter (the hole) was a small extension off the foxhole. The entrance was narrow, you had to crawl in, and you could only stand up once you were farther inside. War turns you into an animal, both hunter and prey. A lot of people found it hard to go back to being normal humans."

"I get that," Rafa says.

"There was a booby trap. The Germans were walking in the dark, in no man's land, then suddenly they stepped on something, it goes off and everything flashes with a ghostly white light. On our side, in the bushes, we saw the German patrol, standing there blinded by the light, and pulled the trigger on our machine guns. It was a light trap."

"That hasn't changed much," Rafa says.

"You know what was worse than the planes dropping bombs, than the flash grenades, than the howitzers? The mines. It was the worst sight: a platoon on a minefield. There was nothing worse than disarming mines, our own mines, after forgetting where we'd planted them, or the Germans'. Mines are cowardly things, it's like fishing with dynamite."

"War is war," Rafa says. "Talk about Monte Castello."

João talks about the battle of Monte Castello, it wasn't a walk in the park, it was a turning point. But he gets lost. He asks Rafa for his collection of American war films. He changes the subject.

“There were rations. Three kinds: K, the assault ration; C, the combat ration; B, the operational ration. The K ration had three small boxes for three meals, breakfast, lunch, or dinner. Each box had a can of cheese, pâté or dehydrated soup, plus cookies, instant coffee or lemonade mix, chocolate, cigarettes, matches, a Halazone tablet for purifying water, a spoon, and a can opener. That food contained nine hundred calories. The C ration had three thousand eight hundred calories worth of food, and B had four thousand calories. To this day, when I hear people talking about rations, I remember that I was an animal,” João says.

Rafa laughs to himself; that’s why he makes these small piles of food, packing them into tablets.

“What’re you laughing at?” asks João.

“With today’s weapons, bringing all the favelas together, in a united movement, I could take Monte Castelo with one foot behind my back,” Rafa says.

“All right,” João Amorim says. “But you’d be just like the Germans.”

BETH RAMISHPATH

Will Guile Xangô just sit there at Luiz's bar all night, doing nothing? He's going to sit there doing nothing, like when he was in the passenger seat of that car. He'll listen, sitting there, content, he'll listen with affection to her voice talking about travel plans and how to come up with the money for the trip the two of them might take, and he'll listen with immense tenderness, sitting there, content, next to her. And then he'd stop hearing her voice and see that she'd slowed the car down while her gaze was fixed on the Black man walking along the sidewalk, and he followed him with her, but without her noticing, the tall, thin, Black man walking along the sidewalk, and sitting there, absent, he realized that, for her, he was no longer there, he was already sitting in oblivion. The man walked like a prince between the cars, with his elastic orixá gait, and continued his walking on the other side of the street. He was blocked by a red bus and disappeared, but he was still walking in her mind, and she sped up the car in a small, deep silence, and asked, "What were we talking about again?" And he didn't look back and just sat there, listening to her talk about the trip, the money, the weekend, her best friend's husband dying of cancer, and he said, "Dying must feel terrible for the person dying but like a relief to others." Then she said, "How about we eat something?" And he sat there thinking about the dead, he was going to say he wanted to go home, like they had been, but he said yes, and she made her way back as she talked about squid, crab shells, Japanese food, and then she parked the car in the lot and they crossed the street and went into the restaurant, and he was sitting there with the menu in his hands and she was sitting there in front of him with the menu in her hands, knowing that every time the door opened she would be watching, waiting for the tall man to come in, while he sat there, as he is now, sitting at Luiz's bar, doing nothing.

But it's impossible to sit in silence at Luiz's bar, and Monstrinho is standing in front of the jukebox and the coin falls in and the machine spills out that "every woman is born to die from love." Cezinha, the waiter, starts planting beer bottles, wine glasses, a sober look, a wry little Jehovah's Witness chuckle on the tables. "I love you," pours out of the jukebox. "I don't love you"; "I loved you once"; "I'm making love to someone else." Guile Xangô thinks, "We're always making love to someone else." But then he realizes that it's not always, actually almost never. "I'm leaving," someone says. "This is hell." A woman's voice: "I don't get it. He touched my belly and cried. But he doesn't believe the child is his." A glass breaks and Dafé starts beating Léo, dragging him from the bathroom to the sidewalk. Léo slams into a parked car, opens his arms, and lets out a laugh, his nose dripping blood. Léo loves getting hit.

Guile Xangô leaves and is now sitting at Nelson's bar looking at the woman as she shops at the grocery store between the snack bar and the Umbanda house. From his seat at Nelson's he sees the woman's thin body, full of youthful energy, and determines that her name is Beth Ramishpath. For a long time, months, looking from his spot at Nelson's into the little market between the snack bar and the Umbanda house, he's been watching the woman do the same thing, making the same gestures, and she takes her time shopping, and it's amazing that she always leaves with a small bag. So much time fits in such a small container, and she goes on and disappears up Sampaio Ferraz, out of sight. It's strange that he only ever sees that woman there, and from his spot at Nelson's, never at Luiz's at two in the morning, never at Miguel's newsstand buying the Sunday paper, never on the metro at seven in the morning, never at the bus stop to Ipanema at nine, Copacabana at ten, Jardim Botânico at eleven, never at the Church of the Divine Holy Spirit after mass, never at the pagode joint listening to Dão and Nei Batera. Only there, and from here, at dusk, from across the street at Nelson's.

Do you remember when you asked Nelson who she is? No one knew. You never thought to get up, cross the street, and shop next to her, a can of cat food, hearing her voice, smelling her and calling her by the name he'd given her: Beth, Beth Ramishpath. He never thought to follow her and confirm whether she turned onto Sampaio, got onto Professor Quintino do Vale toward Lázaro Zamenhof, then disappeared, vanishing into thin air, up there, in front of the beauty salon where Brechó and Lúcia work. Never.

Now he imagines many lives for Beth Ramishpath, he wants to make her come down the steep steps of womanhood, from whore to saint, from secretary to businesswoman, from slave to princess, from cleaning lady to manager. But she resists all this, doesn't show herself, doesn't let herself get kidnapped and slips through his dream fingers; Beth Ramishpath evaporates, before his eyes, just like she is right now.

Nelson's bar starts to fill up and Guile Xangô still doesn't want to talk. He buys a liter of vodka and decides to walk up Travessa Carneiro and listen to Mirtes's stories. "After midnight the gates of hell open wide and that's when everything happens," Mirtes said, remembering her days as a beautiful woman. "And everything happens, I told him, I was young and polite, so polite I was a virgin, a student of something. He laughed, a little embarrassed, and I think he wanted to say, 'You know more about that than I do, after all you work in a hellhole.' That's what I would've said to him if it were me. But he said nothing, drooling with love, entwining his soft fingers with my calloused ones. He said that I had the hands of a fairy. Couldn't he see I had rough, strong hands? He couldn't; he also couldn't see who I was behind the painted-on mouth, the makeup, the hairspray, and everything else. 'You're lost,' I said, no mercy. 'I'll destroy you.' And he laughed, happy as can be, believing it was a declaration of love."

Guile Xangô is back in the car. They went to her house and now he was here, pushing his way in, always with that same canine adoration. He managed to get here after quavering and clinging to her body in the hallway, swearing he wouldn't let go of her, even if she screamed. He stayed there holding her, trembling, until she said, "Your choice, either we're going to be friends or we'll do what you want and never see each other again, your choice."

The funny thing is that, in the thousand and one times he had sex with her, after climbing over the barrier of his self-control, of his awe, she would say, among the thousand and one things, that he'd made up what she was going to say, that she would surrender exactly with those words, with the threat that he could only leave after making her die of pleasure and scream at him, "If I'd known it would be so good, we would've done this long ago, no one has ever loved me, fucked me, destroyed me like this," and he would leave, willing to fulfill his part of the deal, and she would run after him, and call and send messages, and now he was the one who didn't want her, and then she would say she couldn't live without him anymore.

Among the thousand and one things he imagined, he also fantasized about what was happening: her pleasure, her indifference, this favor, this indifferent charity, this icy distraction, like someone painting their nails while reading a magazine, and she's a surgeon and he's in a coma, under general anesthesia, and she's the coroner and he's the corpse, he thought these morbid, violent things, he the dagger and she the wound, he the tower and she the plains under a sheet of clouds.

He'd suffered all the humiliations, gone through all the embarrassments to get here. So many had gotten here without effort, and he knew all the details, some that she'd shared herself, but before that, things he'd heard from the visitors, and it hurt, until he began to put himself in the place of the other people there, here, and really listen to the details. But nothing hurt as much when she, abandoned, clung to him that day (it was a Saturday, it was night, it was raining, it was cold, it was her birthday), she, abandoned, only he had come, and she, crying and saying she was a whore, he was the only one who made her feel like a virgin again, and therefore, he could not be like the others, and then the doorbell rang and she dropped him like a bag of used clothes and opened the door and her friends burst into the house with a big cake and drinks and gifts, and she screamed, played, danced, sang, drank, and he left without her even noticing or caring, he went home alone and slept for more than twenty hours straight.

And now he's here, inside her, and she's opened her mouth, and he's expecting a moan, a word, but she turns her face to the side without bothering to hide her yawn, and he's starting to lose control, and she feels the danger, her body feels the danger, she's thinking of saying something, but it's coming, it's coming, and the doorbell will ring and no door will open, the phone will ring and no one will answer, a Scorpio with a Virgo, a unicorn with a sphinx, it could all have been so wonderful.

THIS DREAM HAS SOME TRUTH TO IT

Beleco, just Beleco, I don't need another name. I'm not a saint. If you think you can get me out of this mess I've found myself in, think again. There's no fixing me. I've done everything wrong. Everything you can imagine. This is how it is with me: I keep doing it. Sometimes I regret it, but by then it's too late.

Glue? I've sniffed it. And much more. I'm no saint.

I'm from the streets, from the chaos, my home is wherever I end up. But I used to have a home. I had my father, my mother, and seven other brothers. I'm the seventh. My father left us. My brothers also left one by one. I was the only one who stayed with my mother. Since I didn't have a nice place to live, I spent most of my time on the streets. I stayed out there with everyone else, in the middle of the crowd, in the chilly air, sleeping all huddled together under the awning and in other corners.

Until that massacre. They got about eight of us at once. They had the bullets flying. It was like popcorn around here. Russo, Caveirinha, Pimpolho, Paulete. I'm not dead because I wasn't there. But I was on my way. I had gone to take care of something, and I heard the shots. I appeared on TV, but with my face covered with a blanket. You'd have recognized me.

It was because of that massacre that my mother showed up and took me back home.

I'm not an idiot. I spent three and a half years in school, learned to read and write, and was good at numbers. At the end-of-year play, I had the roles of a mythological figure and a talking beetle, of course one at a time, everyone laughed, clapped. I was good at it. Then it started raining like crazy and apparently wouldn't stop.

I know how to get by. I've done all kinds of things. I've peddled candy, shined shoes, sold popsicles, cake, run errands for people. I was a guide for a blind scrooge. I've watched Mr. João Guerreiro's cattle, that loser. I've carried bundles of dirty and clean clothes. I've carried pails of water and charged per bucket. I've weeded people's yards, charging by the meter and by the hour. I've sold birds, which is the best business if you have the patience to wait for those bastards to fall into the trap. I didn't.

I've sold guavas, mangos, bananas, oranges, garlic, onions. I've sold fabric and sausage door to door. I've hunted snakes to sell to the science institute that collects the venom, but I wasn't good at that. I was bitten by one and nearly died. But it wasn't even venomous. I've sold roasted peanuts, popcorn, kites, and organized kite fighting tournaments. I've caught frogs. I wanted to be a baker, but no one would let me. I wanted to be a bus fare collector and people laughed at me. I proved I could do math, I multiplied, subtracted, divided, added, did the square root, cast out the nines, and they laughed at my size.

I've carried bags for ladies at the supermarket. I've woken up at dawn to wait in line at the public hospital and sold my seat to people who arrived at nine. There are people, fathers and mothers, who make a good living just doing this.

I wanted to tally up the gambling numbers, but Mr. Paulo Gonçalves, the bookie, told me, "You're smart, but you can't just show up here every afternoon and get paid." "I don't want that, I'm not a beggar or a drunk."

I've done everything. I fell off a horse once. I was run over by a car. The car almost ran over my head. I was going to smash it in: *Pfft!* Every now and then, one of those improvised shows on top of a truck came into town. They do talent shows and dances, hand out prizes, give out gifts, liven up the place. The show starts with the local kids, then the local grown men, and at the end it's the professionals' turn. They're not professionals at all, they just do bad imitations of radio and television professionals. It's a shame.

I won the amateur competition singing "Amada amante." I almost fell off the truck, but I also won the first dance award for moves to some hard rock and I won some prize cash as the night's breakout star. Even I was amazed at myself. The guy who ran the show, someone named Neuzenir Dutra, said I had good luck, complimented me, asked for a round of applause, and promised he would take me with him next time. I'm still waiting, to this day, sitting on the toilet, so I don't get varicose veins.

That massacre was why my mother showed up and took me home. I've already told you. There are wild animals and domestic animals. My mother, a housekeeper, is a domestic animal. She's been a maid her whole life. She washed other women's husbands' underwear. She washed, ironed, and changed other people's children's diapers. She cooked other people's food on other people's stoves. She cleared dirty plates from other people's tables. Her whole life. When someone came and asked, "What do you do?" She answered, "I'm a maid." When someone asked me, "What does your mother do?" I answered, "She's a maid." There's no way around it.

When I got home, she'd say, "I'm no one's slave." And then we had cold food, showered with ice-cold water at two in the morning. I think that's what made things happen the way they did. I'm sure if the others hadn't lived off her, including my father and brothers, the shit wouldn't have rained down so hard. We could have gotten an umbrella at least.

But we didn't have one, and it stunk. The two of us were left alone, me wandering the streets, and her killing herself in other people's houses. Things got worse after one of my brothers, her favorite, was found dead. That's when she started to really lose it. I couldn't do anything. She would curse me out, spit in my face. We fought a lot and I had to defend myself. It was like she was drunk. She was a different person, not herself. But she never drank anything. Maybe she was crazy. Who knows. I don't know. So no one would get upset, I would wander around, trying to figure out what to do. I'd get home in the wee hours of the morning, dead tired. I'd only go home to sleep, or I wouldn't go home for months at a time.

Every now and then she would act like some kind of diva. She would sing songs from God knows when, cry like a baby, pray and sing and sing. Then she would fall asleep. But every single time, she would wake up just in time to go to work. Even the clock stops sometimes. She didn't.

The last time I came home she was much worse. So much worse one day I woke up in chains. "Now you're going to stay there. Mommy will be back soon." She locked the door with the key and left. I screamed all day long, help, get me out of here, stuff like that. The worst part was that I knew people could hear me, I could hear the kids running, the fags talking, the tramps gossiping, but not a single son of a bitch came to my aid. I had no idea they hated me so much.

That night my mother came home and put a plate in front of me, leftovers from the rich guys' houses she always brought home. Pig slop. And the worst part was that the plate was right under my nose, and I couldn't even move a finger, a single hair. She didn't even notice. I started speaking softly, "Think about it, Mom, I'm your son, Mom, I only want what's best for you, Mom, get me out of here, Mom, let me go, Mom." But she didn't care. I ended up losing my patience, yelling that she was a doormat, a slave, a crazy woman, I ended up cursing her and she didn't even care, speaking to the walls, singing that a tiny grain of sand was just a poor dreamer, one of those songs from long ago she liked to sing because her mother sang them to her, and now she sang them to me.

I kept telling myself, "I can't believe it," I fell asleep and woke up, "I can't believe it." And to this day I still can't believe it. She sang, then expanded like a deflated balloon, and fell asleep. But, at the same time every day, the alarm clock would squeal inside her head, and she would wake up. She would take a shower, get dressed, and leave. "Mommy will be right back. Stay there." I think she was holding me there because she didn't want me to die in a massacre. She meant well.

That went on for a long time.

I got so weak, so weak I started to see things. Children started to walk all over me. There was a party out there and things were moving very slowly. Objects drifted with the lightness of a feather. The sun would stay still in the sky for hours and hours. The sky rested on the tip of my toes and the sun was right there.

The children would float. The children would fly everywhere, up and down. They would jump on my belly and do somersaults. The grown men also wanted to fly, but they would fall right down. The children would fly and wage wars in the sky. Wars of paint, tomatoes, and mud. Whoever got hit by a tomato would come falling from above, spinning, spinning, shouting, "Raaaaaul!" And they would fall on my face. They would fall right into my eye.

When the mud, tomatoes, and paint ran out, the children dipped their hands into the sunset and threw sunsets at each other, slipping on the colors. It was the biggest mess. I was left shining with colors.

Then night came and the Moon came out of my chest and hung there. The children would fly to the Moon and come back. They would go to the Moon and jump back to Earth. I was the Earth. Some flew to the stars and disappeared. They would never come back, and I cried because they would never come back down from the stars.

I think it was my sadness that started blowing this wind from the end of the world.

The wind from the end of the world that put away so many men. So many men blown out like candles. You could see grown men running away. They ran away like rats. They ran away like cockroaches. Poor things. Then the wind from the end of the world blew stronger and stronger and stronger, and all the men started going out. Millions of them. And I was covered in ash.

The children came down from the Moon and started to pull me out from under all the ash. They said the wind was a dragon. Invisible. A dragon made of wind. They said it was time. It was time made of wind. A wind-time. And when the wind-time blew, the grown men went out and turned to ash. The kids kept walking and arguing all over me. Wiping the ashes off me. I didn't understand anything anymore. I didn't know who I was. And I didn't know any of those kids.

I was so thin that all I had to do was pull myself a little and I would be out from the chains. But I didn't have the strength to do it. The plate was full of food and fat white worms. The worms crawled all over me, I couldn't think about what would happen if they got into my mouth, into my ears, my nose. I wouldn't even be able to chew the worms if they got into my mouth.

I don't know when my mother got it into her head that I'd left. She beat me with a stick, I didn't feel a thing. She threw me in the tub, bathed me, combed my hair, dressed me. "Come on, you pest, you thug, you little shit." But I couldn't stand up. She picked me up like a feather in her arms. I think we got on a bus. We got off the bus. We walked through a creaky gate. She threw me into some bushes, put a dog collar around my neck. She tied the leash to a tree. I don't know. It wasn't even necessary. I stood there looking at the trees, the sky showing between the leaves, listening to millions of little prickling sounds. The sky was high high high.

I don't know how many times she came to see me, I knew she was coming by the sound of her footsteps. Until some different footsteps arrived, a woman leaned over me and screamed. Everything was a rush. I think they put me in a car or an ambulance. I ended up in a hospital, tubes in every hole. After a while they removed the tubes, I started sucking on a bottle, then I started eating with a spoon, chicken soup, orange juice, baby food, sick people food. A lady came to visit me, I think she was the boss. I didn't give a damn.

I'd barely put on some flesh when they threw me in a huge group home—just like that. Everyone was a pervert in that shithole. The guards said I was lucky, that they were going to pay for my schooling, that they were going to adopt me. I pretended to believe them. Before a month had passed, they started beating me up like they did with the others.

I was a little weak, but I wasn't dead. I ran out of there. No, I didn't run away; I left through the front door, with the visitors. I was tired of being locked up.

I went back home and there were other people living there. I went to talk to Seu Paulo Gonçalves, the bookie, and he told me he'd read everything in the newspaper. I'd been in the news, and I didn't even know. He also told me that from that day on I could consider him my godfather. He got my house cleaned out, got me some money, and I told him that I was going to think seriously about this godfather thing.

Then I went to talk to Dr. Sérgio, who was a lawyer and my friend, and he also already knew everything. He drove me to the crazy folks' home where my mother was. I talked to her, but she didn't recognize me. She was a mess, pumped full of medicine. Her doctor said she had a mania for being a maid, she was always picking up trash, cleaning things. I asked Dr. Sérgio what I could do to bring my mother back home. He told me to think about myself, that I wasn't even responsible for myself yet. I told him I knew a lot of grown men I didn't respect because they were much more like children than I was.

I don't ask for any favors. But when I ask, I ask loudly. I wrote to the president of the republic, asking him to give me my mother back and help me find a way to take care of her. You can pick and choose your maids, but you can't do anything about your own mother. To this day, no one has written me back.

I thought, "It's over. There's no way out. I'm going to grow up and go crazy. If I grow up. There's no way out."

But then one of those days I had a really crazy dream.

It went like this.

I was a boy who lived in a cage because I didn't have a home. I had two wings, I was covered in feathers. I had a red beak, and I sang all day long. I already said the dream was crazy. And I sang all these songs on the radio. I sang a lot. I sang in every language. And I was all the instruments. I was music itself. Everyone liked it, everyone stopped to listen to me sing.

I escaped from the cage.

It was then that I met a girl who was coming along the road. She was very happy because she had four huge feet, two big flapping ears, and a snout. The girl and I became friends, and we went along the long road.

In the middle of the road, we met an orangutan. He had nothing: no shoes, no clogs, no sandals, no money in the bank, no job. He was just an orangutan, and he was always complaining because he liked oranges and didn't have money to buy crates and crates and crates of oranges. He was an orange-utan.

The girl was a big eater too and she had this idea that we had to make money. "It's easy," the girl said.

"Easy?" I said.

"How?" asked the orange-utan.

The girl grabbed the orange-utan by the snout and said to me, "You sing and we dance."

So we went to the city and I started to sing and the two of them started to dance. All the people gathered around. We made piles of money.

But then came the Rat King who owned the streets and was a huge rat. He said very curtly and loudly, "No talking, no singing. I want to hear silence." And there was total silence. Not a single woof. But I couldn't stop singing. So I sang.

The Rat King roared with rage. And I sang. So he locked me up in a dark hole. But even down there I couldn't stop singing. And I sang and sang and sang. The Rat King roared and roared and roared with rage. And I sang. Until the music started to dig and dig and bring light. The music pulled me out of the hole.

I got out and met the girl and the orange-utan. They were in a brand-new car, and they shouted to me, "Come on, come on, come on, you're late!" We were going to perform on a TV show. I sang and they danced.

We got rich. Very rich indeed. Our house had about forty rooms. A huge swimming pool for the girl. Endless strawberry bushes for the orange-utan. A three-story golden cage just for me. My mother took care of the place and things were sparkling clean.

I know it's crazy, but I even started learning how to play the guitar. I don't know, dreams are such a lie, but this dream had some truth to it.

QUARRY

your golden hair Margarete
your ashen hair Shulamit
—Paul Celan

1. Vigil

The two helicopters are up there filming the favela. Buzzing. Rumbling. On the first day, those who had to hide did so. Those who didn't owe anyone anything just stood there watching. What do they want? Are they scoping out the favela? Preparing an invasion? Do they want war? "The police are the only government entity that goes up the hill," they say.

They came back the next day. And the next, and the next, and the next. On the fourth day, no one cared anymore. Only the children: "If I grow up, I'll fly up there and shoot them down." "I'll grab a bazooka, and boom! And they'll fall to the ground, and boom!" "If they were hummingbirds, I'd throw stones at them." After that, even the children got tired.

From up there, you can map everything. From above, the brown roofs, the windows looking in all directions, the greens, the reds, the blues, the alleys, the narrow streets, the white church towers, the slabs, the zinc, the cardboard, the plastic, the aluminum frames, the glass, the exposed bricks, the fish skeletons of open TV antennas, the pirated dishes for paid TV channels, the hustle and bustle, the hubbub.

An anthill, to those who don't care much for people who insist on surviving, some even with great effort. An active hive, vans, cars, motorcycles going up and down. A human termite mound. But the most astonishing landscape is the quarry. Much has been stolen from it, there are marks from the blows of giant machines, of dynamite explosions, but what's left is still an imposing presence, a massive and powerful body. There are houses and mansions built up high, looking precariously balanced, but there is no record of them collapsing. The quarry teaches these houses consistency, and they resist. The quarry also teaches the residents resilience, thicker skin, permanence.

On the sixth day, the two helicopters had become an old tree, a bus. Even when they disappeared, they stayed up there for some time.

2. K-9s

Pedrão and his wife wake up to the sound of their daughters screaming. He grabs the gun from under his pillow, but Dentinho is at the bedroom door with a rifle pointed at Pedrão's chest. "You're smart, don't do anything stupid," Dentinho says. Pedrão throws the gun on the bed and runs to his daughters' room, followed by his wife wrapped in the blanket. The five of them stay there, holding onto each other, Pedrão asking them to calm down and swearing on the inside that he'll do something stupid, he's not going to let it go, but he knows that the best thing to do is negotiate. He racks his brain trying to figure out what mistake he made to deserve this, standing naked, surrounded by his women and eight thugs he's never seen besides Dentinho, inside his house.

And Dentinho explains that this is exactly the house he wants. "You don't have to go far, it's just for a few hours. Then you can come back. And that's good; it's been a long time since you've gone out, Pedrão, and the girls need to see other places. Now, five minutes for everyone to put on some clothes and go for a walk. No need to bring anything. And you don't need to worry, Mrs. Ana, you'll find everything in its place. And you girls, don't cry. Sorry we were rough." Pedrão tries to argue. Dentinho shouts, "Cut the chitchat!" The daughters shout, "Let's get out of here, Dad, let's get out of here!"

Now they're inside a van. The man behind the wheel is a professional and Pedrão wonders how a man that age who looks like that could be stuck with Dentinho, a smug nobody. The other two are a little younger, but also professionals. Pedrão clears his throat. "Don't make it harder than it has to be. Everyone on the ground," says the man behind the wheel. One of the men hands out black masks and shows them what to do. Pedrão and his women obey; they pull the knitted ski masks down to their necks and are now in the dark.

The van turns on Maia and Pedrão hears voices, laughter, the roar of motorcycles, the noise of roller skates and skateboards on pavement, and almost understands Guile Xangô's love for that street, though he knows that no help will be coming from there.

They leave Maia and are on Barão de Itapagipe. Pedrão feels calmer when the van gets to the Central Air Force Hospital. He hears raised voices, and they go back the wrong way, go down Paulo de Frontin Avenue and enter Xangai's junkyard, the bankrupt garbage company.

They jump out of the van and climb up a twenty-step staircase. The sound of a key in an old lock. A carpeted floor, a musty smell. Another door opens. "You better not play the hero. Every hero is a dead man," the older man says. The door closes with two turns of another old lock. Pedrão takes off his mask; he's in a windowless room, the floor covered in worn green cloth, the walls painted black. He looks at his women, hooded, holding hands, the youngest wearing a white sneaker and a blue one, and takes the opportunity to cry in silence before they take off their masks. "This is what we are: trash."

3. Wrong Time

Dentinho lets out a "fuck this" and pushes Afonsinho into Pedrão's house.

"I thought you were going to stay on the road for good," Dentinho says.

"This is my spot," Afonsinho says.

"Not anymore."

"I can't live on the road."

"There's not enough room for the both of us here."

"Can't we let it go?"

"What?"

"Wow."

"I don't know what you're talking about."

"What is it?"

"See? I've already let it go. You haven't."

"We've always been brothers. More than brothers. Remember that . . ."

"No."

"But . . ."

"If you stay, I'll have to put you to bed."

"Then let me talk to Mom."

"Didn't they tell you?"

"What?"

"She went back home."

"I never thought you . . ."

"You never thought. You do and then you think. That's your problem."

"I'm going upstairs."

"You're going downstairs and lying down."

"And who are those guys?"

"Friends."

"You never had any friends."

"You came at the wrong time."

"I'm going up."

"You're going down. You're the unlucky one."

Dentinho is sitting next to Afonsinho's body. The other five don't say anything. They're waiting in ambush, all focused on their mission. Dentinho wants to talk, but he knows it would be a sign of weakness. "There was Cabrita, a young mixed-race girl, looked almost hand-sculpted, I won her over, I went to the Halley, she was taking off her clothes, I went to her still dressed and she was moaning, 'Come on, come on,' and I went, I couldn't come and my dick wouldn't go down and I only managed to finish when the sun was almost up, I wanted it too much. Then I forgot all about her." And he knows he's lying. And he thinks to himself without even meaning to, "A month later you heard she was having an affair with Afonsinho, your brother, your blood brother, and when you showed up at Afonsinho's, she was the one who opened the door, yeah, and you started yelling 'Judas! Judas! How could you do this to me?' and you yelled 'Judas! How could you?' shouting at her and at Afonsinho who was farther inside the house, and she gestured as if to say, 'This is my business, don't get involved,' and turned to you and said, 'Now it's my fault for being hot?' And you never forgot the gesture or the words. And that's when you started to get a little colder, to think before you acted. And then they found Cabrita dead, her face slashed open with a razor, a broom handle up her ass, a soda bottle up her pussy, and a bullet to the heart. But you'd only planned the slashed face, the rest came later. The bullet was for love. And from then on, you did things only a monster would."

Dentinho prefers to think about the day he took acid. The guys decided to race cars at the top of the hill, a ball was tossed high and so he got ready to take it to his chest and then he saw the moon, the full moon, then the moon came falling, falling and he shot the moon in the chest. He felt something so immense that he sat on the ground and started to cry, and the kids didn't understand anything. Then he got up, locked himself in the shack and stayed there by himself. He only left after two days, and he never drank, snorted, or smoked anything again. But he didn't forget it. And that is the best memory he will take from this world, high, shooting the moon in the chest.

Rafa looks at the clock and says, "It's time." Dentinho comes out of his delirium and kicks Afonsinho's body. "The party is about to start," he says.

(Knocking on the door.) "Get off me. These men. Get off me, get out of me, what have you done? Do you owe something?" (Knocking on the door.)

"Who is it?" Micuçu asks, gun in hand.

"It's me, Kleber."

"Fuck, you're still awake at this hour?"

"It's me."

"I know. It's Klebinho. He's four years old and really strong. What do you want?"

"I want a pacifier."

"Wait a sec."

"Do you have one?"

"I do. But it's pink."

"I want it."

Micuçu opens the door to give Klebinho the pacifier and comes face to face with Dentinho and Rafa.

"This is mine now," Dentinho says.

Beleco is showing off to the kids, playing Russian roulette. Rolling the drum of the old .38 and pulling the trigger. Until Dentinho takes the metal to his head and shouts, "Enough!"

"Pull that trigger," Beleco shouts. "Pull that trigger!"

"I still need your head," says Dentinho. "Let's go."

"What's good?" Beleco asks.

4. Fireworks

I'm the fireworks guy, lighting up a Roman candle every time there's a cop around. By the time I was old enough to understand things, I had six brothers and a sister, who was the oldest and took care of us boys like a mother and was even more of a mother than our mother, and she sang, cooked, gave us beatings and affection, and even bossed our real mother around, who was always at work and drinking and weeping and sad and bringing men home on the weekends.

I'd stolen some roller skates and was there sitting on the road, holding onto Dafé's bike, and there were four more bicycles on the road, provoking the cars, me in skates following behind. Everyone screaming, that chaos, flying.

Then Dafé swerved around a hole as I was following him, and my hands let go of his bike, and I was on my own, trying not to fall, and I managed to get my balance back as the car got bigger and bigger and I didn't even feel the impact.

When they took me home, I thought I would be lying down there forever. When I got up, I found out that one of my legs was shorter than the other and that it was going to be like this from now on.

My sister left home, and my brothers started finding their way out. Everyone disappeared. I became a reject. I couldn't even steal. I became the fireworks guy. I light them all up.

I was going back to my post when I saw two shadows and hid. Manaus was passing by with Rafa, and Rafa was saying that he had some weapons he wanted to exchange for Manaus's, the ones he got from the fancy house, and Manaus was saying it was important to have his own arsenal, to no longer rely on Dentinho.

I found it strange and followed them through the shadows and found it even stranger when they went into Pedrão's house. There was no music playing inside, even though they always had those Jesus songs playing until an ungodly hour. It was then that I heard a muffled scream. I didn't even think about it; I took a Roman candle from my bag, lit it, and it exploded up against the outside of the house. I saw Beleco through the back window and an officer with a knife in his hand running after the kid.

I ran to the alley and lit up three more rockets, now high up the hill, and I didn't understand what was happening when the shooting started up there, on the enemy border. My concern was down here, at Pedrão's house, as I watched five officers leave the house, one of them with a bag hanging off his back, a van appeared, and the officers escaped, safe, free.

Up there, the shooting was still going strong. Until it stopped and I saw my team taking four officers onto São

Roberto and I went with them and saw the officers asking to be let go, but the only answer they got was bullets, and then they were thrown into a trash can, doused with gasoline, and lit up like a bonfire.

After that I stayed behind them to the quarry and eight officers asked for forgiveness, they begged, but my guys were angry and started throwing them down from up there, one by one. I don't know what Dentinho was doing with my people, but he was there, encouraging them, and he even shot at the last boy they threw over the edge, but he missed. Then Dentinho looked at me and asked, "What're you looking at?"

"Nothing," I said.

"Want to learn to fly like them?" It was a gentle threat, but the boss joined us and praised me for my service, thanked me for the warning. And then I pulled him aside and said there was something strange going on at Pedrão's house.

And then my people quickly ran downhill, burst into Pedrão's house and found Manaus's gang, all but Beleco and Dafé, and all headless. No sign of Rafa. The boss figured it out right away: the showdown up there was just a diversion, to distract us from what was going on here at Pedrão's. "A professional job," the boss said. He told us to take the bodies to the car and get on the road; those dead men didn't even deserve getting burned at the quarry.

I didn't say anything about Rafa, but I felt a shiver pass through me. Dentinho looked at me and laughed his hyena laugh. I looked down. I only know how to light up fireworks, but if I want to live much longer, I better learn some new trick, and fast.

5. The Moment of Truth

He has no memory of the city of Manaus, he was only born there, it says on his birth certificate. He wishes he could go see the city, the forest, but not that much. He likes it here.

His father, mother, and six siblings. The main person in his life was his uncle Bide, his father's brother. He was a musician. Whenever Bide came to visit his brother, he would bring records, candy, food, invite the neighbors, and throw a party. He did this once a year, but the whole family looked forward to it. Not even Christmas was as worth the wait.

He was eight years old when Bide said, "You're brave. I remember you as a kid, fighting with your older brother. He would throw you against the wall, you would hit your head, laugh it off, and go right back to fighting. Some people are born with courage."

He never forgot. Maybe he hadn't even needed to say it. Despite being small and frail, he commanded respect on the street. They called him Cachorro Louco, but it didn't stick. So they called him by his name instead, Juscelino. When he was born, his mother thought he'd make it big in life. And so she named him Juscelino. Manaus came later.

Once when he was ten, he was playing futsal on the court. His uncle was the referee. He was running with the ball between his feet, looking at the ball, looking at the goal-keeper, and then he wasn't seeing anything at all. He was spinning around and around and the first thing he heard was his uncle's voice, "It's ok, it's ok." It took him a while to get it. He'd been stabbed with a pair of scissors. His knees hit the cement as he fainted. "If this is dying, it's not bad." That's what he thought. And he never forgot it. That was how he wanted to die: total wipe-out.

When he was thirteen, uncle Bide came to get him out of the shelter for juvenile delinquents. Up to that point, he'd only ever committed petty theft. His uncle thought he could yell at him, and it would be over. He didn't last two days at his uncle's house; he took all his money and the black pistol he kept in his drawer, at his bedside table.

Now he's waking up here. They're handcuffing him and forcing his head against the kitchen table in Pedrão's house. There in the living room, also handcuffed, are Beleco, Micuçu, Panda, Nélio, Pilau, all of his men. He doesn't want to feel pain. It would be nice to be able to black out again. He always thought he'd do this himself, that he wouldn't give anyone else that pleasure. And Dentinho's laugh is what hurts the most. He hears the explosion outside and is able to see Beleco take advantage of his killers' hesitation and escape.

6. Silver Showers

The shooting is going on up there. The streets haven't been paved here yet: it's the valley, the valley of death. Rafa's mother ran away from home and is drinking at Raimundo's bar, talking loudly, something she never does. She knows that Rafa is up there, and she gets scared and gives everything away. "He wanted to be a soldier, my son. He was born in Caxias. He was always introspective, quiet, reticent. He was born to my fourth husband, so to speak, because I never got married, we just moved in together, he was his first son after five women. I don't know exactly whose son he is, I suspect it's one of the two, the bus driver or the late-night passenger. I don't know which one. I stopped having kids after him, I already had a son at home to watch over us. I got my act together because of him. I thought he was just another kid to feed, but he wasn't. He weaned early. He didn't cry for food like other children. He looked at me like he understood. One day I hit him, and he didn't cry. He was three years old and was at the bedroom door watching me fuck some random guy. He looked at me like a man. No finger in his mouth, no pacifier, standing there, watching. I yelled, 'Get out of here!' He stood there, I hit him, he didn't cry. I even wondered if he was crazy or stupid. But he started playing with other children, no one made fun of him. He liked to fight and was good at it. He was bossy. The other children always did what he wanted. He had the will. At school, he was always the best. He read. He only liked war books, war movies. All he thought about was serving in the army. Then he joined the army. During an exercise, they threw a grenade into the middle of his platoon. He threw himself on top of the grenade to smother it and save the others. I don't know exactly how it happened, he never told me, I heard it from other people. He was promoted to corporal, a hero. He wanted to fight in Africa, to be a UN soldier, I don't know, he wanted to be a soldier anywhere. But then they discharged him, they dismissed him, and he didn't tell me the reason for that either. He never told me anything. He left the barracks and said he was going to fight the war his own way. He's an expert at weapons and God knows what else. He doesn't snort anything, doesn't smoke, doesn't drink, doesn't gamble. He doesn't talk to me anymore. What he really likes to do is to shoot."

Drunk, misty-eyed, Guile Xangô told whoever would listen that it was common in lots of places to burn the dead and it was getting popular here too, crematoriums were the big business of the future, saving space in cemeteries, which by the way were already taking over the living parts of big cities, and that seen from above, all cities looked like cemeteries, every large building photographed to scale was a grave, a tombstone, a mark of death. All cities grew around a cemetery. The metropolis was born out of the necropolis.

Fine, Guile Xangô, shut up. Soon you'll be talking about the barbecue as a ritual that takes place every weekend, in backyards, in the suburbs, right here in Maia and all over the city, on the edge of soccer fields, on balconies, on rooftops, by pools, millions of people waiting for the coals to get hot, the most advanced using electronic grills, everyone putting meat on a skewer, salt in their left hand, a sharp knife in their right, everyone gorging themselves on red meat.

Cut it out, Guile Xangô. This here smells different. Don't run away, Guile Xangô, it's human flesh, it's people being burned alive inside tires. And there's no point in arguing that somewhere, or in the future, they're going to discover the nutritional qualities of human flesh. No one is going to eat that meat. Be for real.

The smell of burning flesh begins to take over Maia. Bullets are still flying back and forth. Tracer bullets cross the sky. News spreads that eight bodies were thrown from the top of the quarry. Ashes begin to fall.

6. If You Want to Cry, Go Ahead

Pedrão hears the hurried footsteps and tells his women to take cover in the corner. He looks for something to defend himself, but he only has his own bare hands. Someone kicks the door, which gives way after the third attempt. A man comes in and Pedrão wrestles with him. "It's me," Vavau shouts, freeing himself from Pedrão's arms. "Let's go." Pedrão sees his women clinging to Vavau and feels angry, jealous, and relieved.

He's only able to pull himself together when he sees his taxi parked outside the abandoned junkyard. It's a cloudy day. Vavau is driving and says he's taking everyone to Vovô do Crime's daughter's house. "You'll stay there for a few days until the dust settles." Pedrão wants to complain, but Vavau asks him to shut up, for the love of God. Rute comes out of the kitchen enveloped in a delicious smell. "You all need a bath," she says, and takes Pedrão's women to the bedroom. "That's all we managed to get out of there," says Rute, showing them bags of clothes. "They cleaned it out, took everything." Pedrão's women cry pitifully.

"I want to see my house," Pedrão says and walks to his taxi. Vavau pushes him into the passenger seat. "As far as I know, this fucking taxi is still mine," Pedrão shouts. Vavau grabs the steering wheel and looks at his friend without saying a word. Pedrão looks down and says, "I know what you're thinking." And the two go back in time.

Pedrão is trying to face down the two criminals and gets shot in his own taxi on the corner of Sampaio and Haddock. He howls, *"Ai ai ai!"* The greengrocer runs. At Nelson's bar, some run to hide in the bathroom while others run to get help. Pedrão screams in pain, *ai ai ai*, with his hand on his waist. Guile Xangô and Vovô do Crime are the first to arrive. Guile Xangô gets behind the wheel while Vovô do Crime tries to push Pedrão into the back seat, but he resists, his eyes rolling wildly, looking like he's among enemies. They surround him and try to convince him he better go to the hospital, or he'll die. He only settles down when Vavau shows up, despairing. He hugs Vavau, who asks him to "calm down calm down calm down" and leads him to the back seat and tells Guile Xangô to step on the gas. Vovô do Crime wants to go but Pedrão groans, "Not him, no, no, no." And Vovô do Crime says, "I hope you die," and gets in the car. "I want to see you try to get me out of here." And tells Guile Xangô, "Just drive this piece of shit." The car takes off, the tires squealing, Guile Xangô is nervous, takes some wrong turns, but arrives at Souza Aguiar followed by a line of taxis. Vovô do Crime makes a fuss, shows off his ID hoping for preferential treatment, but it's Guile Xangô's smooth talk that does the trick. He knows a doctor there, he's well connected, and the pressure from the other taxi drivers also helps open some doors. Vavau hugs Guile Xangô, and they don't leave until midnight, when they know for sure Pedrão is out of danger.

Meanwhile, on the corner of Sampaio and Haddock, taxis continue to arrive, and drivers gather around the pool of blood. The police arrive, and there's a conflict between the police officers and the taxi drivers. A picture of the commotion appeared in the papers.

"You're my only friend," Pedrão says, getting out of the taxi and walking into Nelson's bar. Vavau orders a shot of cachaça and drinks it all in one gulp. "You'll need one too—not one, two," he says to Pedrão.

They walk up to the house and with each step, people join them like a little procession. They stop outside the house: windows, doors, roof tiles, everything ripped off. Pedrão walks in with Vavau right behind him. There's congealed blood everywhere, carpets covered in blood, it looks like the entire house has been bleeding horribly. Pedrão walks through the entire house, this place where he thought he'd be happy forever. From one of the windows, he looks at the small crowd outside, looking onto his misfortune. He's sure that many of them out there participated in the looting. His furniture, his stove, his women's stereo, his TV set, their TV sets, their jewelry, their dolls, everything is now scattered across other people's houses, sold at a bargain price, exchanged for a pittance to bankroll some bastard's addiction, and he thinks about shouting at them, but Vavau is already shouting, "Get out of here, you sons of bitches, vultures, you scumbags, this isn't a movie." And he comes down on the small crowd with a club. The crowd disperses, some laughing, "Serves you right," others lamenting, but everyone happy; it's better to see someone else in deep shit than to be up to their own necks in it.

"You have nothing left, Pedrão, your house is haunted. And there's no point in going up there to complain because no one will want to hear it."

"I still have my taxi, I'm healthy, and I haven't given up yet."

"That's what I call talking like a man."

"And I have a friend."

"If you want to cry, go ahead."

THE MIRACLES, THE CRAZY

Every afternoon, between three and four, a bird singing, *Bem-te-vi,* punches its card at work, a very helpful creature. They say that a thrush appears on Sampaio Ferraz from time to time. But no one has any proof, and the witnesses here aren't exactly reliable. There's a real bird that sings sometimes near Nelson's bar, but not quite; it's a cuckoo, the cuckoo from the antique shop. No one has ever gone into that shop. It's even possible that the thrush is a real bird too, but no one ever goes into the antique shop.

The traffic, which sounds half like a river and half like wind, has become part of the soundtrack to the days and nights in the area. The hustle and bustle of the farmers market, on Wednesdays, comes and goes. In the early hours of the morning you can hear the dogs barking, talking to each other, and the chorus of roosters crowing to their hens, shouting for help, trading moonlight for morning. And there are always gunshots. Three in a row, never just one. Other times it's a shootout, gunfire, explosions. The strange thing is that the corpses no longer turn up after the showdown and the burning flesh, that smell clinging to memory, the buildings, the ashes on the roofs. And when one appears, no one has ever seen anything, nor do they know who it is. No one sees anything anymore, just like you no longer see a homeless person sleeping or dying on the sidewalk, or the people without wings who are thrown from the top of the quarry.

But some people here become paralyzed and rust. The refined, polite guy opened the snack bar and planted a coin in the sidewalk. Everyone, at least once, has bent down to pick up a coin like that and made a fool of themselves. Only the really bad guys have never bent down. But there's this old man who owns ten apartments in the building by the newsstand. He's all stiff, with arthritis, arthrosis, arteriosclerosis, and he always leaves the building at four in the afternoon to get some sun, when there's sun, and he stops in front of the coin and makes that terrible effort, bending over, bending down, creaking, and trying to pick up the coin. Every day, every day, every day, he bends down, he creaks, he stands there struggling to get the coin out and he can't, so he gives up, stands at the traffic light, crosses the street when the light turns green, goes and sits by the metro vent to get some sun with the other old dinosaurs.

At first, everyone laughed and some even gathered to watch. Then they got used to it. Until the day when one of the old man's granddaughters took a hammer, made a hole in the sidewalk, pulled out the coin along with a piece of cement and threw it all at the refined and polite snack bar owner. He got down behind the counter, yelled back and called the girl crazy, along with some other things, so then she started hammering on the glass of the counter and traffic stopped, the guard came out of the post office and walked up to her, security was already there, and the priest came, and she handed the hammer to the guard and hugged the priest, and the priest took her home. And that was that. The polite snack bar owner put cement over the hole, but the old man still keeps stopping in the same place and looking for the coin, and he doesn't bend down anymore because the coin is no longer there, but he keeps looking, and then he gives up, stops at the traffic light, crosses the street when the light turns green, and goes to sit by the metro vent to get some sun with the other old sclerosauruses.

The priest knows all the homeless people in the area. He never refuses their requests. He once went so far as to give all the money from a baptism to a woman with a child in her arms, even though he knew she was a professional beggar.

He doesn't like it when a beggar says, "God will pay you back double," or things like that. It took him a long time to get over the idea that he was lending money to God, out of pity or a guilty conscience. He would give to the void, automatically, without expecting anything in return. A way of humbling his own needs.

He likes beggars who lie imaginatively and get lost in the middle of their story, "My wife is sick, my three children haven't eaten in three days, I need to buy medicine for my mother, I was well off, then my wife left me, I need to find a job to get my mother out of the nursing home, I need money to buy medicine for my son, to bury my mother," and other tall tales. He doesn't like drunks who ask for money to buy bread, "I'll only give it to you if it's for booze!"

He likes Túlio. He's from the south and is a proud man. From seven in the morning until five in the afternoon, he stands at the traffic light begging from drivers, cursing, banging on windows, punching doors, kicking tires. At six he goes into Nelson's bar and orders a beer to drink under the awning. At seven-thirty in the evening, he has dinner. Then he drinks until ten, lines the sidewalk with a cloth, and goes to sleep. Túlio is proud, complains about the warm beer, the cold soup, demands respect.

The crazy girl spends the day begging in bars, at the supermarket, at the post office. All she has is a smile with buck teeth, all of them perfect, and her nickname is Mônica, after the cartoon. She stands there smiling, her hand sticking out. And one rule: she doesn't accept coins, only bills. She's mute, can only scream and grunt. She walks like a duck or as if she were on a boat, balancing herself this way and that way.

When she gets serious, her teeth still look like a smile, but her eyes are glazed over, they look inward (they seem to be afraid of what they see) or they seem to be thinking (it's a dark sadness, almost like mourning, the two eyes frozen).

She's always waiting for the priest. When he appears, she walks beside him. In her hand, a ham and cheese sandwich. People laugh, say things. She gets serious, her open mouth full of teeth, bread, cheese, and ham, and her gaze is still, her other hand on the priest's shoulder. She must be thinking about marriage, and the whole street is the church corridor, and the altar is there at the gas station, before the Xerez wine bar.

Then there's the man. He wants to confess. He's small, with ears that stick out, a big belly. He drinks and cries because his mother and father rejected him. His two brothers were tall and handsome. They did things to him, the short one, and his parents didn't even care. Where are those two idiots now? In jail for assault, fraud, kidnapping, drug trafficking, and other shit. And him? He graduated from college, he's a chemical engineer, his parents live off him. "But do you think they thank me? Not once." They love to pick on him because he doesn't have children.

Now he lives off his businesses, he has five stalls at the market, he travels to Paraguay and Argentina and smuggles clothes, watches, cigarettes. He hangs out at bars because he likes to drink, to have a good chat. When he drinks too much, he cries and tells everyone how his mother and father rejected him. He's singled out the priest and won't let go.

It's Guile Xangô's fault, he decided to carry the world on his shoulders. A joke, a dirty trick, turning the bar into a church. "He's your son, Father, deal with it, the whole world is yours."

In the darkness of the confessional, he's forced to hear about all kinds of abuse. "I was just a kid when they asked me for a blowjob for the first time. It was at home. Being a kid sucks. I thought it was normal. Later when they asked me to do it with them, I thought that was what they meant. I was a virgin until I was nineteen, can you believe it? I can't believe it either, but it's the honest to God truth, I swear. And I didn't like it," says Dafé's girl, one of them at least, grimacing. "It's not even an addiction anymore. It's a madness. Like thirst, you know? Dry mouth, dry throat? It's the same thing.

Do you think it's gross? It just came to me, this thirst thing. This idea stuck in my head. But that's it. You know? Not for nothing, but that's why I have a thing for you. With you, I can always talk, say whatever. Ideas flow," and she stretches out her hand as if to caress his face.

Her name is Lucinha. She tells Guile Xangô, asks him to help stop her daily pilgrimages. "You're going to have to share this madness with me," Guile Xangô says. And he says that she confesses to everyone. "One day she said to me, 'You are so, so, I don't know, so . . . sweet!' And I said, 'If you call me sweet again, I'll beat the crap out of you!' I looked at her sharply and then relaxed my gaze and laughed. She burst out laughing, covered her mouth with her hands, her body shaking, two big tears pooling on her fingers. 'You make me laugh. Do you know, you're the only guy who makes me laugh like that?' You have to make her laugh," Guile Xangô says.

The day is not going well, an hour after the final and Brazil lost, but it's only Saturday morning. Her youngest son is there, running in front of her, he's six years old and still can't speak properly, he stutters, but he's happy because he's going to spend the weekend at his aunt Lana's house, her sister, Lucinha. The boy isn't all right in the head, he's afraid of everything, and she doesn't know how that happened.

By her side is Luciana, her daughter, fourteen years old and already a grown woman, taller than her. Lucinha goes into her sister's house and Lana starts giving advice, and then she's kissing her nephews, offering them sweets, telling stories. Lucinha pulls her sister away, says she's nervous, tense, and needs something to calm her nerves. Lana takes her sister's pulse and gives her some pills, that will help.

Lucinha is out walking with her daughter. She notices that the men are looking only at the hot young girl. How had she not seen that before? She gets home and João, her man for the past six months, is in the kitchen making food, a talented man, a companion like she's never had before.

"Let's take care of this right now."

The three of them go to the bedroom. Lucinha locks up the entire house. She swallows all the pills with tap water. She closes the bedroom door and sits in the chair she brought from the living room, puts the gun she borrowed from Pardal Wenchell on her lap. "I'm not even here."

João is embarrassed or a little dizzy (he must have had something to drink at the bar). Her daughter doesn't care. She quickly takes off her clothes and lies down on the bed. How could she not have seen that she was already a woman? João takes off his clothes too. The two have sex. Lucinha realizes that her daughter is good at what she does. When she gets going, she fucks like Lucinha isn't there. Even worse, they both give their best to impress her, to hurt her more deeply, to even the score once and for all. They're both there. João isn't looking at her.

Her daughter looks at her and makes a gesture, a request, why doesn't she join in too? She's seeing for the first time what's been going on for five, six months, from the start. She herself asked for it. João covers his eyes with his arm. Her daughter throws her right leg over his body. They're both right there. She doesn't need to imagine anything anymore. It's like this: just like this. Lucinha doesn't know what to do. "I'm scared of myself, that I'll do something crazy, Father."

I was skinny and only knew how to fight standing up, and he knew that and fought me, he was taller and stronger, and then in the middle of the fight I bit his ear off. We were kids, and after that fight I messed up a lot, and we keep running into each other to this day. When he was younger, he used his hair to hide the ear he didn't have, but now his hair has fallen out, there's only a little bit on the top of his head, and he's chosen to embrace his baldness and the ear he doesn't have. We'll even talk, we've been talking for years, but it's never easy. Every time I go into a bar and he's there, I drink, pay, and leave, I walk away. He always says it was cowardice, and it wasn't, but there are people who believe him, and every time I see that ear he doesn't have, I make a point of remembering and telling him that I can't be good because no one will let me.

I want to be good. The old woman from Bahia, the Baiana, left Nelson's bar in the rain, she couldn't cross to the other side of the street, so I went after her. The street was a river, the water was almost up to the Baiana's shriveled breasts, and so I put her on my back, she screamed, and I crossed to the other side and left her in her house, and she screamed that she was going to stab me. I went back to Nelson, shivering with cold and smelling like sewage, and everyone was laughing at me, and now, three days later, the Baiana is telling everyone that I tried to take her by force, that I hurt her, and everyone's laughing, and I'm leaving because if I don't, I'll beat the Baiana to death. And that's why I keep saying that no one lets me be good, and on top of that, because of that, I got this nickname that pisses me off, this nickname, Bombom. Bombom my dick!

Klebinho was kicked out of daycare. He kept wanting to suck the other boys' dicks, he asked the other boys to suck his dick, he wanted to put his dick in the girls' holes, everything. His mother is a prostitute and works at home.

But before that he was innocent, at least for about three months. (He still is, but who will listen?) He found his own shadow. He saw his shadow on the wall and sat there fighting with it. What's your problem, kid? His mother would tell him to stop, and he wouldn't listen. His mother threatened him, and he kept going. His mother mocked him, and he didn't care. Klebinho took his shadow off the wall, put his shadow on the ground, kicked it, hit it. He lay down on top of his own shadow, out of breath. Then he got up, looked at his mother, wanted to know if it was time to go to school, and asked the priest, "Are you here to get me?"

While women line up and subject themselves to a humiliating search to enter the prison, she climbs onto the small bench at the square, with her back to the Ismael Silva statue, and stands there looking at the ground. Up there, from one of the barred windows, someone watches Pedrão's daughter and jerks off, and she knows and lets it happen; and she does this every Thursday, skips class and stands there, and all this because her best friend told her that her brother had the hots for her, saw a picture of her, and fell in love. He was in jail, and if she stood there, she would make his life better, and so she skips class and stands there, being looked at by someone she doesn't even know, though she can't even know for sure she's being observed, but still she stands there. She doesn't pay attention to Beleco, who's nearby feeding corn to the pigeons to turn them into balls with wings he can kick one by one.

Few people know the story of Granola, who died of love for Dedé, took a lot of Viagra to try and satisfy her and ended up dying of a heart attack or embolism, he died of love, but so many other people are dying or letting themselves be killed by love, that sneaky criminal, they should ban love as a dangerous drug or prescribe love only for those who are terminal, lock up everyone in love, put an end to romantic love, life would be much easier.

The priest picks up the girl and sits her on his lap, the embarrassed hostage of the gaze of the prisoners' wives, who are drinking in the bar across the street. He puts the girl down on the ground and they walk hand in hand. Beleco kicks a pigeon and laughs. "He's laughing at me," the priest thinks. "They're laughing at me," the girl's cold fingers between his feverish hands.

YOU DESERVE MORE

It's not jealousy, I'm not jealous of anyone, Vovô do Crime thinks, pissed off, at Luiz's bar. I simply can't. I can't watch futebol, volleyball, or basketball with this idiot. He has to explain everything. Take an action movie. There's the hero and the hero's friend. But there's not a single scene where the hero and the hero's friend are together, side by side, and he explains that the hero has no sense of humor and that the producers filmed humorous scenes to intersperse with the hero's fight scenes on purpose. And who cares about that? Let us watch the damn movie, Guile Xangô!

Same with the soccer match. The championship final is playing and he's giving a lecture on talent and teamwork, saying what everyone already knows. Lourinho is capable of doing whatever he wants with a ball, dribbling, knee-ups, neck stalls, never lets the ball fall to the ground for more than an hour, and all this while drinking beer, smoking a cigarette, that old dog. But on a soccer field, in a pickup game, he's a total idiot, a pathetic athlete. Lourinho can't even be trusted as the goalkeeper, he owns a poultry farm, raises chickens. And then he brings Periquito into the argument, Periquito who decided to take a ride on Rafa's Harley, right here at Luiz's, on the sidewalk, and the damn bike crushed Periquito's head. Nobody understood that shit, much less the arguments, but people pretend to pay attention, after all, he's the one paying for the beers.

He buys for everyone. He's the father, the provider, a bore, he has no self-awareness, everything he says comes out of a book, he's like an encyclopedia, he reads five newspapers a day, four magazines a week, and he's addicted to the internet on top of that, always with his sites, the web, his languages. Undefined personally, a failed guru, a wise idiot, a hen-like fox, the king of rats—no, that's Vavau—the king of the blind, because he can see with his eye of an asshole, that's right, the king of Cuba, the king of *cú*, of ass, of Syracuse, of the asshole, the Asshole King!

But it's not quite like that, of course. It's hell here, but not everyone does what the Devil likes, and the cool ass lover has already baptized half a dozen godchildren, and what does he do next? He takes the kids to fly kites at the square by the metro station. But he doesn't do it like everyone else, fill the sky with kites of all colors, and it's so pretty to see over a hundred kites high up against the huge red sun, a sight worthy of a photography award. But no! The idiot has to find a way to make the kids like model airplanes, that's right, model airplanes, the planes roaring high up, doing acrobatics and taking all the colorful beauty from the poor kites, and it was a good thing when Beleco got drunk on cachaça and started shooting at the little planes, trying to shoot them down one by one, and everyone was scared shitless, and he acted like a hero, huddled on top of his godchildren, the rooster protecting the little chicks from Beleco's errant shots. The great Beleco!

But let's cut him some slack. And let's go back to three a.m. on that anonymous day, as the angelic-looking boy pulls a gun from his waistband and brings the muzzle to his forehead, asking him, "Which one is Vovô do Crime, tell me who it is, who's Vovô do Crime, old man?" And a voice says, "That's Vovô do Crime." The boy puts away the gun and apologizes, "My name is Xande. I'm Cirinho's brother. I just don't like it when they make fun of me and call me Bebê do Crime because of you. But if you ever need anything, I'm there." Vovô do Crime takes off his shirt, wraps it around his head and shouts, "Vovô do Crime!" then walks away, down the hill, maintaining his posture. On the asphalt, he turns the corner and pukes behind the newspaper stand. He walks down the street, shivers as he comes face to face with the Church of the Divine Holy Spirit, at four in the morning, in the light rain. He goes back in time: here's the Estácio de Sá square, which used to be called Bica dos Marinheiros, Caminho do Rio Comprido and, farther down, Mataporcos. He goes back. Behind him, the light goes from green straight to red. The asphalt bleeds. And he screams, his arms open:

Lord, hear my voice
We are sons of bitches,
Sons of unknown parents
We are whores and faggots
Thieves cowards addicts
Bloodthirsty killers going at it
Innocent innocent innocent

Lord, hear my prayer

We are all scarred
In the spotlight
Our life is hanging by a thread
Our life is hanging by a threat
The executioner sharpens the blade
Our soul panics

Lord, hear our cry

We don't know where to go
We have no roof and no bed
We reek of pain
Our hands and pockets are empty
Hunger has shattered our teeth
We are fucked
Lord, hear our pain.

He remembers those words to this day. He spent five months pestering Nabor to put some music to the verses. Nabor, Dão, anyone who showed up with a guitar under their arm, except Nonô. And now he thinks, like a poet, "People come and go. It's hard to capture a face with just one look, a shadow of sound. No one remembers, no one knows, no one has the name of lightning. You walk among ghosts."

And he gets angry again. On the day he was shouting the verses, that idiot must've been up in the tower with the priest. He spends entire nights with the priest up in the church tower reading Saint Augustine and snorting, sniffing coke, the two of them, the priest and the poor old fucker, guests in the clay house where God is so often betrayed. The world has room for all ideas, and it has room for all the spirits who come to serve their sentence here in the penitentiary of creation.

And then he explodes, "Let's be radical here, he's trying to buy everyone, he has his godchildren, he has the support of Mirtes, that's it! It was Mirtes! It was Mirtes who nominated him to get the ring from the movement's leader, the license for fine people, why didn't I think of that before? Mirtes nominated him to receive the Nobel Prize in general mischief, and it's my fault, because I don't suck up to Mirtes, I'm the one who introduced the idiot to her, to the movement, to everyone and their mother! A politician! Not a guru, not wise, not a sage, not anything: a jerk, a politician, the Siddhartha of the arcade, the prince of shit, the crapshit Machiavelli. An asshole!"

Vovô do Crime smiles, victorious. The security guard thinks it was at him, that the laughter was for him, and asks permission to sit down, puts the glass and the beer bottle on the table and says, "I've been onto you for a while." He says he also likes to read. He's about forty, almost fifty, he's done everything, he was a manager of a big company, it went bankrupt, "You wouldn't remember the name," and he starts talking about politics. He swears the violence is too much and details a plan to exterminate all the criminals, a crooked tree must die crooked, and he would take all the murderers, rapists, drug dealers, kidnappers, degenerates, thieves, with him, and push them all out of a plane into the high seas and anyone who managed to swim to some beach deserved a second opportunity to die, maybe with a shot to the back of the head. And after that, for the new criminals, it would be terror, they would be killed on the spot, and that way Brazil would be happy. The money spent on the criminals in prison would be invested in cleaning up the slums and sterilizing all the poor women and giving vasectomies to the poor men, and lots of education, lots of health, lots of housing for everyone. That was his formula for an admirable new Brazil, full of small, happy families and free of violence thanks to a new, vigilant and efficient kind of terror.

Vovô do Crime tries to tell him, just to play devil's advocate, terrorizing people always ends the same way: whoever proposed the guillotine as a solution for a perfect society gets their head cut off, and he sings a samba that he thinks is by Noel, "and the inventor of the guillotine ended up without a neck," something like that. Terror is like a mad dog: it bites everyone, indiscriminately, and makes everyone suspicious, angry, and thirsty for blood. The security guard doesn't like this argument at all, says, "You don't understand what I'm saying," then goes back to describing his plan: he would catch all the murderers, all the degenerates, and then Vovô do Crime shouts, "Who here doesn't understand?" then grabs the bottle by the neck, "Who here doesn't understand, you bastard?" and breaks the bottle over the exterminator's head. The security guard starts screaming, blood soaking his shirt, then threatens to pull his metal piece, but the "let it go" gang takes the opportunity to beat up the security guard while Dafé and Vavau hold down Vovô do Crime, who kicks gratefully and screams, "I should've hit Nabor as payback for the bottle he broke on me, but I think an asshole like you deserves it more!"

VAVAU

This life is a strange hotel,
Which we almost always leave dazed,
For our bags are never packed,
And our bill is never paid.
—Mário Quintana

Vavau moves a checker piece forward and feels a wave of anger wash over him as Marcelo Cachaça captures his pieces one by one and then makes another king. He controls the urge to turn the tables, to punch the bums just hanging around watching the game, making fun of him. With a restrained and gentlemanly gesture, he breaks up the match, rearranges the pieces on the board, gets up and makes room for another player.

Leaning against the counter, he's still furious, even more furious because of the anger he's feeling, and stays there, stormy and distracted, listening to Macacão and Fernando talk about when they used to keep the scores for *jogo do bicho*, the only job they could get after getting out of jail. Macacão, who in two days will shoot himself in the right ear because of his gambling debt, all for a love that turned into a senile passion, listens to Fernando talk about the Colonel who bet on the same box every day, big bets, two to three hundred bucks. One day he placed the Colonel's bets, but didn't get the carbon copy, no proof, and pocketed the money. Late in the afternoon, the Colonel arrived, furious; after five months, they'd finally hit the jackpot, and Fernando ran away, a price on his head, and only managed to escape because his mother knelt at the powerful boss's feet, begged for forgiveness, and paid for the loss with the paltry savings from her disability pension.

Vavau never understood how anyone could like gambling. Pará, who was his best helper, could spend hours on those slot machines, "sucker machines" is more like it, and he was so addicted that he needed bank loans to keep up the pace. Pará bet on pinball, horses, Formula 1, wrestling, spitting contests. Vavau sent Pará away when the crazy guy used one of the cars in his old workshop for a job and brought the car back with more holes than a sieve, telling a story equally full of holes. He cut in and said, "Pará, this wasn't the first, or the second, or the third time, you know? But it was the last, our paths split up here, I'm not going to ask you to come to your senses because I know you're already up to your neck in this shit, and there's no turning back."

He orders a cognac and drinks it along with his anger in one gulp. A wind blows dead leaves on the sidewalk, the yellow leaves falling, and the wind sweeps them across the asphalt, and there's the terrible sound of the leaves dragging along, the wind drawing yellow curtains, and an agonizing yellowish dragging sound on the asphalt that shines black under the lampposts.

He would like to understand the mechanics of the wind. The wind comes from the south and herds fat clouds down the green mountain slopes and envelops trees and houses and streets and entire cities in the all-encompassing embrace of a pregnant sea, and it booms and flashes and machine-guns everything with the strength of billions of drops of water per cubic millimeter per second. The flood turns the street into a river in twenty minutes.

He pays the bill and leaves the bar. A lot of water has come down. The rain has stopped, but the streets are still flooded and full of mud and trash. He tries walking around the corners, there's no dry spot to be found. The doormen of the buildings use hoses to clean the sidewalks. Men and women scrub the soaking wet cars with mud marks up to height of the rearview mirrors. The main street and the side streets are filled with rainwater and mud. The wheels of the buses pop plastic bottles and it sounds like gunshots. He gets to the Xerez wine bar and is trying to find a way to the parking lot when he sees Assassino dragging himself painfully through the mud. "Do you need help?" he asks. The other man holds out a large plastic bag and leans on his arm. They go step by step and Assassino says that it's his varicose veins, in the morning everything is fine, but at night he can't walk because of the pain. "You're my neighbor?" he asks. It's not really a question, it's a statement. Vavau says, "Yes, my brother, I'm your neighbor, I work at the parking lot." And they crawl, like crabs, to the Royal Inn. At the door (it's a swinging door, like in old western saloons from the movies), Assassino says that he'll be fine from there, it's thirty steps up the stairs, but there's a handrail. "God help you," he says, and

Vavau hands him the plastic bag and he laughs at the stupid pride of Assassino, who doesn't want to be seen arriving home with the help of a neighbor, of a brother.

Vavau crosses the street in water up to his knees, goes into the parking lot, takes a shower and goes to sleep. At dawn, he dreams. There are thirteen of them and they're all inside a room in a luxurious building downtown. The fact that there are thirteen doesn't worry any of them. The floor number is also thirteen. They arrive at the room where numbers are being drawn. After decades of good luck, lady justice finally decided to take off her blindfold and look at them, throw all thirteen in the same boat, wrap up the thirteen in the same package, they're not at all comfortable. That's why they're there, thirteen on the thirteenth, waiting for the young lawyer.

More than anyone else, they know their own nature. The Eagle won't have anything to do with the Lion, the Cat doesn't like the Dog, the Tiger despises the Ostrich, everyone despises the Donkey, the Monkey and the Bull distrust the Snake and the Butterfly, and no one understands why the Camel and the Bear are among them. The Eagle speaks and everyone listens. The Lion speaks after the Eagle and everyone listens. Everyone hates the Eagle and the Lion, who won't turn their backs on each other, that's the only thing the two of them agree on.

Every man for himself. Each wanted to defend himself alone. It had always been like this, and each one always knew how to fend for himself, keep himself safe from the others, one against the others, all against all. Each man for himself. Why change the rules of the game?

Then he comes in, Vavau, the young lawyer. He doesn't really know why he's there. They had always had everything: judges, police officers, politicians, journalists. Why were they there shaking with fear when he, the young lawyer, came in?

Vavau puts the briefcase on the table and says, "I'm the Devil's Advocate." Everyone bursts out laughing. He waits for the laughter to end and starts shouting to the Eagle that his lover is going to use up all the fortune he's amassed in two and a half years: yachts, apartments, houses, cars, everything. And the Eagle starts to cry like a child on the Lion's shoulder, who also cries. The others get on their knees and beg Vavau to tell them what will happen to them in the future. And Vavau shows on a blackboard how they'll be defeated by their wives, their lovers, their sons and daughters, their sons-in-law, their daughters-in-law, their entire family, the masters of ceremonies, the standard-bearers, the queens of the drum section, the Bahian women, and they cry their eyes out. The only way out is to hand over the points to him, the young Devil's Advocate, all the points, and they agree happily, and Vavau wakes up to the sound of the first cars entering the parking lot, in a clean and shiny world, brand new.

5X1

Jeans, sneakers, hair up in a ponytail, sunglasses and a Flamengo number 10 jersey. She exuded energy, was bursting with health. He envied her youth.

She got off the ferry that connects Niterói to Rio, a bloom of desire in the middle of the small crowd. She crossed Antônio Carlos and got to Sete de Setembro. He went down Rua da Assembleia. On Rio Branco he had a direct view of her sunglasses, of her determined profile, her red lips. He thought about saying, "You take the metro at Carioca, get off at Estácio station, take the other metro on line two and get off at Maracanã station."

Everyone turned to look at her. The group of street cleaners: "That's too much woman for me!" A group of street kids: *"Flameeeeengo!* Go *ooooff!"* Flamengo-off.

Fans of the Flamengo soccer team gathered at Amarelinho. Three of them surrounded the girl. She smiled, performed elegant capoeira moves and continued through Floriano Square. Boos and applause. The applause was for her, and she clasped her hands over her head and raised an imaginary cup.

She knew how to take care of herself. She ended up at Mahatma Gandhi Square and, on Passeio Street, stopped at a stall in front of Cine Palácio, bought some chewing gum and headed toward Sala Cecília Meireles. Bye!

Guile Xangô thought, "Landfill, Museum of Modern

Art, spending the Sunday lying on the grass, reading the newspapers next to the Monument to the Dead."

At the Republic of Paraguay, she hesitated. A bus with Flamengo flags: "Go go go!" She had a moment of indecision, "Go go go!" And he, to his own surprise, got on behind her. She joined in, shouting war songs. She was not shy at all.

Maracanã stadium erupted. Guile bought a ticket for the stands from a scalper. What if she went to the seated section? He was determined to stay close, and that wouldn't make sense. He thought about reselling the ticket, buying a seat. He was surprised by the number of girls wearing shirts for the rival Vasco soccer team, and beautiful girls at that.

He went in and out of bars, ate a burger and dragged around the stadium the same feeling of abandonment he'd had every day in recent years, the bitter grief of a separation, the bars, the drinking. Why was he losing himself there? He decided, despite himself, that he was going to stay. He bought a Flamengo shirt. Fans were roaring and shouting all around him.

The gates opened. He walked toward one of them and felt like he'd been punched in the chest when he saw the girl wearing number 10, up front, with the mass of Flamengo fans between them. He felt relief and admiration when he realized she was nobody.

The girl stood in the middle of the stadium ring, in the neutral zone. A group was forming around her. He hadn't given up the idea that he was there to protect her, but that was stupid; she didn't need it, she was part of the delirium, of the immense collective solitude. A red and black circle closed in around her and the wave grew until it crashed far away against the other black and white shore.

It had been a while since he'd been to a game, since he'd disappeared into a crowd. How many times had he walked out of there under the cold rain of defeat? And how many times had he floated in the arms of victory, high on happiness? But one day, he started feeling like giving up, a tiredness no one could save him from. Perhaps it was that moment, about eight years ago, that he began to truly die.

The stadium was packed, songs and war cries echoed the battle between two giants. Flamengo's fans had taken over half the stadium. Vasco's fans were also singing, but it was safer not to listen to them. And the girl was still there, invincible, cheering alone, shouting, raising her arms, turning her body into a waving flag.

Fear and frenzy, fourteen minutes into the second half. Vasco invaded their half of the field, the forward kicked, the ball went past the goalkeeper and he stood up to watch the play. He even saw the silence fall over the Flamengo fans like a power outage, a blackout, but the ball was grabbed right by the goal line. If that ball had gone in, the fate of the match would've been different. And her life too. Number 10 stood up and shouted the name of the hero of that play. Everyone shouted with her.

Two minutes later, the explosion. He saw the girl jump desperately in the middle of the crowd. Arms grabbed and mouths kissed. And she grabbed and kissed back and shouted, "Goal goal goal," three times, and howled.

It was through her, at the thirty-minute mark, that he saw the second goal: she jumped high, floated, punched the air, first with her right hand, then with her left hand, and fell into the arms of the fans, dozens of hands touching her body, squeezing, grabbing, mouths drooling over her curves, and he saw her rise to the surface of that assault, jumping, screaming, goal.

The game ended and the fans were there, sweat, screams, tears. She slipped out of the excitement of the hugs and came pushing her way toward him, she clung to him shouting, "We're the champions, damn it, we're the champions! We're the champions!" He didn't scream at all, and let himself be carried away by the anguishing gift of being able to press her against his enemy body. She screamed, and other fans came to cling to the two of them, "We're the champions, damn it, we're the champions!" When the collective hug broke, she said, "Let's go."

They left Maracanã jumping, howling, hugging, and being hugged, "We're the champions!" He started shouting what she was shouting, her warm hand in his cold hand, until the crowd dispersed, and suddenly, the two of them, just the two of them, were walking down the street while cars honked their horns in a crazy chaos.

"Right here," she said. They went into the hotel and she asked, "Do you take credit cards?" He vaguely realized what this was about and his heart raced as he said, "I'll pay." He was pulled up the two flights of stairs and as soon as he closed the bedroom door, she started taking off her clothes and saying, "I've been checking you out since this morning, you're into it, aren't you? OK, you brought me luck, you deserve the cup and you're going to take the cup, you'll never forget this day, man, I'm going to finish you off, you'll see, I'm going to finish you off." And she went all out for him. And she screamed and swore viciously and was determined to finish him any way she could, with her arms, thighs, a hungry mouth, and she swore and swore that she was going to end him, "I'm going to finish you off," and he thought, "Come on, she's going to finish me off." He didn't want to hold out, but he tried to keep himself in check, to remember that he was experienced. What he had to do was play defense, not get carried away by his enthusiasm, defend against her attack as best he could, stay on his feet, on his feet and not fall, not fall, give away his life, his defeat. And when she moaned, saying that she was going to finish him off, and then she just moaned and came, came crashing down on top of him, he almost couldn't believe it; he had held out, he had played defense.

He waited for her tiger heart to switch to a kitten heart and then he turned her around, and then he mounted her, and then he saw her tight smile, the sweat running down her beautiful face, and he started to invade her pitch very slowly, happy to see the astonishment in her eyes. The game wasn't over yet, it was his turn to tie the game, to turn the game around. Invading her pitch, he gave orders to the midfielders to keep their marking, asked the defenders to advance and the forwards to stay on the wings and waited for her to come again and she came, she came strong, one more time. He waited a little longer until he saw a spark in her eyes, the spark of someone who recognizes the value of their opponent, that warm and warming spark. Only then did her goalkeeper come out majestically from under the goalposts and cross the field with big, calm steps and enter her area. And when the ball came falling, in the last second before the whistle went off, already in stoppage time, when the ball came falling, the goalkeeper put her head in, and he saw that he'd scored the goal. She closed her eyes and opened her mouth in a silent scream.

He woke up to the sound of the door slamming. He thought about running after her but preferred to wallow in that epiphany. He slept deeply, dreamless, far beyond himself. He woke up another person and opened the window to let in the traffic, the voices, the wonder, the redemption, and the morning sun of a foreign city by the sea.

OLÍVIA

Guile Xangô guarantees that everyone here has a little knot. It might go by another name: blockage, impasse, dead end, extreme situation, paralysis, blank. There was a disaster and you got stuck there, crashed, traumatized, and no longer able to live, vegetated. You died there, even as you continued living. A knot in the thread. The knot prevents you from creating an emotional bond with anyone else. You no longer give yourself over, you no longer want to be available, open.

There's Olívia, so skinny she's translucent. She invites you to her house. She welcomes you, you talk, drink, smoke, all that. Then, when you start to exchange confidences, she takes out the deck of cards and starts playing solitaire. She closes the door to her world and plays solitaire until the sun is up, ten, fifteen hours straight.

The knot? Her man, Paulo, who went out to receive a loan from a bank with some other friends. It was the last one, he swore, he wanted to give her a decent life, to stop all the little scams in shopping malls and supermarkets.

Everything went fine inside, but when they were leaving, they came face to face with a patrol car, the alarm had gone off. There were six of them, two managed to get away. Three died and her husband was shot half a dozen times. He went to the hospital, survived and then went to jail. With the robbery and the other exploits he'd been planning, he got twenty years.

She's still waiting for him to come back.

Rafa was carrying the money bag in his left hand, the machine gun in his right, walking. The car stopped a little ways ahead, the doors open. He got in. Paulo followed. And then he heard the gunshots. He saw Paulo falling and the men in uniform there, shooting. The other three were running away on foot. He started shooting at the uniforms, keeping an eye on Paulo, and Paulo signaled for him to get out, and tried to say something else, but he couldn't.

The car took off and Paulo was there on the sidewalk, with the uniforms closing in on him, and he wasn't going to be able to keep his promise. "If anything happens to me, don't leave me in their hands," he said, but now he was there. But he would keep the other one: to leave Olívia in a good place.

Rafa hid at Ruth's house for a while. The room stank. Clothes, books, newspapers, magazines, beer bottles and cans, liters and liters of wine. He turned on the TV, turned it off. He watched the movie inside his head: Paulo falling on the sidewalk, the others falling down. He could've fallen next to him, gone back. He even tried to, but Pará pulled him into the car. "Let's go, let's go, let's go." Pará had a grudge against Paulo.

He opened up the bag and emptied it on the floor. He started counting. Almost a million. Why not one point five million? Why not two million? He counted again. Why not three million? He put everything back in the bag and looked for a place to hide the bag. He looked and couldn't find one. He put the bag under the bed and tried to sleep. The movie kept playing. The light was emitting a rotting odor. It was on. Paulo went to look for a way out and didn't come back. He wouldn't come back. Tomorrow they'd say he had fallen, that he was in the trash, it was always like that. The sun rotting you day and night. The light in the room stinking when it was on. Until it burned out. Or someone turned it off. Paulo had already turned it off. It stank.

Pará comes into Raimundo's bar and the silence falls. He drinks a shot of cachaça, his hand shaking, the liquor drips down his chin over his bare chest. He talks. He talks. No one listens. Everyone is focused on the checkerboard where Guile Xangô makes the wrong move and Marcelo Cachaça the right one. The game is neck and neck, but it's almost impossible to beat Marcelo.

Pará continues to talk to no one about his time as a soldier. "We'd found a bank. Lana had brought the weapons on the road. Lana was our mule. The best. No mule was better than Lana. And then we set up the bank, with the men behind us shooting up a storm. We got into two cars. Eight men in two cars, three wounded. The idea was to leave the cars at the entrance to the favela and run up the hill . . ."

Guile Xangô had managed a tie with Marcelo Cachaça, and that was almost a win.

" . . . and me, the three of us, stayed down there on the asphalt, me, Rafa, and Paulo ambushing the officers while the rest of the gang stomped through the favela carrying the bags. Three against more than thirty. Three against a battalion. For God's sake! Thunder, thunder, thunder! We stopped the whole uniformed gang. It would never have crossed their minds that we had the guts. But we did and we stopped them. Ten minutes of fighting, but for me it was an hour, ten years. And I didn't want to leave. I had run out of ammunition, but I kept shooting. I didn't want to leave the fight. Believe me. I was shooting without ammunition. And we stopped the officers, the three of us, me, Paulo, Rafa, and we walked away making fun of them."

Guile Xangô makes a smart move, and everyone enjoys seeing the reigning champion teeter at the center of the ring and start to collapse.

Vovô do Crime regretted having taken Guile Xangô to meet Marinha, his daughter. Half an hour in, the two were already like childhood friends, and two hours later, they were hand-feeding each other. Vovô do Crime thought it was all so cheesy, disgusting even, and went to sleep swearing he'd never met a worse guy than Guile Xangô.

Usually, he got home to some warm bread just as his daughter was leaving for work. The two of them would have coffee in the kitchen while they talked about something or other. His daughter had already given up on begging her father to come to his senses, and he'd already given up trying to convince her to abandon that miserable life as a civil servant in a corrupt and inefficient state, murderer by omission, cannibal on principle, kidnapper of humanity, Robin Hood in reverse, stealing from the poor to give more to the rich. They grumbled about the little things in their lives or the big shit going on in the city and the country. The daughter would leave with a kiss, and the father would go to bed to sleep with the black cat he'd taken off the streets and let make its nest there.

Vovô do Crime would wake up around two in the afternoon and follow an unfailing ritual: feed the cat, roll his first joint of the day and, sitting on the toilet, smoke and empty his bowels, then drink a coffee, and smoke some more leaning out of the apartment window.

He did everything like he usually did, but with a sensation of heartburn in his soul. Guile Xangô came to lean out of the window next to him, and they stayed there in silence. The day was clear and calm, but you never know. Never, ever. An armed group came out of the bank across the street carrying bags of money. Three of them got into a parked car. Another car arrived to pick up the other three. Shots rang out from inside the bank or from the corner and one of the men with the bags fell onto the sidewalk. The first car was already far away. The second one sped off, leaving the injured man. Police cars started to arrive, surrounded the area, and went after the robbers.

"Damn, today is my lucky day," Vovô do Crime said. That was the third robbery at that bank in less than two months. The other two times he hadn't seen anything and even thought about hanging a banner in the window, asking the robbers to let him know when the action was going to happen, so he could watch it all from the best seats in the house. Now he didn't need to ask anymore.

He took a deep drag on the joint and watched the police throw the injured robber into the back of the police car, and he started to think he was unlucky after all; the other two times the job had been quick, clean, and perfect. In an automatic gesture, he passed the cigarette to Guile Xangô.

The police car took the injured man away. "Isn't that Paulo they're taking?" asked Guile Xangô.

Olívia was happy. Paulo was happy. They woke up, smoked, had sex, and slept again. She woke up again, went into the bathroom, and stood there looking at the city shining under the Sunday sun, a day so wonderful it made her want to cry, to die, to pray, and beg for the world to stop and for it to be just this, this happiness, this sunny Sunday. Then he came and hugged her, and they stayed there, breathing in all the sweetness, the goodness, the beauty.

They went down the hill and the magic continued. They did some shopping at the supermarket (out of professional habit, she grabbed two kilos of steak and half a dozen packets of noodles). They came back along Sampaio, she with two bags, he with four. They stopped at Nelson's and had a beer. Then at Luiz's, two more. Everyone could see that they were happy. On Maia, a small black dog started following them. Olivia wanted to chase the dog away, but Paulo said, "Leave him alone." They stopped at Raimundo's, had another beer. They went out and the dog followed them up the alley.

Now she's busy in the kitchen making food while Paulo watches TV and talks to the dog. He asks, "What's his name?" She doesn't know. She'll think about it. Paulo is there, getting tangled up with the dog on the rug. He needs to wash the rug. Buy a real rug. Paulo likes children and animals. Animals know he's a good person. That dog knows. He is like a son.

The two of them eat and Paulo gives the dog a piece of steak. Then she clears the table, washes the dishes, and Paulo calls out, "Come lie down, white girl." The two of them watch TV. The dog falls asleep at Paulo's feet.

On Monday, she gets out of the shower and goes to work. He wakes up and asks her to sit next to him on the bed. Paulo promises that he'll leave that life behind, that he'll help her leave that life behind too. "Let's leave it all behind," he promises. When he explodes inside her, Olivia screams, "I want a child with you, let's make a child, let's make a child!"

When she comes back, it's already getting dark, the house is empty. Except for the dog, who peed on the carpet, shit in the kitchen, and tore up the couch. She kicks the dog but stops herself; it's Paulo's dog. She puts the dog food she bought in a dish and the dog eats it all. She doesn't have a name for him yet, but with all the shit he leaves everywhere, he could easily be Cagão.

It's daybreak, Paulo hasn't returned, and she hasn't slept. She takes a shower, locks the dog in the bathroom with a bowl of dog food, leaves a note stuck to the mirror. Then she writes on the mirror with lipstick, "I love you," and puts the date on it. She chats for a bit at the neighbors', she needs company.

She goes back home, and the house is still empty. The dog peed and shit all over the bathroom, hasn't eaten anything, and looks at her like she's an enemy. She kicks the dog.

She doesn't want to sleep, but she blacks out with the

TV on. She wakes up to the sound of the rain. She puts on the first clothes she finds and goes down to the street in the rain. She's passing by Raimundo's bar when Pará waves her over, "I want to talk to you." The two go into the mansion and Pará tells her, "They were leaving the bank, everything went wrong, Paulo fell, he's either dead or in the hospital." She stumbles out of the house, a taste of vomit in her throat, and all she can think about is finding Guile Xangô. Then, as if by the power of thought, she bumps into him on the corner of Maia and Sampaio, and she doesn't need to say anything, Guile Xangô says, "I know, let's talk." They sit at the back of Kadhafi's bar, Guile Xangô telling her what he saw, Olívia sobbing on his shoulder. On Tuesday, Guile Xangô says he knows where Paulo is, but they won't let Olívia see the injured man. She manages to get past security, goes up and down the stairs, he must be in there, where there's a police officer at the door. She talks to the police officer, and he says, "You better work hard, he lost, you lost." She doesn't give up. She talks to a nurse: when he's out of danger, he'll be sent to prison to await trial. Paulo runs the risk of spending the rest of his life in a wheelchair.

She's walking up Maia when Pará whispers something in Guile Xangô's ear and hands him a bag. Guile Xangô catches up with Olívia. They get to her house and Guile Xangô opens the bag and shows her bundles of new bills, new money, freshly printed, and says, "It's yours." Olívia closes the bag and throws it on top of the cupboard. Guile Xangô brings her a glass of water and two pills, "Here, drink this." She wakes up two days or two worlds later and finds a note from Guile Xangô, "There's food in the fridge, I bought it at Tia Glorinha's, just heat it up, you need the strength, I'll be back soon." The dog is asleep under the table. Olívia picks him up, goes outside and throws him against the wall of Mirtes' house. He whines, groans, goes limp, and she throws the dog against the wall again. Then she hears Mirtes' voice asking, "Why'd you kill the little dog?" Olívia realizes that she's naked and that the children have stopped playing ball and are now watching and laughing, laughing at her. Then they stop laughing, grab the dog that still shows signs of life and start running because she's screaming something they don't understand, and she stands there, screaming, and they don't look too closely because they remember that almost everyone there eats at her house, but it's the other Olívia who fills plates and plates with food, screaming, "You have to eat it all, you have to lick the plate clean," not this one here, screaming naked. Mirtes covers Olivia up with a sheet, but she resists, wants to fight back and kill her, and then Mirtes shouts, "Help me here, Xaxango, I'm losing my patience, I think Olívia has gone completely crazy!"

ALWAYS

Then this friend of mine comes along and tells me straight out, "You know I love you, don't you?" I say I do. And he says more, "I love you. Always." And he tells me that within five years his whole family had landed in jail: his grandmother, his mother, his wife, his two brothers, his brothers' wives, his children, and his two brothers' children, only Tereza, who was blind and a saint, was left out. "You need to write my story," he says.

There are people around here I don't love and remain a stranger to, and that will never change. It's part of how I live, how I survive in the underworld. There's a woman who now only wears black because I chased her away, and she felt chased away, she called me a lunatic, I don't argue with her.

I'm a man of my word, and words are like a very slutty woman, they're on everyone's lips, your mother's and your father's, so I'm one to keep a man's word, if you know what I mean. I know I smell good, and sometimes I stink badly, but even so I put up with myself, they put up with me, we meet halfway. I don't care. I'm the kind of person who stinks and smells, and one day I'll stink so much that they'll bury me in wreaths of flowers just to mask the stench, and I'll become meat for worms and bones for dogs. Then I won't stink or fuck myself up anymore. Never again.

I'm a man of my word. I love being loved and I even

love those who don't love me. I don't sell or trade my love for anything, nor do I mess with jealousy, I'm no better than anyone else. In fact, I'm a nobody to be somebody else, and I go ahead or else.

"Hoi polloi." Among the Greeks, "hoi polloi" was the crowd, the common people, the lowest of the low.

Idiot. Among the Greeks, idiots were those who only knew how to take care of their own things, of themselves, those on the outside of society. I've never been an idiot in the Greek sense, I'm gregarious, supportive, even promiscuous. But none of that keeps me from being an idiot in the modern sense, and they use me and abuse me, I don't care. Screw them. Bite them.

I'm alive. I live on the street and in the bedroom, in hotels and bars, I have sex, I don't have sex, I get soft, I lie with truths, but I don't cheat, that would be too much. I live among Greeks and Trojans, faggots and mermaids, nymphs and godfathers, and I shit on them and walk on them, and I love them, and I hate them. I'm human.

The only thing I can be proud of right now is drinking all the drinks and not throwing up on the person sitting at the table next to me.

So when this friend, in front of everyone, hugs me and tells me he loves me, I accept this love with humility, even though I know I still don't know myself well enough to love myself completely, and then he kisses me, hugs me tight and whispers in my ear, "Do you love me?" And I hug his arms and shout to the entire bar, "Always."

(The best phrase I've ever heard about love—of anyone, your neighbor, yourself—is the following: "I loved you," "you loved me," and "we fucked up.")

Forever yours or else!

AT THE INTERNET CAFÉ

"Well, the opinion of the bubble . . . "
"A bubble has no opinion."
—Machado de Assis, *Quincas Borba*

"I died again," says the boy with big green eyes, punching the video screen and demanding Guile Xangô's attention as he restarts the game. Guile Xangô sees on the boy's screen a man armed to the teeth, blowing up cars, shooting other armed men, running through the streets of an unreal city, jumping over fences, running into a warehouse full of enemies tucked into a huge maze of containers and getting killed by a man who shows up out of nowhere. "You died again, kid," says Guile Xangô. "My name is Cristiano," the boy says and wipes his face with the collar of his blue T-shirt. He's sweating profusely despite the cold air conditioning. "I can't sleep. Since my sister died of tuberculosis everything is a party to me," Cristiano says as he restarts the game for the tenth time.

Guile Xangô downloads his emails, deletes unwanted messages, reading most of them absentmindedly, taking pleasure in the virtual encounters. His diplomat friend is leaving Switzerland for Brazil and writes:

"It's three in the morning and I'm posting this message without editing it. We know very well what the word Switzerland means to most people: perfect clocks, precise schedules, trains on time. So, yesterday was a day to remember. We boarded the proud inter-city train, still shiny, at almost six o'clock, trusting the local precision that often borders on boring: boarding the double-decker was scheduled for 6:02 p.m. We noticed the AC wasn't working. The result was a terrible trip, with temperatures over thirty degrees Celsius and the windows sealed with glass . . . Sauna carriages. We were going to Zurich to see a performance by Maputo's Avenina theater group. The writer Mia Couto adapted Schiller's *The Bandits* and staged the play with a group of former street kids. We couldn't even get past Bern. The entire train network in the country was down. We had to take my car. I had to drive. Really drive. To try to get there on time, I averaged a crazy speed of about one hundred and twenty kilometers per hour. We arrived in Zurich and got stuck in an insane traffic jam. The clock ticked with Swiss precision. And we still had to find the right location, catch the right tram (fortunately, the trams hadn't stopped). We thankfully found a parking lot near the central gare (in Switzerland, the gares have replaced cathedrals and squares in the urban planning of cities). Then we went looking for the trams. We arrived after the performance had already started, I'd estimate we were about forty minutes late—worthy of African and Latin American delays combined. I could see Mia's delirium in all its glory. Today my spine is flaring up, reminding me of my real age, offering complaints about the excess in my life. But the nightmare is over. The trains are running again, sucking up the electrons that never stop flowing, incomprehensible—to me, at least—through the power grid that proudly connects all of Switzerland. The gears turn. Forever?"

Guile Xangô googles "Orson Welles" and replies, "I really like Orson Welles's quote about Switzerland, 'In Italy for thirty years under the Borgias, they had warfare, terror, murder, and bloodshed, but they produced Michelangelo, Leonardo da Vinci, and the Renaissance. In Switzerland, they had brotherly love, they had five hundred years of democracy and peace, and what did that produce? The cuckoo clock.' Everyone always attributed that quote to Graham Greene, who wrote the screenplay for the film *The Third Man*, in which the brilliant star of *Citizen Kane* uttered this line."

Lylee sent songs. The muses have become skinny models, but Lylee remains a muse ahead of the curve. She makes music on the internet. Her Japanese (or Javanese or Filipino) virtual friend wants to know what the place she's from is like. So Lylee captures and processes the sounds from the bells at the Church of the Divine Holy Spirit, the sounds from the bars opening (steel doors being rolled up, the spoons clinking in coffee cups, the hot oil browning pastries), the sounds from Miguel's stand (early morning voices discussing that day's news), then the sounds of traffic, waking up the beggars on the square, the metro running under them. And then the sounds from crowded bars (drunken voices, loud TVs, slot machines, jukeboxes). The barking of the K-9s. The street on market day. The internet café. The kids banging on the shoe shine boxes, "Want some shoe polish?" and always asking for a real, a "hell," a "help," and the sound of real gunshots and fireworks all at once. And her guitar and voice like a siren's in this sea of detonations.

Guile Xangô lets the muse's presence take over his mind. Rolling Stones in Rio:

"To get close to the stage you better have a lot of strength. Youth. Passion. I got there at seven in the morning on Saturday and there was already a crowd. I stayed and made a little pile of sand. I stayed guarding my little pile of sand until nine that night. When the old guys came in, the crowd went into a trance. I tried to defend my little pile and I couldn't. I could only see the backs of the guys in front of me jumping up and down. So I started walking away from the crowd and the VIPs, there in their pen, near the stage, making fun of each other. I also saw that stupid sign, 'mick jagger make a son in me,' a disgrace, all wrong. A guy was selling cans of beer and shouting, '*é o mico jegue*: he jumps like a monkey and he's ugly like a donkey.' A boy next to me, saying, 'I didn't think he'd be so old.' I took the metro and went back home. My beloved was there worried sick watching the show on the muted TV and she hugged me so tight, nearly crying."

He clicks on a post from Lylee:

"The artist is always searching for that stroke of genius. That breath of intelligence that makes them special among so many human beings on the planet. They're vain, the good ones know they're good and seek 'perfection,' genius, recognition. The artist themselves is a selfish being. At times they have the feeling that they're the only one on the face of the earth and that they don't come from human parents.

Sometimes they're ashamed of their egocentric and selfish depression, but it's impossible for them not to absorb the pains of the world and their own pains, even if they're imaginary. Many pains are chimeras, in a space of astral adiposity. I'll let my unconscious voice flow, who knows, when I can't psychograph, I'll let some force that governs me take the direction of my thoughts, take the reins of my writing? Everything you write, you write until you lose consciousness and go into a trance, allowing every spirit to speak through you, overflow, come to its senses. Sadness, melancholy, why do they haunt me, keep me from moving on with my life, keep me from realizing my dreams, from dreaming and doing? Sadness is like being tied down by yourself. Meds can't help it. And in between these great oscillations is the human being, idiotic, questioning as always.

"But I truly believe we humans are nothing more than thinking meatballs. That's what we are: meatballs. We have to drink water to hydrate, if we don't hydrate, we don't even have sperm to fertilize and produce other meatballs. We sweat, we expel almost everything we eat, we eliminate liquids, we're moist, if we don't shower, we stink. We rely on the air we breathe, we rely on the earth, we rely on each other, otherwise we die. We're very dependent. Any catastrophe can kill us. We'd have better chances of surviving as a group, that is unless there's an epidemic spread by other groups of meatballs to annihilate us. We are rubbish. Skeletons stuffed with blood and flesh, relatives (distant, but relatives) of worms, bacteria . . . That's all we are.

"On the other hand, much more complex than what I've been saying, we are sublime when we are truly cordial and, when I think about it, the human body, the meatball, is a miracle, where each little piece has its function and works in favor of the whole in the most perfect synergy. That's what we think (thinking meatballs): how there's something divine, a bit of divinity in the existence of every being inhabiting the planet!"

Guile Xangô laughs. He googles "singing whales, Josephine the singing mouse Kafka," and writes back:

"You're absolutely right. What do whale songs and waves have in common? Quite a lot, and these waves have nothing to do with water. In a studio in Northern California, an engineer uses waves—the kind used to process digital signals—to transform the calls of ocean mammals into movies that visually represent the waves, and still images that look like electronic mandalas.

"Among whales, certain sounds and patterns are unique to different species and even to individuals within a given group—a sort of auditory identity. When we see what whales are doing with sounds, or witness what they're capable of doing, it becomes clear that humans are not the only artists on the planet.

"If humans could hear ultrasounds, canaries would be in serious danger of losing their jobs to unlikely competitors: mice. They emit a sound that is in no way similar to that of birds. Like a good tenor, rodents emit syllables that can contain leaps of almost an octave above or below on the scale. It's like the animal lets out a C and then immediately jumps to a higher B (skipping past the D, E, F, G, and A). Everyone learned from Josephine, the mouse singer, from Kafka."

Guile Xangô types out the recipient and sends the message.

The internet café was packed, all the computers were busy, people were waiting. Most of the boys like Cristiano, who's no longer by Guile Xangô's side, are fighting mortal combats on adrenaline battlefields.

Sibyl sends a message:

"Nerval: the Dream is a second life. We cannot determine the precise moment when the self, in another form, continues the endless work of existence. In the secret, empty underground are pale figures in the shadow of limbo—and then the picture becomes fixed, and a new light illuminates everything and makes bizarre shapes appear—the world of the Spirits opens up to us.

"Egology: Many of your selves have already gone to study the geology of the holy fields. Some came back mute, others as saints, many less than that, all completely different. When will you come to your senses? When will you have the courage to complete what you started, to not give up halfway, to not run away from me?"

Etc. Etc.

Guile Xangô deletes the message. And regrets it immediately. He types in the recipient. He writes, "We love each other—and we screw each other. Forget. Forgive." And sends it. With a pang in his heart.

The group of visual artists from Gomo is promoting a

spectacle with painting exhibitions and rock band performances, trading in brushes and artifacts for guitars and drumsticks. Guile Xangô responds, "You have to make a scene. Get on stage. Show up. Don't let the ball drop. Piss in Duchamp's urinal. Etc." He doesn't like what he's written, but he's not in any position to sit there polishing inspirational messages and manifestos. "Add more water to the beans, I'm on my way." And he sends it.

Macy, an old war veteran and friend of Lylee, sends poems. One of them:

and then the shadow told me

and then the shadow told me:
you are to blame for all the mistakes I make
you are to blame for all the betrayals I betray
you are small talk and a barfly
you're wimpy, dumb, soft, less than
you force me to do everything I don't want to do
you mess me up
you are the bad angel
you are the worst
you make me feel sorry
you make me sing out of tune
you make me feel guilty for everything I do, and I've already said that
you make me lose out everything I dream of, and I don't deserve it

you make me despair
you stink

and then I asked:
my soul's shadow in my cat's eyes,
my shadow in the sand,
shadow, what do you want me to do?

and then the shadow told me:
I want you to go blind deaf dumb,
I want you to die

and then the shadow fell on me
and I drowned
and night fell.

Guile Xangô writes to Macy, and hits send, with a hint of ill will and another hint of jealousy, "I think it's time for you to put all your texts together and publish a book. It's time to face the music, to swim, to let day break, to come out of the shadows."

Guile Xango's time is up. Half a dozen boys and girls watch him like a flock of vultures in a garbage dump. Guile Xangô makes a gesture and asks for more time. The boys and girls growl at him as if he were a cockblocking worm, a police officer doing a traffic stop, impeding the flow of cars. Guile Xangô deletes the boys and girls and thinks, "In twenty years, this internet café will be more out of date than pay phones."

He feels like a dinosaur. He feels as exiled as Lylee. "I was born in the year of the drunken storks, when all the children were switched at birth." Who said that? Guile Xangô opens more emails, reads, googles, replies, sends, while the new generation deletes his presence.

It's already night. Guile Xangô leaves the internet café feeling like he's carrying someone else's exhaustion. He says to himself, "I prefer the street, the street, the eye to eye, but I still can't escape the virtual circus. How many bar conversations have I had in my head for days on end, without understanding or only to understand months later? Even someone's brain can become obsolete. And why this attachment to one's own body, to one's own ideas?"

Shadow. That idiot Macy knows a little bit about stuff. And so many people live in the virtuous shadow of being kind! Like Maria's Índio: he was happy, had a house, a car, children, then he stopped being happy, lost his wife to another man, got drunk on too much cachaça, went into Maria's bar like a cat and stayed there, and now lives in Maria's shadow, filthy like a rat.

Celsão and Celsão's rabbit. The day the rabbit was stolen, he almost died from the pain, after feeling nothing for his own brother's death. And Celsão with his ironic refrains and his face, his mask, half Friend of the Jaguar, half Joker, "My mother's cow died. My father's donkey died. My sisters' chickens died. My brother's dog died. To hell with them! But why did they steal my rabbit, which was much better than all of them together?"

Sheila, who got out of jail. "I'm an irresponsible thief. I know I've got the plague, I take all those chemicals to survive for just a while longer. And what did the thief here do, the crazy woman? She stayed up all night from Friday to Sunday, drank everything, smoked everything, snorted everything. I'm a danger to others and to myself. I have to go back to jail. My only problem is the line for the shower. Nine hours in line for five minutes under cold water, the other women putting pressure on me. You saw my cell, all tidy, beautiful. I have to find a way to get back there. If I stay out here in the big world, I won't last another year."

She bumps into Lana and her baby stroller with Ester inside. Lana is all everyone talks about these days. She spends her nights pushing the blue stroller around the bars, defending her right to be a mother the way she wants with tooth and nail, in between sips of beer. The baby laughs, healthy, happy. "I'm coming from the doctor's and we're both fine. She's well fed because she's nursing, but I'm hungry and who's going to nurse me?"

They sit at Graça's fish tank, the new spot on Sampaio. It used to be a cool dive, but they added on the dining room next door, which used to be a shoe store and some other thing, and now it's a decent place to have lunch until three or four in the afternoon, a cozy place to chat until the early hours of the morning. There's Toinha smiling like a pretty Maria, wearing a seaweed necklace and a small star on her forehead shining above her eyebrows and her honeyed eyes. At the slot machines, players press buttons, screaming, hoping to hit the jackpot, betting on the figures and numbers. In the fish tank, there's a starfish near to the clock that's always stuck at twelve: the second hand turns, the hour and minute hands don't move. Whoever comes in here will die of stagnation and of being stuck in the stagnant water of time. But the windows save everything. Just pull back the curtain, open the window, and there are the Portuguese cobblestones that mimic, in their fake way, the Copacabana boardwalk. Here, the only breeze blows from the canal on Presidente Vargas Avenue, the old mangrove canal with its smells of fears and failures. Like those of the Captain, the king of thieves, lying there on the Portuguese cobblestones drowning his sorrows and days of glory with increasingly deadly doses of cachaça that he drinks out of a small, round bottle.

Guilê Xangô and Lana drink and talk suspended in the still time of the fish tank. At some point, like in an astral moment, Guilê Xangô talks about Cristiano. Lana is surprised, "But he died, he was buried the day before yesterday."

"But how, if he was right next to me just now, there in the internet café, sitting next to me?"

Lana tries to explain with perfect patience, "Cristiano was a good boy. He acted like a saint for three years. The saint in him may have been strong, but his mind was weak. It always had been. So his sister died of tuberculosis, that's what they say, she died of neglect, really, she was sick and didn't take care of herself, like everyone else here, and he abandoned the saints, or the saints abandoned him, and Cristiano joined the movement. 'Since my sister died, everything is a party to me,' he kept saying."

"That's what he told me just now," Guile Xangô said.

"It wasn't a party at all, and he didn't say anything because it was over, it was over, it was over," Lana continued. "He wasn't interested in anything else. He just wanted to play soldier. And then he fell in the alley when the enemies invaded. He was the first, he was in the front line. He fell. That's all he wanted. And he got it. No one's going to bring him back. Not even you."

Guile Xangô listens, he doesn't believe it. Lana starts to lose her patience, "It's not for nothing, my love, but you're so stressed that you're seeing things that no one else sees."

Guile Xangô says goodbye to Lana and goes to spend the night at Tiãozinho's crowded bar. It used to be a fabric store, but the entire block near the Paulo de Frontin overpass where it crossed Haddock was condemned by the city. On the other side of the street, the buildings became storage for the trash pickers, and one of them is now an evangelical church. On this side, it's in better shape, there's even a sauna, a stationery store, a shoe store, and now Tiãozinho's bar, the last refuge for the sleepwalkers who can't go home before the sun's up.

The virtual games continue to play in Guile Xangô's head. And there's Sheila, plus Celsão and Índio, as if by magic, all sitting at the same table, they, who were in his mind just now. He looks at the three of them and checks if they're real. Apparently, they really are there, and they laugh, and stand up and hug him to show that they are who they are.

"Look who's still alive and kicking," Tiãozinho says, and he challenges Guile Xangô to a game of pool. While the balls roll, Guile Xangô goes through the moves he'd googled. Geneticists have said, after examining the DNA of hundreds of species of bacteria that inhabit the human organism, that perhaps we're not completely human. Researchers evaluated the posture of healthy people and concluded that seventy-six percent are asymmetrical, with differences between the right and left sides. By 2030, we'll be able to create a supercomputer that's much more intelligent than us. Machines will have self-awareness and the ability to create other machines that are even smarter and more creative, and from that moment on, the world will no longer be ours. Ti Chin-Fu died after spending three months in an internet café, playing games and smoking, eating instant noodles. In Asia, addiction to online games has caused young people to spend days and nights in front of these machines, mainly in internet cafés, trying to conquer a virtual world. But, more and more frequently, the journey is interrupted halfway through when the player collapses.

While playing, Guile Xangô looks at Celsão without his rabbit, at Índio without Maria, at Sheila without her chain. He senses this confused and unreal world trapped in the smoky air, in the music that's always too loud, in the men and women, all there, too alive. Guile Xangô tries playing a trick and shoots in the eight ball instead. Tiãozinho puts in another chip with a victorious smile plastered across his face and the game restarts. It's just a quick move (a spin on the

Samsara Ferris wheel), the chance as good as getting struck by lightning, a stray bullet, a ball that hits the backboard and falls capriciously into a pocket. It's take it or leave it. The loser takes home the prize. Cristiano has every right to want to stay in the game.

UNDER THE HOSPITAL'S SHADE

Nabor is dozing off, sitting at the bar under the shade of the Military Police's central hospital. In his field of vision (which is a bit glaucous), he can see Beleco feeding corn to (and kicking) the pigeons in the square, he sees the priest gently taking Pedrão's daughter as she loses her balance at the top of the slide, he looks at the tailless donkeys that pass carrying cardboard and black trash bags the poor will turn into some change. Beleco boos when the priest and Pedrão's daughter leave hand in hand, cross the street, and go to São Carlos as a couple. As Beleco continues booing, he gets tired and walks toward the Sambadrome to make some noise on the hill in Mineira.

"Can I sit down?" Soneca sits down without waiting for permission, her hair white, her tongue sharp. "I'm seventy-nine years old and no one thinks I'm younger than sixty, fifty, I've never had a man, I raised my children at Praia do Pinto, today the oldest works at the Central Bank, the youngest at Eletronorte, I hate Brasília, my daughter paid for a plane ticket, but I'm not crazy enough to fly in one of those things, I prefer the bus but the bus takes too long so I never go there, they're the ones who come visit me, they wanted to give me a cell phone but I don't like it, I'm from a time when idle hands were idle, today people are just lazy, there's no idleness, no real malandros anymore, just a little shame and a lot of cowardice." Soneca is still sitting down but Nabor already knows her diatribe by heart and it won't be long before Soneca talks about Getúlio's death, she'll say what she always says, full of reason, and Nabor hopes he won't be like that when he gets older, always telling the same story in the same tone of voice, over and over.

The two old men are sitting in the shade outside the Military Police hospital, on the yellow chairs and tables with a beer logo, the chairs are actually comfortable, they haven't seen each other in sixty years, the two old men, a dog and a cat, they tolerate each other now, getting old sucks, you no longer have any convictions about anything and the only certainty is the past, the life lived and remembered, and another certainty is death, but let it not come so soon, let it not come now.

Back in the day there wasn't a bar here, or Nabor, or Soneca. Right across the street was the police station, the sixth or eighth precinct? And now it's a tenement. The First Baptist Church of Rio de Janeiro was already here ("It looks like a fake Greek temple," Guille Xangô said the other day), and to the right of the church is the prison, which was the women's correctional facility where Soneca once had a cell, but she's trying to forget it, to remove it like a tattoo from her skin, and they're planning to tear down the prison to build a new city, to clean up the city center, like they've done before.

Between the church and the prison there was a large house that was torn down to make way for the Rádio Manchete building, which today is just another tenement, taken over by the poverty that flows into Rio from far away, thin parents and their even thinner children, and Angolans.

The Military Police hospital looks like a castle where soldiers wounded in combat are taken in patrol cars, ambulances, all red and piercing. ("This is the beginning and the end of everything, Nabor. The hospital for men of the law, the jail for men without law, the church for men of faith, the radio station full of deaf-mutes, and the bar where people get drunk on laws, on faith, on words," Guile Xangô says in that tone of his, his way of complicating what everyone already knows, they're so sick of knowing it it's become like pissing, breathing, shitting, but it's contagious like a cold, and even Soneca is trying to trying to separate idleness from laziness when it's always been the same shit, what's changed is the know-how, "And even I'm coming down with it," Nabor thinks.)

"I hate the Sambadrome," Soneca says. "I hate it, I'm from a time when we used to parade around Praça Onze, in the middle of the road, cordoned off, I made my own costume, today everyone is parading around for television, and they killed the drum master, they put him in the microwave because he didn't want anyone from the movement dancing to his drum, back in my day we didn't have microwaves."

"Who do you think you're talking to, Soneca?" Nabor asks. "I'm from the same time, I know there used to be a Singer tailor shop where the supermarket is now, I know that the streetcar used to go up São Carlos, then turned onto São Roberto, went down Laurindo Rabelo, São Diniz, and came back along São Carlos again, I know that where there is asphalt today there used to be only mud, I'm from that mud, the bush, rain barrels, buckets of water on our heads, straight-edge razors, people dancing the pastorinha."

"I worked with Dorival Caymmi, a beautiful man," Soneca says. "Oh, don't start, Laurita," "Don't call me Laurita," "I know who you are, Laurita," "Don't call me that," "I know, Soneca, I know your past," "And I also know your past," "It's a dark one, Soneca," "You're still unbearable, Nabor," "I didn't invite you here," "But I'm here," "You can leave if you don't like it," "I'll stay, it's a public place," "The table is mine," "Then buy me a beer," "You buy me a beer," "I'll pay, my son works at the Central Bank," "Pay and leave me alone, Laurita."

Cars are starting to pull up outside the Baptist Church and the well-dressed parishioners get ready to praise the Lord. Women and children hold onto bags and packages at the prison gate. The poor people from Manchete help park the churchgoers' cars and sell juice and pastries to the anxious and shaking prison visitors while children beg for money at the church and at the prison.

The cops' relatives park their cars on this side of the street and go up the ramp to visit the hospital. The delivery men park their motorcycles next to the bar and go up the ramp carrying pizzas and bottles of soda for the doctors and nurses.

And the garlic, hammock, and peanut vendors start to circulate. The seller of sentences. The girls selling candy and chewing gum. The Chinese with their trinkets.

On São Carlos, fireworks begin to go off amidst bursts of machine gunfire and rifle shots. A congressman wanted to bulletproof the hospital windows, but the state vetoed it, it was too expensive to protect the wounded cops, and lawless men and boys continue to shoot people down here. They machine-gunned Piranhão, the city hall headquarters built just above this area, and Piranhão is right next to the post office building, in the line of fire for the samba schools that parade at the Sambadrome and appear on TV.

The fireworks go off, the Baptist church's bell starts to ring, a convoy of patrol cars and police vans drive away, red lights flashing and sirens blaring. The Caveirão, the armored police car, parks next to the bar and masked soldiers with rifles and machine guns come in and out with bottles of mineral water and cans of Coca-Cola.

Nabor lets out, "You never danced at the Elite, Getúlio Vargas wasn't killed by his brother Benjamin, you never worked for Caymmi or Dr. Roberto Marinho, and Pixinguinha didn't write 'Carinhoso' for you, Laurita."

Soneca leans back on her chair and lets out a scornful laugh, "Sarney ate at my parents' house in Maranhão, he ate with them, he fought with my brothers, and you've never cooked at the Copacabana Palace, you didn't cook for Frank Sinatra, and you're so old you think Eros Volúsia was hotter than Vera Fischer, and she wasn't."

And Soneca keeps going while Nabor thinks about malandro bohemians in silk shirts, flared pants, heeled boots, Panama hats, silk scarves around their necks; he also remembers how opium, cocaine, and heroin could be bought at the pharmacy for less than a glass of beer, so cheap there were already fake malandros in those days, "And I wanted to go to war, to kill Hitler, but my Germans were Black like me, wretches like me, I wanted to go to war, but I was already in prison as an enemy right here, and I wanted to kill Getúlio and I wanted to avenge Getúlio, and I had nothing to do with killing or avenging a father who wasn't even mine, I didn't exist, I still don't." Nabor thinks without listening to a word Soneca is saying right now, "Without Getúlio we wouldn't have salaries, retirement plans, we'd be sleeping under the bridge." "The world is doing nowadays, we're the ones still dying," Nabor grumbles.

The sky is turning violet, and the bar is full of police officers, prison guards, prisoners' wives, dancers dressed in the red-and-white colors of the Estácio samba school. The boys on the other side, Madame Satã's kids, are making a racket, all muscly, "fit," as they say, and demanding respect. The girls with free bodies, all difficult and all easy, drink and smoke like they're happy men or boys, and this has been going on for a long time, it didn't start happening today, everything has changed under the indifference of the skies, clouds, suns, deaths, hangovers, cigarettes, dreams.

The slot machines light up full of numbers, figures, animals, laughing at the suckers who're paying for Laércio Bicheiro's good life, sitting like a sultan surrounded by five women at the table in the back, all sweaty, covered in rings and necklaces, the piece of shit. "Enough with the malandros, enough hedonistic bullshit," Nabor thinks. "And what's this talk about the Mandelas? They're there too, but there's only one Mandela and it's going to be hard to find another. Little shits! Little shits is what they are!" Nabor laughs, "Are you laughing at me, you old slob?" and Nabor laughs even harder, "You can find a fake Mandela anywhere, they think they're hot shit, they're posing, taking the piss, but they're what they've always been: just another crop of malandros, scumbags!"

The jukebox has a screen showing videos and it starts to overflow with forró, funk, pagode, hip-hop. "I hate that music, back in my day . . . " Soneca says. "Our time is over," Nabor says watching a young couple of dancers dancing to that hammering sound, to words that sound like rain on the roof—*You do what we say and we'll do what we want to, We're fuckin' up your city and we're fuckin' up your program, Fuckin' all your bitches we can fuckin' give a goddamn*[4]—and Nabor doesn't understand any of this, no one there understands, but they sing and dance, they mimic the sound without knowing what it means—*Man, you just caught your wife cheatin'! While you at work she's with some dude tryin' to get off?! Forget gettin' divorced! Cut this chicken's head off!*—and Nabor feels marooned, at sea in this brave new world, in this promiscuity of bodies and gestures, of lawmen's mothers and daughters drinking next to lawless men's mothers and sons, of samba dancers dancing to words no one can understand, all indifferent to the explosion that's still smoking on São Carlos, "Calm down, sir, it's all right, you'll be fine," Nabor listens and doesn't even realize that he's going up the hospital ramp

4 The words are from Eminem.

carried by two nurses in a makeshift stretcher made out of the bar table, while Soneca holds his hand and prays:

> You are fire
> I am water
> You set me on fire
> And I extinguish you
> At two I see you
> At three I scare you
> In the name of the Father
> And the Son
> And the Holy Spirit
> Go to the one who sent you
> Tell him you didn't find me.

And Soneca says, "I love you, Nabor, I've always loved you," and Nabor holds back his laughter, and the pain in his chest gets worse, it feels like the hospital, the church, the jail, the city hall, the Sambadrome, everything is falling on his chest and, in the middle of the earthquake rubble, he still manages to gasp, "Stop messing around, Laurita, enough of this, woman, we've lost."

GUILE XANGÔ'S POEMS

GOOD DAY

The birds sing without a conductor
They have cleared the traffic accident
A good day like any other
To blurt out confessions
To talk shit
To show off
To shout from rooftops
To put your foot in your mouth
Not to think, suffer, weigh down
To plan a third suicide attempt

ORPHEUS XXI

Drunken binge false loneliness sex and sense dieting
And the angel was there on the other side of the mangrove canal
Smiling at him like he was Murilo Mendes himself
He raised his hands and tried to shout make contact
But the moment passed like a crowded bus

He locked himself in his room logged on to the computer
Google searched got annoyed a primal anguish

Fueled by pizza whiskey beer and more anguish
After four days of copulation in the spider web
He slept woke up no knowing who he was slept again
Brought into the world a state of transcendent mess
Woke up tidied the house easier than tidying up a life

He boards the metro at Estácio toward Copacabana
Three women catch his attention tall young blondes
Sky-blue eyes he doesn't understand what they're talking so much about
They arrive in Copacabana only the four of them still in the train car

He follows the women to the exit the women stop
He comes closer they speak in a language he doesn't understand
The three look at him with immense pity and walk away
He goes back to the underground world of the metro
It's too early or pointless to try living a life that makes any sense

FATHERS AND SONS

Dudu walked down São Carlos and didn't give a damn about the happy voices that greeted him as he passed by, the shouts coming from the windows of houses and bars, he walked down the street without touching the friendly hands offered to him, without returning the hugs and smiles. He walked from Salvador de Sá to Haddock Lobo, went into the supermarket, picked up a bottle of cognac, paid the cashier, crossed the traffic light between Salvador and Haddock, sat down on a bench at the square, placed the bottle on the reinforced concrete table, and put his head between his two hands.

Everyone knew what had happened.

Dudu's youngest son came into the house with a machine gun and said he was going to join the movement.

Dudu tried to convince the boy, he had given him everything, the very best, he was doing a technical degree in graphic design like his father, he had a guaranteed job ahead of him.

Dudu was desperate. "What did I do? Where did I go wrong? Was it too much love? Are you scared people will call you a daddy's boy? A spoiled brat? Do you think you're more of a man than me? Then you better hit me where it hurts! I never hit you, I never laid a hand on you, do you want to hit me, do it, do you want to be more of a man than me? Put that gun away and let's settle this man to man!"

The son didn't let go of the gun, "Dad, you're cool, you're the best father anyone could have, you're the coolest guy I know, but there was no way, I'd already made my decision, and you'd better get out of here, I'm just starting out, I can't protect you."

Dudu was even more desperate. "Then you're going to get in trouble. You'll never be more than a soldier. If you're going to get into this to be a small-time criminal, a petty criminal, you'd better stay, we'd all better get out together, I'll get out, your mother, your sister, let's all get out of here."

The mother tries to kneel down at her son's feet, but Dudu won't let her. "Don't kneel at his feet, he didn't deserve that. Now go, son, and see if you can be the best, the best criminal in the favela, the biggest criminal in town, the king of illicit activity, isn't that right? The king of the movement."

The son smiled. "I'm not promising anything, Dad. I'm out of here!"

The older sister clung to her brother, but he wasn't moved, he was determined. He was gone.

The son was gone. The mother packs her things, says she's going to disappear from that cursed place, cries, she's going to run away from this house, leave the favela, she's going to live with her sister, she's going to take her daughter with her, she's pulling her hair out. The daughter clings to her mother. They cry together.

Dudu looks at the house built with twenty years of sacrifice. He punches the wall. His punch breaks the mirror. He lets the birds out from their cages, but the birds don't leave, they fly around the living room and bedrooms, resting on the furniture, and the daughter lets her mother go on packing her bags while she puts the birds back in their cages. "And me?" says the daughter. "Are you going to release me too, throw me away?" Dudu and the daughter hug each other, the mother leaves, dragging her bags. "I'm going to stay," Dudu says. "I'm going to bring my mother there and come back," says the daughter.

Dudu is left alone and thinks about breaking everything, setting everything on fire, but he can't. He can't cry, he can't burn down the house, he can't wrap his head around any of it.

He walks down the hill, his hand wrapped in a handkerchief, and now he's down there at the square.

Vovô do Crime appears with two plastic cups, asks for permission, opens the bottle, pours two shots and toasts with Dudu. Soon after, Guile Xangô arrives with a bottle of whiskey and cans of beer.

Little by little, other people and friends appear. A bass drum, a cavaquinho, and a guitar appear too. Someone plays the old samba-enredo that Dudu wrote and that was disqualified because of the truculent stupidity of the samba school president, but which everyone still remembers.

They bring snacks and more beers. Did someone steal the hot dog van? It's there and everyone eats, drinks, and dances.

Dudu drinks, but he can't get drunk, he can't talk. No one knows if it's a party or a wake for a living person, but there's no shortage of food, moon, or stars.

Now it's the middle of the night, a boy plays alone at the skate park, three beggars sleep on the metro vent. The favela shines peacefully under the serene sky. "Let's go home, Dad," the daughter says. Dudu listens, but keeps replaying in his mind, as he has been since the moment he sat down in the square, every word he said to his son. Maybe if he'd found the right words he wouldn't have left, and he continues to search for the right gesture, the magic word.

"Let's go, Dudu," Guile Xangô says.

Dudu shifts his daughter, who is asleep on his lap. "I was born here, I grew up here, I'm the only one still alive out of all my childhood friends. I thought I had won, I was proud of that, and when I was closest to being happy my son killed me."

SMART TALK

Pedrão comes into the Chinese restaurant with Guile Xangô and orders a pastel and sugarcane juice. The cheerful mixed-race girl is at the counter, holding a candle for the Chinese boy, teaching him words that he repeats, paying no attention to the customers. She says goodbye and walks to the van and mototaxi stop. She talks to a biker, dodges his naughty hand with a graceful twirl, climbs onto the motorcycle with the lightness of a cat, her thick thighs with their bleached hairs, and looks back at the restaurant (the Chinese boy has been watching her the whole time), makes a red lipsticked pout, puts her hand with its bright red nails in front of her mouth and blows him a kiss, and the kiss hits the Chinese boy right in the face, who blushes, a faded lipstick stain on his cheeks.

Pedrão, who's watching everything attentively and enthusiastically, is ready to say, "This could only happen here," and turns around to say that "not even the Chinese have an out," but he sees Guile Xangô surrounded by the old girls from the easy life, Elza, Miriam, and Gaúcha. You watch one thing and miss the other right behind your back, Pedrão thinks. Guile Xangô caresses Miriam's swollen face and purple lip ("I'm not Míriam, my name is Miriam"), who explains with great difficulty that she'd gone to the dentist, her front teeth were loose, she was scared to death, "I can't wear dentures, but the dentist said it was OK," she should file a report at the police station, "but I told him straight out that I was there to take care of my teeth and that I already knew how to take care of myself. The dentist was pissed and didn't say anything else, and he just stood there fiddling with those torture instruments, angry, open your mouth." Miriam says that, while she was waiting to be seen by the angry dentist, she had written something to him, Guile Xangô. She rummages through her purse, remembers something, and takes a piece of paper from her generous breasts, "Only you understand me," and leaves with the other musketeers.

His hands full of his Chinese pastel and a glass of sugarcane juice, Pedrão waits for Guile Xangô to explain the situation, but the smart guy backs out and starts to say nothing at all, saying that in the beginning there was chaos, plus the butterfly effect. Like this: if a butterfly flaps its wings in China, it can start or stop a terrible storm in the United States. In other words: the small and the big, the near and the far, the sky and the earth, everything is connected. So, the crowd is there around the boy who was hit in the head by a stray bullet. No one knows if the bullet came from a police officer's gun or a criminal's. The boy is there, dead, in a pool of blood, and the crowd stands around him. Until the mother, a girl of fourteen or fifteen, arrives, makes her way in, throws herself on top of the boy, picks him up in her arms, doesn't know where to go, starts rocking the dead boy, and suddenly: she screams! The crowd also screams and runs down the hill screaming, and stops traffic and sets the buses on fire, and closes the shops. Like this: the complex web of events. And he says, "For want of a nail the horseshoe was lost; for want of a horseshoe the horse was lost; for want of a horse the rider was lost; for want of a rider, the battle was lost; for want of a battle, the kingdom was lost." One more thing. So, you're going to catch a plane, you end up arriving late because the taxi driver got out of the car to fight with a biker who cursed at him ("That's not my style," Pedrão thinks), you shout that you're late, but they keep arguing, more taxi drivers and bikers show up, the police show up, the commotion gets bigger, traffic gets more congested and you want to get out of here on the back of a motorcycle (Pedrão doesn't say, "I don't like this story at all"), but you have your suitcases, you're forced to go ahead with the taxi ride, and you arrive at the airport in time to see the plane you were going to catch explode in the sky.

"Did that really happen? When? Where?" Pedrão asks, but Guile Xangô has already picked up the pace and started talking about uncertainties, plots, free will, deviation, bias, elective affinities, out-of-tune essences, coincidences, fractures and fractions, the networks and the fabric of the networks. And, like a bolt of lightning from the blue sky, "Laplace's demon" appears. Guile Xangô takes a piece of paper out of his pocket (he doesn't notice that Miriam's scented note is there on the restaurant floor) and reads, "This is an entity that could have full knowledge of all facts. It can see the present state of the universe as the effect of its previous state, and as the cause of the state that is yet to come. An intelligence that, at any given moment, knows all the forces by which the natural world operates, the position of each of its components, and that also has the capacity to submit all this data to mathematical analysis, that can encompass in the same formula the movements of the largest objects in the universe and those of the smallest atoms; nothing would be unknown to it, and the future, like the past, would be present before its eyes."

Pedrão makes an excuse, "I have something to do" (and he really does), and he leaves, still a little dizzy from so much wasted time and conversation. He walks into Luiz's bar, orders a beer, and reads Miriam's note. "My dear, all I see here are small, narrow-minded, closed-minded people, demented minds, people who don't understand, people who suffocate me. But whenever I'm suffocating, drowning, I look for my best friend. A friend who always listens, who only knows how to say good, beautiful things. My friend is open, has a spacious heart, is warm and gives me comfort. It's a nice place to live, where you can breathe with an open chest and not have to suffocate anymore. Always yours, Mimi Valente." Pedrão reads it twice more, laughs, thinks, "The bastard, the quiet fucker, Laplace's demon my ass, the warm one that gives comfort, a very alive man pretending to be dead—" and, out of nowhere, Pedrão feels shame for having invaded a friend's privacy like a petty thief, and then he acquits himself, "Friends can't keep secrets. Be careful: you're under surveillance."

"Everything okay?" Shao Lin says, patting him on the back with a level of intimacy he'd never shown him before. Shao Lin is the craziest of the waiters, always drunk, a native of Paraíba with Chinese eyes, and always speaking Chinese, mumbling, and it takes Pedrão a while to find out that Shao Lin is saying that he came from Ceará as a boy, started out as a janitor, became a waiter, and was the General's favorite waiter. The General would come into the bar at nine in the morning and order a whiskey while he read the first newspaper. He would order a second whiskey and read the second newspaper. He would order a third whiskey and read the third newspaper. That would happen until noon. Then the General would order a fourth whiskey and wait for one or another friend. Friend 1 always came on Mondays, Wednesdays, and Fridays and would stay until six. Friend 2 always came on Tuesdays and Thursdays and left at six. Sometimes they both came together. They never missed a day. The General was the only one who talked and drank, and 1 and 2 listened and didn't drink at all. From six to seven the General drank alone. At seven fifteen, Shao Lin would call him a taxi and walk the General outside. The General had a tab, which he paid at the end of the month.

The General liked Shao Lin, gave him big tips and advice, battle strategies on how to do well in life. When Friend 1 died, the General said that Shao Lin was going to leave the bar and work at his widow's house. Shao Lin went. It was a huge apartment, full of rugs and curtains and a huge gun collection. Shao Lin's job was to take care of the old cook and the maid, and serve the widow from Monday through Saturday, and her three daughters and five grandchildren at Sunday lunches.

In less than three months he won over the widow, fired the cook and the maid, and started to rule the house. The widow called him her son. Eventually he moved in. He convinced the widow to buy him a car and took her for long drives around the city. Between seven and eight o'clock he would take the car and pick up the General at the bar and take him home. When the widow had a stroke, her daughters put her in a home and kicked Shao Lin out to the curb after three years of devotion. They accused Shao Lin of a bunch of things, including selling half of their father's gun collection. The General defended Shao Lin and he got away with it. He bought a bar and never saw the General again. Now he's there, bragging, making light of everything, and Pedrão wants to ask if the General only ever drank and never ate anything, but he's almost certain that Shao Lin is telling a story he heard from someone else.

Shao Lin goes to the back of the bar and comes out with a wedding cake box. "Look here, this is my gift for the General," he says.

The city center favelas full of cardboard shacks came after the first wave of police presence (the UPPs, the so-called Pacifying Police Units hadn't come yet), like a flood, a torrent that came down from the hills and the outskirts and crawled under awnings, occupied corners, flowed into the steel doors of banks, clubs, theaters, trendy bars, and churches. There, whatever evidence was still left, the ruins of a face that was once young, the curse on a name, the hangover after getting sober, the fly on a criminal's three-legged horse's poop, there the scum took shelter under the rubble of senselessness, colorlessness, loneliness. A homeless man passes by with a shopping cart full of dogs, and Pedrão stops: the man curses, the dogs bark.

They park in front of Neve Shalom, in the Fátima neighborhood, and Shao Lin grabs the cake. There they are, the General and a friend with his arm in a sling.

The General asks Shao Lin to take the cake back to the taxi and leave it in the trunk. Pedrão gets out with Shao Lin and does that. They stand on the sidewalk. The waiter comes and asks them to enter, General's orders.

They sit at the table and Shao Lin falls asleep almost immediately. The General and his friend talk about violence and moral duty. They talk about the Green Amazon and the Blue Amazon, about the defense of the national territory, about tactics and strategies, about weapons, natural disasters, the living, the dead.

During a lull in the conversation, Pedrão manages to talk about the attack on his house. That piques the General's interest, and he asks for details. Pedrão gets lost in the details and doesn't hear when the General says, "What a coincidence," and starts looking at him with suspicion, even anger, and then Pedrão starts to mix up his words, to feel intimidated, to get angry with himself for feeling this way, stuttering, and before losing his train of thought he manages to say, "Do you know who is to blame for all this violence? Che Guevara! He was the one who turned the favelas into Vietnams!" and the General lets a drop of sweat roll down his steely face and emits a thunderous laugh that makes Shao Lin jump to his feet and ask, "Wasn't that the guy's boss?" but the General waves his hand and Shao Lin goes back to sleep, and he says to Pedrão, "You're smart," and pours him a generous shot of whiskey. Pedrão excuses himself, walks across the bar with the glass in his hand, and goes to take a look at the car. It's raining and the downpour is washing everything clean. Pedrão takes a deep breath and opens the trunk.

The General and the Colonel continue their business conversation. At four in the morning they get up, walk through the bar with a martial gait, and get into the taxi. The rain has stopped. Pedrão leaves the two of them in a large house in Sumaré, near Bispo. Shao Lin wakes up in time to receive money from the General. Pedrão gets another wad of bills and is about to leave when the General shouts, "Stop!" Shao Lin takes the cake out of the trunk and hands it to the General.

Pedrão goes up São Carlos while Shao Lin snores beside him. "This night has changed everything," he thinks, "I'm going to have to look at the world with different eyes."

But here, as the sky lightens, Pedrão thinks, "The boys of the movement look at the boys who go to school or work. The soldier boys may envy the ease with which the schoolboys leave the favela, living down there, wandering the streets in absent-minded freedom, going into shopping malls, moving around, mingling with the human herds of the open city. The soldiers look at the boys as if they were sailors on a sea of opportunities. For the soldier, this is a quilombo.

"If it's not a quilimbo fugitive community, it's a trench. And if it's not a fugitive community or a trench, for the boy soldiers here, it's a ghetto. The truth is that two teenage universes coexist here. Those who chose to fight with guns and those who chose to integrate. The difference is between living at full speed (the kids in the movement) or choosing a slow life (the kids who go to school and work, the sailors)."

Pedrão wakes up Shao Lin, who stumbles out toward his house, opens the door and turns to greet Pedrão with an almost perfect salute. Pedrão thinks about calling Shao Lin a great actor, X-9, but ends up just laughing instead.

A car with a PROPERTY OF JESUS bumper sticker stops in front of him. The boy soldier tells the driver to get out and shoots up the car. Jesus's face looks like Che Guevara's. What a coincidence.

Walking down São Carlos, splitting Jesus's image from Che's, Pedrão imagines the General walking through the door—"Honey, I'm home!"—opening the cake box and letting Manaus's head roll down at his wife's feet.

TIGER XANGÔ 2100

What's happened? I remember almost all my reincarnated lives. That's easy enough since they invented memory chips, but I've never used one. In the earliest clear memolife, I was a king like everyone else, so I won't even bother talking about it. Trust me. In the second, a soldier, a sailor, a sorcerer. In the third, a tiger.

This one is very clear, I can smell it. I carried rich people's excrement and threw it into Guanabara Bay. Barrels full of shit on my back. Another name for shit: "wastewater." Ammonia and urea ran down my shoulders, stinging like whips, the sun burning stripes on my skin. Some of my friends were proud to carry the piss of Emperor Pedro, Princess Isabel, the counts and barons. I didn't even care, it all stank the same. I died before the abolition of slavery, but I wasn't promoted to full human. No one was.

I was reincarnated as a trash picker in Jardim Gramacho, in Duque de Caxias, the largest landfill in Latin America, seven thousand tons per day of unimaginable things, including entire human bodies. And hands. And feet. And faces. I lived in a wooden shack; a former tiger living with flies, worms, herons, and vultures. The main advantage was that I was free, and the downside was that I didn't notice the difference.

I only realized it when the city government closed the landfill in 2012. I received a card from the Federal Savings Bank to withdraw the compensation, fourteen thousand reais.

I spent it all in one week on whores. Sometime in early August 2013, I took a bus, crossed the bay, and went to work at an illegal landfill in São Gonçalo. The old Guanalixo, every single day, got four hundred tons of domestic sewage, sixty-four tons of industrial organic waste, seven tons of oil and three hundred kilos of heavy metals like lead, mercury, etc. I earned a few bucks at the landfill, the police came, I couldn't pay the authorities, they arrested me, beat me, I kept to myself.

On August 20, they let me go. I got on a boat, got out at Praça XV, lit a cigarette, took about five puffs, threw the butt on the ground on Assembleia Street, and was surrounded by three government workers: a street cleaner, a municipal guard, and a military police officer. The street cleaner said I was a criminal and asked for my ID. The guard pulled out a computer with a portable printer. The police officer told me that the guard was going to print me a bank slip so I could make the payment. If I didn't pay the state, my name would be registered with Serasa and the credit service. The three of them told me the fine could range from R$157 to R$3000.

I was furious. I screamed, "I'm a tiger! A trash picker! A piece of garbage! Three thousand reais for a cigarette butt? Are you out of your mind! Haven't you read Plato? 'Any city, however small, is in fact divided into two, one the city of the poor, the other of the rich; these are at war with one another.' Whose side are you on? You're just trash like I am!"

And I screamed again, "I want a lawyer and a philosopher! A lawyer from the jailhouse and a philosopher from the bar!"

The three dumb flies were furious. Then the street sweeper hit me with a broom, the guard hit me over the head with his computer, the police officer blinded me with pepper spray—and the mob lynched me.

Take a good look. I have been re-re-reincarnated and I'm circling the Earth on another August 20, 2184, in an old museum spacesuit, with automated navigation and enough oxygen for two hours. The prison freighter that was taking me to Mars, along with more than twenty thousand ex-tigers, was hit by space junk and capsized, and now I'm floating here, trying to undo the damage. I volunteered. I'm a tiger, a bag of trash, a scumbag, a loose screw orbiting the planet.

Down below I can see the Earth: a trash heap. A dump. A landfill. The planet is no longer blue: it's gray and brownish. The color of shit with euthanasia sunsets and suicidal dawns. From here you can see the domed cities where the world's big VIPs now live. Bigvipdomes. The superclasses caged in gated communities like the old shopping malls of the early twenty-first century that were elevated to chic neighborhoods. Seagardens and islands of aircraft carriers, float in the cadaver-colored sea, a tubercular sea. Everything is paranoia, and no one can leave, the sad womb of Gaia. The air is breathable, the temperature is regulated, it looks like a circus, there's eros, emperors, serums, cannibals. There's no shortage of survival drugs. Every domecitizen has computer chips for parallel lives, future memories, scanners for duplicating free lives, dream lives, spirits through mediums. A whole universe of virtuality.

Outside, everything is an immense landfill: billions of

people face the depleted environment, the furious sun, storms, floods, droughts, a killer moon. In 2025, the then existing UN warned that cities had generated two-point two billion tons of garbage. Well, it's increased fivefold, and this is what's happened. Most of the rest of humanity lives off the waste of the few million who managed to secure their princely status. As always. Nothing is lost, everything goes to shit.

I was convicted and extradited for invading one of these domes. I trafficked water and VD-XIX (chips for nineteenth-century human life). It was the trend at the time. I went in there, found the access codes, the garbage men were running over each other without a leader, without a grand master. We were defeated, and they arrested me, tortured me. I lived for a while in VD-XIV, the black plague. I was a rat. It's not that hard to be a rat. Leftovers. Or insects.

I have thousands of egopaths in my hands. Those condemned to the monad, to the nonada, still want to swim like Martians.

Should I fix the prison freighter or not? Should I go back to life on the garbage planet and try, once again, to take over one of the superclass domes? Should I dive off like a meteor man? Should I get screwed? I'm not scared. I know there's another life. A naked life. A prison life. On the moons of Jupiter or Saturn there's still a chance. Any way of living is worth it, the soul, the body.

In an hour or so my oxygen will run out. I've been through this before. I'm thinking empty thoughts. You're not going to make the decision for me.

ALL A LIE, MINUS THE MOTHER AND THE DREAM

It was all a lie, but now it's true. The first loser I took down was in a suffocating spot. I was a kid, ten, almost eleven, I was running down the cliff and the *pow pow pow* coming after me, it was dark, and a malandro came to check things out, and I was stuck in the middle of all the garbage, and he came to take the machine gun, I had the machine gun and a .38, and he came, and I put three holes in him and ran, and the *pow pow pow* coming from up there. What I know is that I came out on top. I thought the dead man would appear in a dream, pull my leg, haunt me and such, and nothing. I'm Beleco; I'm good.

And then there was the day they killed me. It was a job at a rich man's house. We were supposed to come in, grab things, and get out. We slipped on a blabbermouth's spit and then it was done.

It was a big house, something out of the movies. One floor. Another floor. Another one. Three in total. And a window the size of a door. And a swimming pool. And a pool house. And a ton of dogs, but Nélio threw a steak here, a steak there, another steak over there, the dogs fell on their faces and then started gulping, crawling on the green green green grass. Even the birds died.

So we went in, me and five others and Nélio all sergeant-like, yes, yes, no. It was easy, fast: we got in and out, took everything to the van. It was enough stuff to fill a moving truck.

Then we squeezed into the van. We drove until the early hours of the morning and stopped by the landfill. In front of the headlights, a collapsing house, and bushes as far as the eye could see. A car stopped next to us, a Monza. It stopped next to us and some people jumped out, screaming, that's the one, that's it, that's it. That was it.

There wasn't even time to scream, cainjudasforfuckssake. They really went all out. They hit us the way you kill snakes, rats, cockroaches. They hit us in the face, the balls, hit hit hit, and screamed and laughed and spit. They put out cigarettes on our flesh. Then they shot us until we were sieves.

I only survived because I pretended to be dead. I pretended so hard even I thought I'd died.

I survived by a thread, a spider's sticky thread. And I woke up with the ground sucking me down. Sucking me down like I was lying in a swamp. And I kept waking up and dying by a thread. Dying and waking up hanging by a thread of drool. And I kept climbing up that thread until the sun the sun the sun the sun. The sun. And I saw ants carrying little balls of blood. And I saw a dog sniffing the real dead. And I saw my hand holding onto some uprooted grass. It was my hand, but it was so far so distant from me, closed like that, in a fist, holding onto a handful of black earth and grass.

I woke up in the ambulance and I was still pretending to be dead. I was in the wind, a twisted kite, a strong wind, a howling horn and siren wind, a loud wind, and there's nothing nothing nothing holding me back.

LET THE DOGS OUT

. . . so many, I had not thought death had undone so many.
—T. S. Eliot/Dante

The news spread and everyone could talk of nothing else. No one had expected this. Guile Xangô had been promising to show these films for ages and was always delaying, giving excuse after excuse: he was editing, switching from PQD to FGT, from eight to twenty, from thirty-eight to one hundred and twenty, and from millimeters to kilometers, and miles, cutting, the color wasn't good, the sound was terrible, the soundtrack could be improved, anyway, excuses. It got to a point where people stopped asking and dove back into their mediocre lives, sucking up, sniff sniffing, instant snapshots, stray bullets and stray lives, except for those who see everything and are also blind, who hear everything and are also deaf, who say everything but only through silence, as Guile Xangô himself would say.

Rewinding: when he started taking pictures, some people gritted their teeth, at least the people who owed him money, and there was a rumor that he was an X-9, a P2, a spy, a snitch, a traitor, but he had some loyal friends and the resistance fell with each click and each photo developed.

Once he was good, he started using those cool cameras that looked more like some kind of weapon. People thought it would all end up falling apart, and when the movement leader sent a message for him to come on up, his closest friends, Nabor, Meu Bem, Pedrão, Vavau, Ruth, Mirtes, and even Vovô do Crime, everyone asked him not to go, it was a setup, but he went up there full of courage and ended up winning one of the gold, platinum, and diamond rings the commander gave to his ten chosen people. It was a sign of immunity. Guile Xangô became untouchable. For a week Vovô do Crime drooled venom of pure envy in a rage. He bought that ring, it's fake, he's always trying to show off, but then its true origin was confirmed, and Vovô started telling everyone that the ring was meant for him, it was his, and he kept talking until he was talking to himself because no one could stand his bullshit anymore.

At first the party was going to be at the Lima gymnasium, but the gym was tiny and Guile Xangô decided to postpone it. He thought it would be a small get-together, family-album stuff, but the thing grew so much that he was afraid there would be riots. The gym only had one entrance and one exit and a narrow side door. Guile Xangô managed to delay the event, what was supposed to be a killer show turned into a pagode show with Dão's gang. Since the beer flowed freely and was free, people let it go.

Then Guile Xangô decided he could throw the party at the quarry and even said it would be a way to exorcise the boys who'd been thrown off the top and stuff.

The day started off gray, threatening rain, with heavy clouds. The bars were empty, and everyone was holed up waiting for something to happen. The church bells rang twelve times, and the signal came from where people least expected it. From the top of the quarry, they started to unfurl a flag with ropes tied to both ends. But it wasn't a flag, it was a huge white cloth, and a flag: yes, a white cloth is a peace flag. The enormous white flag was unfurled from up there and, down below, a group of young people shouted to bring it down a bit more, higher on the right side, stretch it more on the left side, until two hours later the quarry had gained an immense white square, hanging from ropes up there and stretched with ropes tied to stakes down here. No design, no words, just white. And the sun came out to boot and shone in celebration.

A line of trucks, cars, and vans went up Maia, turned on Santos Rodrigues, and a group of men without uniforms started to set up a stage about twenty meters from the quarry, and another smaller one, about a hundred meters away. Tent after tent started popping up. A powerful and full-bodied sound poured out, music.

The crowd started to grow from all sides when the news spread that the food and drink were free, though no one was absolutely sure who was the source of such generosity on such an ordinary day, on a date not meant for large productions, and, especially, at such an unlucky, even cursed, place. Everyone refused to go straight there, they hemmed and hawed, and many believed it was a trap, if not for everyone then at least for some, those who were already past their time, expiration date looming. A small group of people who were very brave, not to mention thirsty and hungry, decided to check it out, to scout out the terrain, and went to the quarry like cattle to the slaughterhouse, flies to honey. As professional survivors, they believed in the possibility of escaping at the last second.

The children had no such thoughts and were the first to join in with a confident, limitless commitment to the party. They were the ones who exorcised the quarry with their laughter and cries of trusting innocence. Soon spontaneous organizers emerged, and music and dance channeled the childlike energy that took hold of all the young bodies, and the explosion of bodies was a vigorous tide, the pure energy of youth, the announcement that life was a force so powerful nothing would be able to resist it.

At around eight in the evening, images started to appear on the large white flag, photos and videos, fragments of life, memories in motion, some that were to be swept away like dry leaves by the gusts of memory, others that ought never to be forgotten, and they were there, all flashing past at a frantic pace, a river of images, poor and rich, comic and tragic, a tumultuous current of laughter and tears. The crowd applauded and booed the one thousand faces. There were the happy couples, now separated, betrayed loves, drunken nights, hugs, kisses, vows, the cries of protest, dancing, bodies pressed together. The living and the dead. And it came with a chilling sadness, seeing how many were already dead. And how many, how many dead! And what havoc the days, the nights, the early mornings had wrought. But the same river of time had softened its cruel flow a little, and between the narrow banks of life and death, yesterday's children could be seen there, on the big screen, held in warm arms, balanced on firm shoulders, the sons and daughters, the seeds of the tree of good and evil, the survivors.

It was Mirtes's birthday, and she had preferred to stay at home, but the house felt too small. She woke up at eleven in the morning as usual, and as a tribute she had not made in centuries, she remembered her own mother. When she was four or five years old, her mother started seeing things, foreseeing the future, speaking like an old woman, all at once. She got pregnant at the age of thirteen, and using her gifts in a dark little room, playing cards and shells, she managed to raise fifteen children, and they never went hungry. At eighty, she suddenly went blind and mute, but she did not worry that the saints had abandoned her, and a year later she went in her sleep, in front of the TV, the only peaceful death in her family.

The crowd started to come in, to leave, to stay. Mirtes's seventeen children were the first to arrive and she always had a sweet or harsh word to say to them. At each moment her vast body shook with sobs; her birthday was also the day of Cirinho's death, her favorite son. Of all of them, he'd been the only one willing to make a path for the bullets. By the time he was sixteen, he'd gone from lowly soldier to the boss's right-hand man. At nineteen, he had fathered eight children and already had a big body count, he'd stopped keeping track of the number. At twenty, his body was riddled with bullets and his head separated from his body. Mirtes opened the door and once more saw Cirinho's head on the ground out on the porch, one green eye open and the other closed. And she, usually a quiet woman, spoke loudly. The movement leader didn't forget her. Every weekend she got money from him, which helped her raise her children, adopt others, take care of grandkids and great-grandkids, and godparent dozens of orphans and abandoned children.

Mirtes locked herself in her bedroom and opened the small jacaranda trunk she'd inherited from her mother, from which she took out his memorial prayer card ("It's not a prayer card, mother, or a memorial card, or a funeral card; it's a pamphlet," Marquete said a long time ago), printed for Cirinho's seventh-day Mass. That was the first one she saved, and in her life of anarchic passion without method, this was the only collection she ever had, there were over a hundred funeral cards ("When you get stuck on something you are worse than a mule, Mom!") tied with string, organized by day, month, and year. The last one was from Dafé. She took out the little card and read:

Missing my dear friend Henrique
A song: *Love in the afternoon*
It's so strange
Good people die young
That's how it seems
When I remember you
Who left too soon
(. . .)
I remember the afternoons we spent together

It's not always like this, but I know
That you are fine now
It's just that this year
Summer ended
Too soon

And more Legião songs: "A Via Láctea," "Vento no Litoral," "Angra dos Reis," "Música Ambiente."

She remembered the priest's words, read from the same holy card she had in her hands:

"José Henrique,

"Your irreparable loss has left us with inconsolable pain. Only the comfort of God's love will make this bearable.

"You leave behind the happy memories you gave us and the good you did for others. Your memory will be a blessing.

"The sorrow of having lost you will never make us forget the happiness of having had you with us.

'Don't cry, for I am going to meet God and I await you in heaven. I will love you from the other side of life, as I always loved you on earth.'

"We are deeply grateful for the prayers for his most beautiful soul and for the comforting words offered to us.

"Merciful Jesus, grant him eternal rest, welcome his soul with open arms, shine your light on his face.

"We will always remember his smile, his boyish face, his humility, his clumsy funny way that always made us laugh. We will never forget him.

"'I am going to God, but I will not forget those I loved on earth.'"

The Mass was beautiful like all the others in honor of her children and her children's friends, they are all my children, until Vovô do Crime took the microphone from the priest's hands, he was scared to death, the poor priest, and Vovô do Crime started barking those terrible stories about the real Dafé, a bicycle thief in childhood and a motorcycle thief in adolescence, a pothead, a ruffian, a scene maker, and more of this and more of that, I'm told I started screaming and praying to God lightning would strike the head of this father of lies, and I lost my breath, almost had a heart attack, and swore that I would grow out my nails just to rip out Vovô do Diabo's eyes, that demonic piece of shit. I spent almost a year with that pain in my chest, mumbling about that hurt, until Guile Xangô came here and promised me that he would fix everything, that he would pay a great tribute to my son, to all my children, and then I calmed down, the pain went away, the hurt dissipated, but to forgive, really forgive, I don't think I have the will, the strength, and I leave it in God's hands.

Mirtes doesn't want a candle on the cake. She doesn't want a cake. She asked them to take the old armchair to the backyard and she sat there, under the mango tree, drinking and sniffling, welcoming visitors, her closest friends and relatives, the most distant relations and the strangers, looking at the huge white flag covering the quarry, but it took her a while to understand that this was Guile Xangô's doing, that he was honoring his promise, and she felt her heart lighten, fill with a desire to sing and be happy.

Marquete came and said, "Mom, you have to see the party down there, up close, it's the most beautiful thing." And she said, "I'm not leaving here, no one can get me out of here," and then she asked Marquete to take the music outside. Her daughters set up the grill and, sitting down, she led everyone at the party with her shouts.

The quarry party ended, and the crowd took over her backyard and spread out across the street. Guile Xangô handed her a package and said it was for the queen bee of Maia. She opened the package: a huge golden-yellow robe. She laughed, kissed Guile Xangô, and drowned him in a huge hug. Then she took off the dress she was wearing, leaving only her shorts on, shamelessly showing her large, powerful breasts. The fury of desire was long gone, and she put on her robe. She walked around like the priestess of an ancient cult to Mother Earth or some other entity, she danced, and amid laughter and applause sat back down on her throne, puffing, asking for more beer and joy. She grabbed Guile Xangô, and he sat on her lap, and she rocked him amid applause and laughter.

She was still holding Guile Xangô in her arms when she saw Xande walk through the crowd hand in hand with a classy, very thin, and very surprised boy, and introduced him, "This is Bastian, my main squeeze." Mirtes's eyes clouded over with an ancient fog, and in the middle of the fog, she saw Xande still a kid, a little soldier, and the men, the dogs, running after him down the street. Xande jumped over the wall around the house, and the house was just this big house, none of the other neighbors it has today, and the wall was still low, not this high wall with glass shards and barbed wire. The men broke their promise and went into the house after Xande. The Mirtes from back then was in the kitchen, making food, and she stayed in the kitchen. She stirred the pot and kept demanding independence from the men, a peace treaty, they couldn't come into her house like that, they had agreed, but the men were after Xande and turned everything in the house upside down anyway. They searched under the bed, inside the closet, opened Mirtes's trunk (they found some stuff, but left it there), the water tank, climbed up on the roof, made a mess. They didn't find anyone, the kid must've jumped over the other wall that led to the empty yard and hid there among the trash and bushes. They went there, couldn't score anything, and ended up giving up. And where was Xande? Under Mirtes's skirt! Xande told everyone that Mirtes didn't wear panties and that he'd almost died choking on the smell of her pussy. Mirtes got mad, screamed that her pussy smelled great, and swore that he'd been hiding in the oven. But Xande added to the lie: while the men were messing up the house and she was stirring the stew with a wooden spoon, he was there sucking her pussy. She was coming when the captain came in to apologize and say that his men were leaving, and Mirtes had to pretend she was fainting, but she was coming, and the captain even gave her a glass of sugar water. And it was Xande's story that stuck, and everyone liked the idea that Xande was under her skirt doing these things, and Mirtes saw there was no point in screaming and demanding respect, she ended up getting used to it, and whenever she sees Xande, the two of them make up more stories within this story.

Now Mirtes is locked in the oratory telling this to a sleepy Bastian, tears rolling down her fat face, saying, "Xande was the devil, I struggled to get him off his bad path, I couldn't, I never thought he would change, thank you for what you've done for him, for saving my son's life, only God knows that was the best gift I received today."

Pedrão breathes a sigh of relief when Mirtes comes back without Bastian, if the bastard kissed him on the mouth in front of everyone there would be trouble, and he didn't want to ruin anyone's party. "I present to you the world's savior," Vovô do Crime shouts to the crowd and points to Vavau. "The legit father of lies, the true king of rats." And Pedrão grabs Vavau, who manages to kick Vovô, who loses his balance and falls on Mirtes's flowerpots, and Vavau goes over, picks up Vovô do Crime, they hug and kiss. No one notices and the party goes on. No one there would see any scandal in a gesture of contempt, a guilty conscience, a kiss on the mouth.

Around two in the morning, the people from the movement came to make a statement, to make their presence felt, then they fired a series of shots with tracer bullets and disappeared. At six in the morning, Mirtes let her head fall to her chest, a nap, a moment of hesitation, and the dead took over the yard, emerging from all eras, many wearing the same clothes they were buried in, elegant and sad and serious, others ragged and tormented, and then Ciro came too, her Cirinho, but it wasn't really him, something wasn't right, and Mirtes realized that all the dead had their heads switched, Cirinho's head on Dafé's body, Dafé's head on Cirinho's body, and her mother was wearing Xande's head, but Xande was alive, leading a new life, thank God, and Mirtes frowned, this wasn't a carnaval parade, no one goes around changing faces like a mask. And all this mess, this silly nonsense, this unfunny mess could only be the work of that scumbag Parangolé, who died thinking he was the father of all her children, and he wasn't, he wasn't! But there he was, all dressed in white, with a Panama hat, a red scarf around his neck, pointy-toed shoes in two colors, seeking encouragement, walking up and down, moving around, his arms open, his mouth wide open in a smile, piranha teeth and catfish mustache, and there were those Black guys full of themselves, who thought they were hot shit, giving Parangolé a fifth Mandela medal, and the Comadres applauded, and never, never, never! Because that's not how the song goes, and the hostess of the party got up from her throne and shouted, "Enough! That's enough! Enough!" She climbed up the stairs, slowly and imperiously, amid drunken applause and resentful heckling, rejecting everyone's hugs with slaps and shouts, them begging her to stay, stay, stay, it's over, leave me to it, it's over.

Following her lead, a fine rain fell sadly on the people and the trees, and the fine, sad rain turned into a storm, and red mud and garbage stuck to the white flag hanging from the stony wall of the quarry. From her balcony, still unable to separate the living from the dead, Mirtes thundered, "Lock the gate and let the dogs out."

FRANCISCO MACIEL was born in Rio de Janeiro in 1950, the son of a maid and a shopkeeper. He became a manual laborer before age six, when he went to school to escape such work and later managed to enter an elite high school. He studied journalism at university but gave up because he felt "too foolish and unprepared for life," before hitchhiking around South America.

BRUNA DANTAS LOBATO is the author of *Blue Light Hours* and an assistant professor of English and creative writing at Grinnell College. Her translation of *The Words That Remain* by Stênio Gardel won the National Book Award for Translated Literature.

THE WORDS THAT REMAIN
BY STÊNIO GARDEL

Winner of the National Book Award, *The Words That Remain* is set in Brazil's little-known hinterland as well as its urban haunts. This is a tender love story about the importance of literacy—a sweeping novel of repression, violence, and shame, along with their flip side: survival, endurance, and the ultimate triumph of an unforgettable figure on society's margins. *The Words That Remain* explores the universal power of the written word and language, and how they affect all our relationships.

THE VANISHED COLLECTION
BY PAULINE BAER DE PERIGNON

Pauline Baer de Perignon grew up knowing little to nothing about her great-grandfather who was a leading French art collector and patron of the Louvre. In this book she investigates what became of his collection after Nazis seized his elegant Parisian apartment during World War Two. The quest takes her from the Occupation of France to the present day as she breaks the silence around the wrenching experiences her family never fully transmitted, and asks what art itself is capable of conveying over time.

THE HEBREW TEACHER
BY MAYA ARAD

Three Israeli women, their lives altered by immigration to the United States, seek to overcome crises. In the title novella, Ilana is a veteran Hebrew instructor at a Midwestern college who has built her life around her career. When a young Hebrew literature professor joins the faculty, she finds his post-Zionist politics pose a threat to her life's work. This book comprises comedies of manners with an ambitious blend of irony and sensitivity—celebrated Israeli author Maya Arad probes the demise of idealism and the generation gap that her heroines must confront.

DISTANT FATHERS
BY MARINA JARRE

This singular autobiography unfurls from the author's native Latvia during the 1920s and '30s and expands southward to the Italian countryside. In distinctive writing as poetic as it is precise, Marina Jarre depicts an exceptionally multinational and complicated family. This memoir probes questions of time, language, womanhood, belonging and estrangement, while asking what homeland can be for those who have none, or many more than one.

NEAPOLITAN CHRONICLES
BY ANNA MARIA ORTESE

A classic of European literature, this superb collection of fiction and reportage is set in Italy's most vibrant and turbulent metropolis—Naples—in the immediate aftermath of World War Two. These writings helped inspire Elena Ferrante's best-selling novels and she has expressed deep admiration for Ortese.

UNTRACEABLE
BY SERGEI LEBEDEV

An extraordinary Russian novel about poisons of all kinds: physical, moral and political. Professor Kalitin is a ruthless, narcissistic chemist who has developed an untraceable lethal poison called Neophyte while working in a secret city on an island in the Russian far east. When the Soviet Union collapses, he defects to the West in a riveting tale through which Lebedev probes the ethical responsibilities of scientists providing modern tyrants with ever newer instruments of retribution and control.

WHAT'S LEFT OF THE NIGHT
BY ERSI SOTIROPOULOS

Constantine Cavafy arrives in Paris in 1897 on a trip that will deeply shape his future and push him toward his poetic inclination. With this lyrical novel, tinged with an hallucinatory eroticism that unfolds over three unforgettable days, celebrated Greek author Ersi Sotiropoulos depicts Cavafy in the midst of a journey of self-discovery across a continent on the brink of massive change. A stunning portrait of a budding author—before he became C.P. Cavafy, one of the 20th century's greatest poets—that illuminates the complex relationship of art, life, and the erotic desires that trigger creativity.

THE 6:41 TO PARIS
BY JEAN-PHILIPPE BLONDEL

Cécile, a stylish 47-year-old, has spent the weekend visiting her parents outside Paris. By Monday morning, she's exhausted. These trips back home are stressful and she settles into a train compartment with an empty seat beside her. But it's soon occupied by a man she recognizes as Philippe Leduc, with whom she had a passionate affair that ended in her brutal humiliation 30 years ago. In the fraught hour and a half that ensues, Cécile and Philippe hurtle towards the French capital in a psychological thriller about the pain and promise of past romance.

THE BISHOP'S BEDROOM
BY PIERO CHIARA

World War Two has just come to an end and there's a yearning for renewal. A man in his thirties is sailing on Lake Maggiore in northern Italy, hoping to put off the inevitable return to work. Dropping anchor in a small, fashionable port, he meets the enigmatic owner of a nearby villa. The two form an uneasy bond, recognizing in each other a shared taste for idling and erotic adventure. A sultry, stylish psychological thriller executed with supreme literary finesse.

THE EYE
BY PHILIPPE COSTAMAGNA

It's a rare and secret profession, comprising a few dozen people around the world equipped with a mysterious mixture of knowledge and innate sensibility. Summoned to Swiss bank vaults, Fifth Avenue apartments, and Tokyo storerooms, they are entrusted by collectors, dealers, and museums to decide if a coveted picture is real or fake and to determine if it was painted by Leonardo da Vinci or Raphael. *The Eye* lifts the veil on the rarified world of connoisseurs devoted to the authentication and discovery of Old Master artworks.

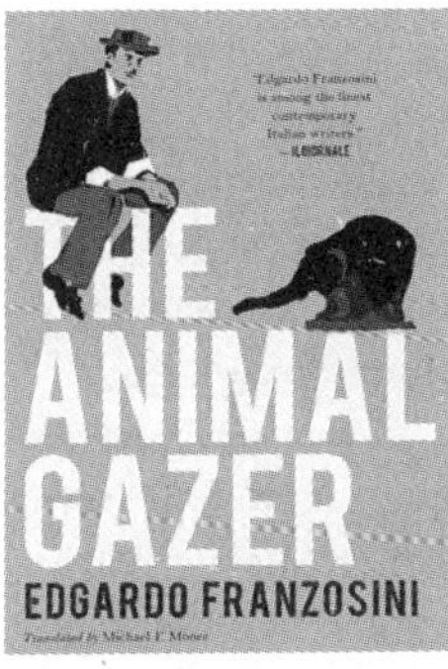

THE ANIMAL GAZER
BY EDGARDO FRANZOSINI

A hypnotic novel inspired by the strange and fascinating life of sculptor Rembrandt Bugatti, brother of the fabled automaker. Bugatti obsessively observes and sculpts the baboons, giraffes, and panthers in European zoos, finding empathy with their plight and identifying with their life in captivity. Rembrandt Bugatti's work, now being rediscovered, is displayed in major art museums around the world and routinely fetches large sums at auction. Edgardo Franzosini recreates the young artist's life with intense lyricism, passion, and sensitivity.

ALLMEN AND THE DRAGONFLIES
BY MARTIN SUTER

Johann Friedrich von Allmen has exhausted his family fortune by living in Old World grandeur despite present-day financial constraints. Forced to downscale, Allmen inhabits the garden house of his former Zurich estate, attended by his Guatemalan butler, Carlos. This is the first of a series of humorous, fast-paced detective novels devoted to a memorable gentleman thief. A thrilling art heist escapade infused with European high culture and luxury that doesn't shy away from the darker side of human nature.

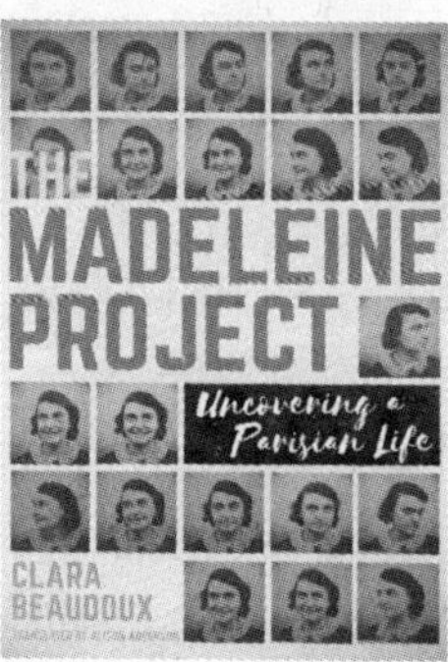

THE MADELEINE PROJECT BY CLARA BEAUDOUX

A young woman moves into a Paris apartment and discovers a storage room filled with the belongings of the previous owner, a certain Madeleine who died in her late nineties, and whose treasured possessions nobody seems to want. In an audacious act of journalism driven by personal curiosity and humane tenderness, Clara Beaudoux embarks on *The Madeleine Project*, documenting what she finds on Twitter with text and photographs, introducing the world to an unsung 20th century figure.

ADUA BY IGIABA SCEGO

Adua, an immigrant from Somalia to Italy, has lived in Rome for nearly forty years. She came seeking freedom from a strict father and an oppressive regime, but her dreams of film stardom ended in shame. Now that the civil war in Somalia is over, her homeland calls her. She must decide whether to return and reclaim her inheritance, but also how to take charge of her own story and build a future.

IF VENICE DIES BY SALVATORE SETTIS

Internationally renowned art historian Salvatore Settis ignites a new debate about the Pearl of the Adriatic and cultural patrimony at large. In this fiery blend of history and cultural analysis, Settis argues that "hit-and-run" visitors are turning Venice and other landmark urban settings into shopping malls and theme parks. This is a passionate plea to secure the soul of Venice, written with consummate authority, wide-ranging erudition and élan.

THE MADONNA OF NOTRE DAME
BY ALEXIS RAGOUGNEAU

Fifty thousand people jam into Notre Dame Cathedral to celebrate the Feast of the Assumption. The next morning, a beautiful young woman clothed in white kneels at prayer in a cathedral side chapel. But when someone accidentally bumps against her, her body collapses. She has been murdered. This thrilling novel illuminates shadowy corners of the world's most famous cathedral, shedding light on good and evil with suspense, compassion and wry humor.

THE LAST WEYNFELDT
BY MARTIN SUTER

Adrian Weynfeldt is an art expert in an international auction house, a bachelor in his mid-fifties living in a grand Zurich apartment filled with costly paintings and antiques. Always correct and well-mannered, he's given up on love until one night—entirely out of character for him—Weynfeldt decides to take home a ravishing but unaccountable young woman and gets embroiled in an art forgery scheme that threatens his buttoned up existence. This refined page-turner moves behind elegant bourgeois facades into darker recesses of the heart.

MOVING THE PALACE
BY CHARIF MAJDALANI

A young Lebanese adventurer explores the wilds of Africa, encountering an eccentric English colonel in Sudan and enlisting in his service. In this lush chronicle of far-flung adventure, the military recruit crosses paths with a compatriot who has dismantled a sumptuous palace and is transporting it across the continent on a camel caravan. This is a captivating modern-day Odyssey in the tradition of Bruce Chatwin and Paul Theroux.

To purchase these titles and for more information please visit newvesselpress.com.